LITTLE BOXES

CECILIA KNAPP was the Young People's Laureate for London, 2020–2021. Her writing has appeared in *Magma*, *Wasafiri*, *Popshot*, *The White Review*, *Ambit* and *bath magg*, as well as *The Independent* and *Vogue*. She has presented BBC Radio 4's *Poetry Please* and she curated the poetry anthology *Everything Is Going to Be All Right* (Trapeze). She was shortlisted for the 2020 Rebecca Swift Women's Prize and won the 2021 Ruth Rendell Award. Her debut poetry collection is *Peach Pig* (Corsair). She teaches creative writing and poetry in a number of settings. *Little Boxes* is her first novel.

LITTLE BOXES

CECILIA KNAPP

THE BOROUGH PRESS

The Borough Press
An imprint of HarperCollins*Publishers* Ltd
1 London Bridge Street
London SE1 9GF

www.harpercollins.co.uk

Harper Ireland
Macken House,
39/40 Mayor Street Upper,
Dublin 1
D01 C9W8
Ireland

This paperback edition 2023
1

First published by HarperCollins*Publishers* 2022

A catalogue record for this book is available from the British Library

ISBN: 978-0-00-844084-8

Typeset in Adobe Garamond by
Palimpsest Book Production Limited, Falkirk, Stirlingshire

Printed and Bound in the UK using 100% Renewable Electricity
at CPI Group (UK) Ltd

MIX
Paper | Supporting
responsible forestry
FSC™ C007454

This book is produced from independently certified FSC™ paper
to ensure responsible forest management.

For more information visit: www.harpercollins.co.uk/green

For Leo. We miss you.

PYLADES   I'll take care of you.

ORESTES   It's rotten work.

PYLADES   Not for me. Not if it's you.

Orestes, Euripides
translated by Anne Carson

But how do you choose your form?
How do you choose your name?
How do you choose your life?
How do you choose the time you must
exhale and kick and rise?

Joanna Newsom, 'Divers'

Monday

Everything changes when the old man dies, quietly and on his terms, as though he had always known that it would happen this way. It starts with this ending.

Then, four young people stare at the mouth of the world, its gaping blackness. They stand beside his wet grave. The vibrant green that summer spills so recklessly everywhere mocks them in the blatant presence of death. Each of them feels something rattling within; they have become unstuck. The three boys are awkwardly draped in ill-fitting cheap suits, inexpertly folded ties, excess material bunched around downward-facing shoulders. Their suits shine in the high sun. The girl is in a black dress that's too short; she tugs it down periodically and glances at her thighs, purplish even in the heat. Though they should be holding each other, as they once would have, they don't. Everything happens in slow motion. The tallest boy, the thinnest with the violent cheekbones, picks up a handful of dirt and throws it on the coffin. The others don't look up. The noise it makes is grotesquely loud. From the top of the hill, they see the town that they both love and loathe shimmering in the hot midday. In the not so far off distance, gulls. Always gulls. Somewhere much further from where they are, laughter, bold and unashamed, carried to them on the wind.

Sunday

Two weeks earlier

Brighton is preening itself, preparing for summer, slowly unfurling and coming to life, getting ready to show itself in all its dirty glory. The daylight is doing something different. It's hard not to smile during the first days of summer in a seaside town. Winter feels crueller, somehow, more dead, the angry grey sea churning and unkind every day for months on end, the air freezing and damp. The exodus of tourists makes the streets seem flat and the stench of wet wood and salt is everywhere. Leah likes it like that. It feels as though enduring her town in its worst months shows she is truly a local. But when summer comes, everything feels sharp, lush, turned up. Leah gets a twist of excitement in her belly each time she leaves the house.

She leaves her flat and begins to walk to work, down the long hill that leads from her estate, up on a hill, set apart from the postcard aesthetic of the town centre. Buses murmur past, quiet as smoke. Cafés are opening up, their doors propped open by crates. In the Laines, there is weather-faded bunting criss-crossing against the sky, rails of second-hand clothing outside the front of shops, tables and chairs, filthy pastel buildings crammed together like books on a shelf. A busker tunes up a battered guitar. There's the smell of something grilling. Gulls. Dogs. Buttery sunshine, still early enough for the air to feel a little cold on her cheeks. Under the bridge by the station, there are rainbows painted on the walls. The homeless crew sit in a tangle of sleeping bags, the unwashed smell of human bodies. Leah stops to say hello.

At a set of traffic lights, Leah watches a group of cold-looking teenage girls feign annoyance at boys with too much gel in their hair and the collars of their polo shirts popped up like stag horns. They're showing off, shoving each other into the road, bored, stomping around looking for something to do. Leah remembers the feeling of being young in the town she has grown up in; the sense that each street belongs to you and your friends alone, and nothing else matters but the small daily dramas that play out in the parks and alleyways.

At the Pavilion Gardens, she feels a tug of fondness for this town. It's easy to forget the parts she loves when she's up the hill in her small flat, separate from the colours and the noise. She thinks of summers sprawled on the grass after school with holes in her tights and biro on her hands, kissing Jay and rolling new cigarettes from the butts of old ones. She pictures Nathan, shirtless, his long back like a muscular fish. She thinks of Matthew, pale and tall holding grease-soaked chip papers, Jay stealing them from his hands, of sharing headphones, Jay knocking Nathan's hat off his head. She thinks, as she always thinks when she walks this way, of the four of them years ago, hot, slightly stoned and a bit grubby.

Outside the Prince Albert, there's a group of people laughing with full pints. They probably haven't been to bed yet, have stayed up all night, wired and listening to low music in some flat, sharing exaggerated stories of childhood, watching the sunrise, waiting for the pubs to start serving. Leah knows the ritual: ignoring the pangs of panic, the unsettling glare of daylight when you haven't slept; mouths ringed red, taking the edge off with more booze before hitting the greasy spoon for soft foods, easy to digest. Beans and white bread with butter.

Everywhere she looks, she has the feeling people are enjoying themselves more than her. They are more interesting, lead more exciting lives, lives filled with international travel, spontaneous camping trips, eccentric garden dinner parties out the back of large houses with candles in empty bottles. They are probably the type of people who make documentaries featuring grainy footage from nineties video cameras. They likely go to the art college and make their own bread. The group on the bench outside the pub take on the quality of talented, chic and spontaneous people, people so far from Leah's reality, people who she wants to be around, as if by association with them she might like herself more.

Leah can't remember a time when she didn't consider herself generic. At school she was right in the middle of things, liked by some, ignored by many, by no means the lower tier of the cruel hierarchies set by teenagers but not in the upper echelons. Some boys fancied her, most teased her, said she was too much, too loud sometimes, annoying, definitely not the right type of shape. She was smart but didn't speak much in

5

class. She was never confident enough in her opinions or her ability to express them well. When others spoke out loud in class, she was struck by how instinctual and articulate they were. They shared observations that had never occurred to her. She did well enough in her exams but played it down. She found it humiliating, the thought that people might think she had a high opinion of herself, that she thought herself bright. She didn't want to be liked for being clever. She wanted to be liked because she just had that unnameable thing, that special quality that couldn't be cultivated or mimicked, which was venerated by teenagers. Overall, she wasn't treated badly. But she did feel distinctly average, middling, never exceptional. She tended towards doubt and always felt slightly embarrassed without knowing why.

When she is around people she sometimes changes who she is, what she likes and how she talks. This makes her feel like she's just a neutral body gliding about. A rational part of her knows this can't be true, that she has the fundamentals of a personality, but more often than not, she can't get this thought out of her head and her characteristics blur, shapeless and indefinable.

Sometimes it helps to write it down. *Good friend*, she wrote last week, then crossed it out because she didn't believe herself. *Good listener.* She crossed that out too because sometimes she drifts when people talk to her. *Likes books,* she added, then put a question mark after it. She often falls asleep when reading and gets distracted by her phone or the TV, which makes her think she can't enjoy books in the way she tells herself she does. She's started keeping a diary but it's hard to remember to write every day and she feels guilty when she doesn't. Matthew tells her she's funny, and cutting when she wants to be, not afraid of talking about tits and fannies, he said. She has opinions, lots of them. She enjoys forming them and could monologue loudly for hours to Matthew or to Nathan. But there are times when she retreats inside herself. She likes the satisfaction of eating leftovers and washing out the Tupperware, knowing there's been no waste. She enjoys stationery shops. Sometimes, when she's sad, she gets swept up in the idea of baking a cake but they always sink in the middle and then she gets irritable. She likes new things, even a new bottle of water makes her feel special, though she can't afford new clothes. She likes knowing about other people's lives, why they made certain choices. It makes her feel she might one day be more in charge of herself, that she might live a larger life. She wants someone to show her exactly how to live, to take her decisions from her hands and sort everything out for her in a matter of fact kind of way. She wonders how people fit in all their living, how their lives seem so much more varied and exciting than her own.

She's been working seven-day weeks lately to give her mum a break from the bills. It's led to a type of numb surrender that a strict routine allows, and in truth she's enjoying not having to think. She's drifting through the town when she hears her brother's voice.

'Here she is!'

Raph is standing with several other men. He's in a high-vis vest with nothing underneath, combat trousers and a belt of tools hanging low on his slim hips.

'Hello you,' she says.

He breaks away from the group he's standing with, inhaling cigarettes, chatting and drinking tea from flasks and takeaway coffee cups. He walks towards Leah with a bacon roll in his hand.

'Want some?' His mouth is full. Little patches of dusty flour stick to his facial hair.

'Close your mouth, you dick, you just sprayed me with bread.'

Raph opens his mouth and flashes half-chewed breakfast.

She gives him a shove, laughs, happy to see him like this. Simply eating, talking, getting ready to work. When he's on good form, charming and energetic like a dog, she wants to be in his presence. There's a kind of magic to him. Around his waist, metal clips from a harness clatter together.

'What you got today?'

'Cutting down a whole fucking bunch of trees, sis.'

Raph smiles wide, showing his teeth, the same shape as Leah's.

'My mate hooked me up last minute. Cash in hand.'

His arms are thin and toned; Leah can see the network of tendons and slim muscles working away under the skin. She feels a rush of love for him, a gratitude that he's here and not sleeping off a hangover on the sofa.

'I'm glad you're working.'

'What do you mean?' Something shifts between them.

'Nothing. I didn't mean anything.' She smiles.

She sees his eyes narrow a bit. They are like sky, changeable. Raph is mercurial. He loves her one minute and hates her the next. When they were children, he'd ignore her for days inexplicably. Then he'd stop as quickly as he started, be back to her brother, the best brother, inventing games for the two of them that would fill an entire afternoon. Nowadays, his moods darken quickly, he drinks and Leah looks after him. This is their way since their dad left.

'I need to go,' Raph says. He's cold. It's clear she's gone wrong in their exchange.

'See you at home?' Leah says.

'Maybe.'

Someone shouts something in their direction and he turns and leaves her standing alone.

Sunday

The morning air is full of salt. Nathan is sitting on the balcony outside the flat he shares with his parents on the fourth floor of his block. He licks his upper lip, tastes the sweat left dried from that morning's run along the seafront. He is twenty-three and there's still not much hair on his top lip. His mum still kisses his head, tells him not to worry. Some boys just don't ever grow much.

His dad is sitting on the ledge of the balcony rolling a cigarette. The sun haloes his grey-tinged afro. His eyes are deep and wise but he is somehow ageless. His silver rings look heavy on his hands as he strikes the match and his gums seem to resist his large teeth, which are white except for the glints of gold in the back corridors of his mouth. One fat piece of crystal quartz is set into the thick silver of the ring he wears on his middle finger.

From the kitchen, Nathan's mum Elena shouts, 'Fuck.' The heat of the small flat dulls her voice into a soft thud and the men laugh. Elena comes out onto the balcony, her heavy fringe flattened to her face with the heat. She wipes her hands on her apron, takes a pull of Benny's cigarette.

Everything in their flat is sensuous. The smell of cooking is constant and so is the music.

'No garlic,' she explains, passing the cigarette back to her husband. With her other hand, she pulls Nathan close to her. His head rests on top of her head.

'I'll make coffee,' Benny says. He passes Elena. He puts his large hands on her shoulders and squeezes them briefly. The family move around each other as easy as water. Their bodies know the choreography of navigating their small surroundings. They touch each other whenever they pass.

Benny comes back with three blue mugs. He passes one to his son and puts his arm around Elena. Most mornings start like this, the three of them on the balcony talking about the day ahead.

Benny is a musician who spends most of his time teaching kids how to play guitar. Sometimes he plays with his blues band in the back rooms of pubs on the weekends and Nathan and Elena go down to watch him, drinking rum until they're singing along and Elena's crying with love for him. Elena looks after community gardens with young lads fresh out of prison who love her long silver hair and her red lips and how she brings them different lunches in Tupperware. She's tired most days, her hands are always filthy with soil but she's got all the time in the world for anyone who needs to talk.

'I need to bounce. I'm opening up today,' Nathan says, drinking the last of his coffee.

'Don't you dare go anywhere without a kiss from your one and only mother,' says Elena. 'The woman whose body you once made a home of, who gave you life!' She gesticulates with her cigarette, her bangles crash together on her arms. Benny's laugh is deep

11

and resounding. Nathan leans his face towards his mother, who holds it in her hands and kisses his cheeks several times.

'Mum, I'm going to be late,' Nathan says.

'All right, baby, all right.' Elena holds her hands up in surrender and positions herself back under Benny's arm.

Nathan smiles at the sight of his parents, his mum tiny by Benny's side, still in her red pyjamas.

'Make the day your masterpiece,' Elena says. Nathan turns towards the stairwell. She and Benny begin ballroom dancing gently in time to the record playing inside their flat. Her slippers shuffle a tune on the concrete.

'Turn the fucking music down,' a voice shouts from the balcony below.

'It's a classic!' Benny shouts back.

'I love you,' Nathan shouts to his mother, who's leaning over the balcony arguing with the downstairs neighbour. Benny holds a fist of her pyjamas in one hand to stop her from toppling over, and waves at Nathan with the other. Nathan passes his best friend Jay's flat on the way out of the building. Jay is standing in the doorway in just his boxers, broad-shouldered, with a stance too wide for the narrow frame, chewing a piece of white toast. Nathan greets him with a touch of his hand as he passes.

He makes it to the ground floor, running quickly down the concrete steps with ease acquired only by treading the same stairs for years and years. He glances over at Leah's flat. He hovers for a second then moves, pulls his jeans up, lights the half a fag nestled in his palm, chipped from earlier, and makes his way down the hill to the pub.

Sunday

From his balcony, Jay watches Nathan's figure disappear down the hill. He surveys his small kingdom. Everything is familiar. The whole town is at the mercy of the sea winds: the peeling white paint of the block, the sparkling tarmac of the basketball court, the things kept on balconies, old bikes and geraniums, the washing and a couple of rainbow flags, the recycling bins in the car park. The insides of flats spill out, people shout out of windows, towels blow in the wind. The best thing is the view of the sea winking at Jay in the sun, and the wind turbines in the distance like strange trees. Jay can already see curls of smoke rising up from the pebble beach, keen Sunday sun-worshippers getting started on barbecues. Jay likes the summer, he likes bounding around shirtless and heady and audacious, the small thrill of seeking out trouble on a hot day in a town full of tourists.

From where he is stood, Jay sees Ron walking his slow and heavy steps past the basketball court and towards his flat, a paper tucked under his arm and a pint of milk dangling from his finger. Jay watches Ron making his way to the shops most mornings. Things repeat like clockwork on this block. You can tell time in this way. Jay likes the routine of it. Ron is always the same, up early, in sand-coloured trousers and a raincoat, cutting a beige figure, big square glasses that reflect the sun. Ron stops, looks up and nods, one tight little nod in Jay's direction. Jay smiles, waves. There's something warm in his chest and he can't quite grasp the cause. It's something about being acknowledged by Ron. He wants to walk with Ron to his flat, put his milk away in the fridge for him. Ron has interesting things to say, little phrases that calm Jay down. Ron likes Jay but does not look up to him in the way Jay is used to. He tells Jay he's got a lot to learn, but this doesn't bother Jay like it might if someone else said it. It feels natural, like some order is being followed.

Jay shrugs off his feelings. Today is important. He pulls on his tracksuit bottoms, grabs his car keys, and makes his way to Mickey's.

Jay has heard the rumours about Mickey. There weren't many people from his school who hadn't heard them. Some people said that the reason he'd disappeared for years was that he was serving time for possession. Other people say it was because he'd been caught selling counterfeit washing powder. There was the rumour that his girlfriend, a young-looking pale blonde girl from Peacehaven, was actually his cousin. Jay had joked that everyone married their cousins up that way anyway, a joke he was proud of and often repeated. Then there was the rumour, in year eleven, that Mickey was gay, which led to him having his head kicked in. Beyond the rumours, everyone knew it was him who drove a stolen Ford Focus into a shopfront in the early hours of the morning with four passengers, one of whom died, and that's why Mickey's left arm doesn't work well anymore.

Jay sits in his car, breathes in and out through his nose. He's nervous and unused to the feeling. His head feels tight, as though his skull is too small. He'd like to speak to Leah. She could calm him down. But he doesn't. He puts the key in the ignition and turns.

Mickey lives in a basement flat in a townhouse in Kemptown that probably used to be nice. It was likely once a cheerful yellow colour, but the brightness has faded now and the wood around the windows is rotten. Leading down to the flat, below street level, is a black iron railing, flaking its paint off in sharp-looking curls. The window is dusty, and the metal blind is hanging at a strange angle. Jay slams his car door shut, itches his nose until it hurts a bit. He walks down the steps and knocks three times on the door. A dog barks inside. Then other noises, an internal door opening, the shuffle of feet, someone calming the dog quietly.

Mickey opens the door. Jay recognises him from school but he looks older and more tired. He's wearing a towelling dressing-gown but patches of it are worn to thin cotton. When he opens his mouth to yawn, his breath smells stale. Jay tries to keep his face neutral.

'All right Jay,' Mickey says. His voice is grainy like it's the first time he's spoken today.

'All right Mickey.'

'Is it eleven already?'

'Yeah,' Jay says, apologetic for being prompt. He hates being on the back foot.

The dog that Jay heard earlier nuzzles at the back of Mickey's knees and makes him jolt towards Jay.

'Fuck's sake, Rocco.' Mickey reaches down to scratch his head.

Rocco looks at Jay with cool blue eyes.

'Come in, mate. Sorry, I'm not with it this morning. I've just woken up.'

The corridor into Mickey's flat is narrow and dark. There are coats and hoodies hung off a row of hooks which Jay squeezes past. Mickey leads him to a living room with wooden floors and beige walls. There's a window where the smallest bit of light is coming through, the bit that can make it in from up on the street. The living room doesn't have much charm about it. There's a chocolate brown sofa with a fake fur throw tossed over it. Jay notices curls of tobacco are stuck to the artificial fibres. There's a low glass coffee table with squat leather legs and on the table is more tobacco, an old cereal bowl and some wet cigarette papers. There's an enormous plasma TV mounted on the wall and a tangle of games console wires and controllers underneath it. There's a practically empty bookcase with a couple of DVDs leaning against each other and a tiny cactus on the middle shelf. The room creaks. Jay hears a refrigerator humming somewhere and footsteps in the flat above him.

Jay stands in the middle of the room. Mickey doesn't invite him to sit down.

'So, how've you been?' Jay says.

Mickey smiles limply. His skin is a dusty texture, coppery stubble sprouts from his face. His hair still holds the shape of some sort of cut or style, but it has grown out a lot. Jay notices a faded-looking tattoo on Mickey's neck. He reckons it's a shakily drawn pair of dice.

'I've been all right,' Mickey says.

Jay has no idea what to say in order to proceed and is glad when Mickey speaks.

'What was it you're after again, mate?'

'Three hundred, I think,' Jay says, deepening his voice, trying to look Mickey in the eyes.

Sunday

Matthew hears the front door close and opens his eyes. Through the crack in his bedroom door, he can see Ron making his way down the corridor in a bottle-green raincoat.

He sits up and looks out of his window. The sun is behind a thin summer cloud, a slight mist is hovering over the sea. He's always been a bad sleeper, too nervous and full of thoughts to drop off easily. Night time seemed to be when all his excruciating or mortifying memories chose to visit him. He'd only managed to get a few hours last night. He presses his soles against the carpet. The room is small, only a strip of floor space between him and the door, which doesn't shut properly. He sits in silence for a few minutes, waiting for his eyes to adjust to the day, lifts his thin arms above his head to stretch. In the creases of his elbows, there are dark patches of eczema, purple in some places, strange shapes like a faded map.

In the kitchen, he flicks on the light and stands by the kettle, yellowed with cooking stains, waiting for it to boil. He takes a mug from the cabinet, the one that is apparently the perfect size for coffee, puts it on the Formica table and spoons one teaspoon of Nescafé instant into it, fills it up halfway and drops in two sugar lumps. His body is bare and almost translucent in the strip light. Thin, silvery stretch marks on his upper arms reflect the glow of the kitchen. He walks to the bedroom next door to his, as he does every morning at the same time.

'Grandad, coffee,' he says.

Ron doesn't look up. The feeling in the room is odd, inscrutable and tense. Ron gestures to the pint of milk sitting on the bedside table. Matthew undoes the lid and splashes in a small amount. He puts the cup on Ron's bedside table, stacked high with newspapers. He waits for a response. The air is big with something strange.

Ron sits on the edge of the bed with his head in his hands. He's still wearing his mac, the day's post in his lap, some of it opened, the jagged lips of envelopes resting on his corduroy legs. He's a man of few words. He moves quietly, peacefully around their flat and is sometimes peculiar in the way he goes for long walks alone at night. He collects facts, weather forecasts, gardening tips and measurements for the things he is building in small A5 notebooks. He sleeps in his armchair often, eats little, can go days without saying much. But this morning is different. He seems disturbed, ragged and unusual. It is unlike him to not be getting on with something. Most mornings he rises before the sun, always without complaint, and keeps busy for hours. There is always something to fix. A watch perhaps that he has found at the market. The week before he took apart an old broken three-bar heater and mended it because he liked the colour of the metal. Often, he's in his allotment, even in the depths of winter.

Matthew notices he hasn't got any socks on with his shoes. His face is unshaven, salty stubble. His eyebrows are iron grey and thick and his hair is pure white, sparse and unbrushed. Ron looks up. His eyes a deep peat, little creases running on the skin around them in all directions, magnified by his glasses. He blinks, slow. Matthew can feel his eyes on him, very aware of his naked torso.

'Why do you do that to yourself?' Ron says and moves his eyes down to the marks on Matthew's chest. It's a plane of DIY tattoos that he'd done with old friends in the Railway Lands, a part of town where steam trains used to pass through, now a place for daytime drinking and bunking off school, a dappled green clearing home to wide oaks and old condoms trodden into the dirt, names of lovers carved into the bark. Matthew glances down, a myriad of shaky lines, names of people he hasn't seen in years. Most of it seems foreign to him now, a different Matthew who drank with older men who made it OK to get wasted on a Tuesday afternoon.

'Put some clothes on, Matthew? It's Sunday.'

'OK,' Matthew is grateful his grandad has said something. He is holding the doorframe gently. He crosses the room and pulls the curtains open.

'Leave them, will you?'

Matthew feels massive in the small room, inappropriate.

'Sure. Do you want the shower first? A shave?' The sound of cigarette paper rubbing against itself. Then the striking of a match. Ron inhales deeply.

Recently, Ron has been spending more time alone in his room. Shaving less, his white hair frequently uncombed. Matthew has tried to put it down to age. Asking about it seems too difficult, humiliating somehow, a concrete mass between him and his grandad. Matthew has always been tentative. He can't think of a way to approach.

'Are you OK, Grandad?' Even this is hard to ask. Matthew picks at a piece of peeling gloss on the doorframe.

'I'm fine.' Ron squashes the cigarette into an ashtray by his bed and rubs both palms down his heavy trousers. He crosses and uncrosses his legs. Matthew notices his calves are shiny and hairless. Old smoke rises in the silent air between them.

'I guess you don't want to talk about it.' Matthew can feel the atmosphere becoming more awkward. He doesn't feel in control of the exchange, like he lacks the authority to be imposing.

'I guess not.' Ron's mouth is one thin line.

'Well your coffee's there,' Matthew tries to sound light, happy, to contribute to some shift in the atmosphere. 'I'll grab the first shower.'

He turns on the shower in the avocado bathroom. He makes it so hot that when he gets in, his hands hurt, his nails feel the pressure of the heat. He goes over what was said, evaluating his weakness. He presses his forehead against the wet tiles.

Matthew has never told his grandad he is gay. He has convinced himself it would be impossible. The language needed to explain it to Ron won't form in his head. The only people he has ever told are his best friends Leah and Nathan. The thought of any official coming out, of sitting across from someone and saying it, waiting for their response, has always felt too excruciating. His mum, who has lived in Spain for years, told him once she's known since he was a baby and it made no difference to her. His dad, Ron's only son, was happiest marooned on oil rigs for months on end and Matthew never found the right moment to tell him. Sometimes he wonders if he'd be a different person if he'd had a dad like Benny, someone deliberate and obvious with his love, who seemed to unravel people from themselves without even trying.

Matthew learned young to hate what he was. Boys at school taught him that, and the television at home taught him some more ways to feel shame. Red newspaper headlines and scandals involving celebrities painted gay men as perverse and disgraceful.

At school, Matthew kept his head down, trying to avoid being discovered, but earned himself the worst label there was: weird. He struggled to make friends with other boys. There were so many things he worked hard to keep to himself: how his favourite colour was purple, how he loved Enya, how he wanted to read Leah's *Bliss* magazines and how when they were children, he preferred sitting with Leah on her bedroom floor as they acted out soap opera narratives with her Barbies rather than be outside on the green kicking footballs into goals made of piled-up jumpers.

Mostly he avoided getting his head kicked in because of Jay. Jay and Matthew weren't exactly friends, but Jay was Leah's boyfriend and so they spent time together as a three, or as a four when Nathan joined. They all lived in the same block, which gave Matthew a certain amount of protection. Mouthy Jay, with his meaty fists, with his territory and cheekbones and smile as wide and long as the Lewes Road, could defend anyone he chose to, and no one would dispute it. Beautiful, bold Jay, the first boy Matthew had a crush on until Caleb came along, though that would remain a secret he would take to his grave.

In truth, Matthew wasn't ever really concerned with being liked. He kept his head down. He was shy and wanted to remain as invisible as possible, unlike Leah, who enjoyed attention when she could get it. The less people knew him, the more realistic his goal was of remaining a peripheral character. Attention made him cringe. Talk of himself he found uncomfortable. He preferred to just get on with it, to enjoy the things he wanted to privately without having to expose his opinions through definitive likes and dislikes. He was much more interested in others than he was in himself. Leah always had to push for him to discuss his feelings. He liked photographs and taking pictures, that was a thing he was certain of. His grandad listened quietly with his hands clasped in his lap the first time Matthew approached this. He'd come home from school after his art teacher had shown him a film camera and a book of photography. Ron gave him his old Pentax. They fixed it together, taking it apart and reassembling it in the dim light of their flat. Matthew took it to the beach the next day. It was Ron who encouraged Matthew to apply to work at the camera shop in town, developing film and servicing cameras. He was good at it.

Matthew met Caleb when he was fifteen. It was the first time his feelings for boys had ever felt right. When he lost Caleb, it felt as though he had been drained of light, his body was weak. He tried to forget Caleb in the Railway Lands and when he was older he would go down to the seafront, meet older men, get into the backs of their cars to try and find what he had lost.

Now, he sees love as something not made for him, some abstract thing like the shape of something at the top of a faraway hill, lovely but never to be fully grasped. He works, he takes photographs, he drinks with Leah, he watches films, he walks on Sundays with his grandad. He would never meet a man for a date, wouldn't want to be seen walking hand in hand back up to his flat with anyone. He has ruled it out. He gets the feeling his life is somehow on pause, the same every day, but he doesn't know how to move and it's easier to keep it this way.

After he turns off the shower, his skin glows with heat. The flat is full of steam; it hangs in the air. He tries to find an inch of space to hang his wet towel. He sits on the end of his bed and the silence is too much, he flicks the radio on, closes his eyes and listens to the voices.

Sunday

Mickey sits with his legs apart on the sofa, his dog's head resting on one of his knees. He scratches Rocco with his right hand and reaches underneath the coffee table with the other, lifting a stack of VHS tapes. He has to bend his arm at an awkward angle, seeing as he's got his other hand on the dog, and Jay thinks he sees a flash of pain cross his face. Mickey puts the tape on the glass-topped coffee table and then massages his forearm vigorously with his right hand.

Everything about his face looks a bit crooked. He seems to have too many teeth for his mouth, but he is sort of beautiful, grey eyes and a soft, rounded brow. A police car drives by fast and Mickey's face is illuminated briefly with blue light. He reaches into the pocket of his dressing-gown with his good hand and pulls out a thin screwdriver. Jay catches his eye and immediately wishes he hadn't. Micky laughs at Jay's discomfort or rather shoots a quick burst of air from his nostrils. His mouth doesn't move. He unscrews the back of the VHS tape, lifts it off and pulls out a sandwich bag stuffed with smaller bags of various pills. Jay notices some are peach-coloured and cut into the shape of clouds. Mickey holds the bag in his open palm.

'You've never done this for me before,' Mickey says. Jay feels like he's on stage while Mickey sits there, legs spread apart, holding the bag in his hand, weighing it slightly like a portion of meat.

'So I'll explain a couple of things.' Jay gets the sense Mickey is playing with him a bit and this annoys him.

'It's pretty simple really.' He chucks the bag at Jay's chest. Jay catches it and is glad he does. The little pills feel lumpy beneath his fingers.

'Start with these. You pay me back two grand in two weeks and you keep the rest. Get creative. Do any deals you like. Three for twenty-five, stuff like that. Don't use your own number, obviously. And they didn't come from me.'

'How many in here?'

'Three hundred.' Mickey screws the back on the VHS. He leans back against the sofa and sighs.

'When you come back, we'll sort out the money then.' Mickey gets his phone out of his dressing-gown pocket and appears to be typing something.

'What's the date today?'

'Sixth.'

Mickey nods and types it into his phone.

'So how long you been doing this for?' Jay says. He wants Mickey to say something that would indicate that he likes him. He is still holding the bag to his chest.

'What?' Mickey is distracted; his phone is ringing. He reaches for a half-smoked spliff in the ashtray in front of him and puts it to his lips. It's conical and burnt ragged at the end. He excuses himself by waving a hand to Jay and walks into the other room. Jay turns the bag over in his hands. It is packed to the top.

From the other room, he hears Mickey's voice dispensing a warning. The dog looks at him. For a second, Jay wants to drop the bag on the floor and run out the front door.

Mickey comes back in and stubs out his joint.

'Sorry, what were you saying?' He's standing right in front of Jay now. They are the same height.

'Doesn't matter. Listen, Mickey, thanks so much for this. Honestly.'

Mickey spends a long time looking at Jay's face. Jay wants to look away. Mickey puts his hand on Jay's chest and leaves it there for a while, a gesture Jay finds unsettling but one he doesn't feel he should disturb.

'No problem, Jay.' He pulls his hand away abruptly and walks back over to the sofa. Mickey flicks on the TV and picks up a game controller.

'Nice one. Yeah,' Jay says. Rocco lets out one quick bark as a huge animation of a man with a gun appears on the TV.

'See you mate.'

Sunday

Leah walks towards London Road. Women in hats and colourful clothes are gathered outside the church by the Old Steine. They talk enthusiastically, holding each other's hands to emphasise a point, laughing.

She sees her mum then, part of a pastel crowd. Jenny is wearing pink linen. Leah walks towards her across the grass. Jenny spots her and raises a hand to wave. Leah smiles. Her smile shows perfect teeth, something she can confidently say she likes about herself. She knows she has straight teeth, that she is lucky in that way. She knows she is tall. She likes to assert these things in her head because they are things she knows, concrete and tangible.

Leah greets her mum with a hug. Her soft body smells of lavender soap.

'Hey Mum.'

'Hi darling.'

Leah wants to shrink back down to the size of a baby and never have to speak again.

'Have you come for the service?' Jenny says, looking hopeful. She runs her fingers through her short grey hair and looks Leah up and down.

'People don't tend to wear jeans really though, love,' she adds, tapering off the sentence with a nervous laugh. She reaches out a hand and pinches the waistband of her Levis. Her thumb brushes against Leah's stomach and is warm. Leah looks down at her mum's broad hands. Short nails and a couple of sunspots. The skin looks a little dry, sore perhaps, from too much washing up.

'You can do anything as long as you're wearing washing-up gloves,' Jenny said to Leah, cleaning out Leah's dad's bedside cabinet after he left.

'Sorry Mum, I'm on my way to work.'

'Oh, that's right.' Leah thinks she looks disappointed. She blinks several times. She is wearing the blue mascara she only wears on Sundays.

'Well maybe next week.'

'Maybe.'

'I know you think that it's silly.'

'I don't think it's silly, Ma. I'm just busy.'

She looks over her mum's shoulder at the bodies filing through the large wooden doors. It makes her irritable, everyone following each other down the path.

'Come, just once, why don't you. Next week.'

'I'm working next week too,' Leah says, a bit too quick, a bit too loud.

Jenny looks down and adjusts her watch strap. The sun makes her cheeks look powdery, a ripe peach. Leah swallows. She hates seeing her mum wounded. There are days when she wishes she believed. It would make everything easier.

The priest comes over then in a cassock that hangs in folds.

'Leah! To what do we owe this pleasure? Will you be joining us today?' He tilts his head.

'Not today, I'm afraid.' Leah smiles, aware of her mum still fussing with her watch strap.

'That is a pity.' The priest's voice is a soft coo. 'I haven't seen you since you were – oh, I don't know, about this high.' The priest holds his hand somewhere around Leah's waist. 'What are you doing now?' A rivulet of milky sweat travels down his forehead.

'I'm a receptionist', Leah says, 'at a clinic, up Elm Grove way.'

'Oh, fantastic! Saving up for something? Uni?'

Leah's mum looks pained.

'Not sure yet. I want to. At some point. Things didn't quite work out at the time.'

The three of them stand in silence for a moment.

'Right,' the priest says. 'It's just us then, Jenny.' His voice is loud and bright above the noise from the road.

'Bye, love,' Jenny says. 'See you at home for tea.'

'Bye, Ma.'

The priest puts his hand on Jenny's lower back and guides her into the church. Jenny beams up at the priest and, for a moment, Leah hates her. She pictures her in the church with her eyes closed and her palms facing up, singing.

It was after Leah's dad left that Jenny started going to church every Sunday and hosting a bible group twice a week. Leah can't remember much about her dad from when he was around, but some things stuck with her. He always seemed to have a different car with something wrong with it. He called himself a businessman. He ate sardines on toast on the weekend sitting at the kitchen table in his dressing-gown with his chest hair showing. Some days, he loved Jenny openly. He was endlessly charming. He'd pick her up in the kitchen and dance with her to the radio. He'd take her out to restaurants. Jenny was happy. She'd ring up Leah's nan and tell her how lucky she was to have a man like that. She told her children all the time how wonderful their father was.

It was normal, though, for him to leave for work and be missing for days. It was normal for him to leave just before the end of the month, when the bills needed to be paid but the bank accounts were almost empty. His trips became more frequent as Leah got older. Jenny distracted her and Raph while their dad was away, took them for walks on the hills on weekends and hid sweets in bushes, on fence posts and in tall grass. She took them to the open market, to the park and occasionally to the cinema. She'd pull out thirty pounds from the cash machine on a Friday and show it to them.

'This has got to last us the whole weekend,' she'd say. She made it fun. She'd give them a fifty-pence budget in the cheap supermarket. She'd divert questions about their dad. When they'd get home to find that Leah's dad still wasn't back, Leah would get under the duvet with Raph on the sofa and Jenny would go to bed.

Leah doesn't remember many details about when her dad officially left apart from the view of him waving up from the car park as she stood on the balcony in velvet leggings, watching. She remembers how he was waving and smiling with a box of his belongings under one arm and his car boot open, like he was off on holiday. She felt, as she grew up, that she had something to do with his leaving, that her entrance into the world was the beginning of him becoming tired of them all. It made her so aware of herself, concerned that she was irritating, needy, fundamentally a bad and intolerable person. Raph took it badly, worse than Leah did. He threw his dad's remaining things off the balcony and shut himself in his room for three days.

After that, there were more women in the house, women from the church who Jenny would call 'real rocks'. Aunts and friends in the kitchen, cooking, diligently helping with piles of ironing, talking in hushed voices very close to each other over cups of tea, stopping and smiling whenever Leah came in. Elena came round a lot. She'd bring clothes for Leah that she'd found in charity shops. She'd bring wine. There was crying in the dark. But in the morning, Jenny got on with things, packing lunches for Leah and Raph with messages of love written on bananas in biro, sitting through Leah's ballet classes, bleaching the kitchen in her pink marigold gloves, making sure they had what they needed in their pencil cases and a good pair of shoes each September. She did what women do; she carried on.

After Leah's dad left, it wasn't uncommon to find Ron at their kitchen table. He redid the grouting in their bathroom. He fixed their broken kitchen chairs. He found Jenny her own second-hand car from a friend and drove it into the car park, taped a metallic red birthday bow to the rear-view mirror. He sat and helped her stitch Raph and Leah's name tags into their PE kits. He baked flapjacks and brought them round in a cheerful tartan tin, brought her vegetables from his plot. And after every visit, he sat with Jenny for a long time, listening.

'You're worth a thousand of him, Jen.'

After school on Fridays, Jenny took Leah to her friend's salon in town at the end of a narrow alley. The door was covered with plastic curtains like a butcher's. It reeked of chemicals that permed and bleached. There was a dim yellow light and rows of ancient ladies coughing under brown plastic dryers. Lyndsey the hairdresser cut their hair for free when they needed it. They would stay until she closed the salon, Leah drinking powdery hot chocolate, Lyndsey and Jenny sharing wine out of plastic cups. Leah, bored and restless, never understood why her mum chose to spend her Friday night sitting on an upturned plastic bin – there were no spare chairs – chatting to Lyndsey. When she met Matthew, when things with Jay started to hurt, it made sense, how time can pass this way.

'You're better than this, Jen,' Leah remembers Lyndsey saying. 'You can do better.'

When Leah's dad began coming back, periodically, after months of being absent, he'd take her mum out. He'd love her again, hard, for a day or two and Jenny would be happy, smiling and singing to herself. He always seemed to have answers to her questions about where he had been, where the money was, how he was making more if only Jenny could wait. He made promises. He was kind to Leah. He played with her, made a fuss about the drawings her mum had pinned on the fridge, said she was a genius. He gave her pocket money and asked her to recite her times tables for him. They forgave him each time, they made space for him. At least he never drank, like Jay's dad did, Leah thought. But inevitably, he would leave again.

'It's love,' Jenny said when Leah asked why. 'It doesn't always make sense. Some days it's wonderful and the next day it's unbearable. We're here for your father when he needs to come back. He's got his issues, but we're his family.'

Raph felt it all deeply. Each time his dad disappeared, he would take himself to the shop and buy three bottles of cheap cider in blue plastic bottles and shut himself away in his bedroom. Jenny went back to church and Leah took take care of her brother, making him huge platefuls of mash to keep his belly full and pillow the drink. On the good days, he'd eat and fall asleep; on the bad days, he'd go out.

Eventually, their dad stopped returning at all.

Leah turns and continues walking to work. A bus hisses to a stop next to the church. She thinks of Nathan. She knows he will be opening up the pub. Nathan and his small, pleasant ears. How he rubs his earlobes as he listens.

As soon as the thought arrives, her phone rings: Jay. The sight of his name on her screen still makes her heart jump a little. It is alarming, even after all the years. Jay. The shape of that name. The slope of the 'J' that mirrors what her stomach does when she thinks of him, the sharp peak of the 'A', the curve of the 'Y', his hand around her neck, JAY. Summoning her. Jay, who walks around town like a soldier going to war. Jay, who she once felt safe with. Jay, who never wears odd socks, who drives too quickly around corners, who can't cook but carefully cuts up apples and dips them into cheap peanut butter. Jay, who smells of his dad's old tacky cologne, who Leah has seen crack a nose with one punch on the seafront and who she has also seen kiss his mother's head while she sleeps on the sofa, cover her bare feet with a blanket. Jay, who loves daffodils and tells her that each spring, who will always stop to stroke a dog, who likes the smell of petrol. Jay and the view of his forehead with his head between her legs. Jay, whose kiss is like a punch, who bites her lip, who snores until she turns him on his side. Jay, who is dangerous, who makes her laugh. She ignores the call. It makes her feel powerful. She makes a detour towards Nathan's pub.

At the Level, some eager skaters are up early, gathered like crows on the top of the halfpipe. Dog walkers are dotted about, launching tennis balls for their dogs to fetch. Homeless men sit on benches talking quietly to each other. Though the town is starting to shine itself up, readying itself for the summer – the theatre festival, the alfresco dining – evidence of pain is smattered around. You do not need to look hard for it: how the town picks up some and holds them to the sun at the same time as it drops others to the ground.

Leah approaches the pub and sees Nathan opening the doors outside, a huge bunch of keys in his hand. He notices Leah as she walks to him, smiles, pulling his face into something even more beautiful, his sleepy eyes shining in the morning light.

'Le,' he says. His voice is slightly husky. Not for the first time, Leah finds herself imagining him with no clothes on.

Inside, Leah sits up on a high stool by the bar.

'Is it too early to drink?' She bites her lip. He laughs. She realises she wants to flirt with him. This happens sometimes.

'11 a.m. is pushing it a bit, I think.'

'Fuck my life,' Leah says, 'I've not given you a hug yet.' She leans over the bar to kiss Nathan's cheek, simultaneously scraping back her red hair into a knot on top of her head.

'Just a tea then?' Nathan says, flicking on the kettle.

'Fine.'

Nathan drops a teabag and some milk into a mug. There are two chips on the rim and the phrase 'Life is a gift' is printed in faded calligraphy on the side.

'I forgot you put the milk in first,' Leah says, surveying him from her stool.

'I don't understand why you'd do it any differently. It makes the whole process much quicker. Like an all-in-one method. A pot noodle if you will.'

'Yeah but the point is, the water is supposed to be boiling when it makes contact with the bag.' Leah prods him in the chest with her index finger.

'Bullshit.' Nathan smiles.

'What do you do when it's dead like this?' Leah says, looking around. 'You must get so bored.'

'I like it. I listen to whatever I want. Read a book.'

'Read these?' Leah points to a damp tabloid on the bar. 'Page three, yeah?'

'Shut up,' Nathan says. 'I appreciate things like light. The way it comes through the windows.' He smiles to show he's joking but she knows there is actually some truth in it. The syrupy glass windows morph the shapes of passersby.

'You idiot,' Leah says, but she's playing. She likes this about him, his own brand of inertia, and how he is full of thoughts. She likes how he goes on long drives with his dad in his white transit, listening to soul music rattle the dirty dashboard. It moves her when he hums to himself.

Leah often talks with Nathan. They read the same things online and discuss them. He's moderate. He turns topics over in his hands like he's examining a penny. He poses questions. He lets her respond, figuring out what she thinks, he gives her the space to feel confident without interrupting. With him, she's more like a person who can figure out what they think or feel. He encourages her. They often reach a conclusion together, or he agrees with hers. Leah always wants to know what Nathan thinks about things, his insights stimulate her. Their time together, their conversations, feel totally private.

There is something flirtatious about the way she and Nathan speak to each other. It's been like this for years. They both know it, but it's never mentioned, like they have entered into some sort of secret agreement. Leah likes pushing it, seeing how far she can go with it. It gives her a kind of thrill.

'I sometimes take tea out to the homeless blokes on the Level,' Nathan says. 'Have a chat.'

This is another thing Leah likes about Nathan. He does things for others in a way that doesn't make him seem like a martyr. It's something his mum's instilled in him. She likes how Nathan is not afraid of touch, how he holds her so securely, drapes his arm around Matthew often, his long hugs with his dad.

Leah's phone is face-up on the bar. It starts to vibrate loudly against the wood. She presses the button on the side to silence it. Jay's name and a picture of him with Leah in a playful headlock flash on the screen. He's beaming and frozen with a knuckle rubbing her scalp like a rough older brother. Jay. Filling every door frame. Jay. Shoulders. Fists. Enormous laugh. Jay in the centre of a circle back at school, everyone looking at him as though he was a God. Jay and his light.

Leah starts rolling a beer towel into a fat sausage. Nathan wipes his hands even though they're not remotely wet. There's a weird silence until the phone goes dark again.

'How's that tea then?' he says. 'Don't lie, you can't taste the difference.' He smiles at her, raises his eyebrows, daring her to laugh. She does and Nathan looks pleased.

'How's Raph?' He always asks about her brother.

'He's back at work. I saw him this morning. Hopefully he won't fuck it up.'

'I have faith.'

'Yeah. Well. Fingers crossed this time. He's not drinking. At the moment.'

'You seen Jay?'

'Yeah', Leah says. 'Why wouldn't I have?' Her voice is shrill and she can hear it.

'Oh. So are you two back together then?' Nathan says.

'Kind of,' Leah says. 'I mean, we never really ended it. Officially.'

'Kind of?'

'We're trying this thing.'

'Oh. Right.'

It started a few months ago. One afternoon, sat at his kitchen table chatting, he started pushing. He'd do this a lot. Wind her up. Sit opposite her, regarding her as though she were a toy, considering how far to go, how far was far enough for him to have fun while still knowing she'd come back. She never tested him in this way, was too afraid of what might happen, that he'd just walk away. But he never feared the consequences.

This idea was new, though. He thought it would be fun, he said, to stop using the label of boyfriend and girlfriend when they refer to each other and to open up their relationship to other people. He spent a great deal of time explaining the virtues of a relationship that was unattached and non-possessive, in his words.

Initially she resisted. He posed an ultimatum.

'You're making things really difficult for me, Leah,' he said. 'I need this. If we're going to carry on being in each other's lives. Which I want. Don't you? Then maybe in the future we can see. A couple years of this, just to try it.'

It had felt as though she had no choice. He dismissed her worries so easily. He was so confident, convinced of his own logic, of the reality he was creating. In his presence, she felt herself shrinking, wondering how he could be so sure. He used her doubts as proof that she was being unreasonable, like there was something wrong with her that she couldn't get on board with it. He made it seem normal, modern and innovative, so much so that she found it hard to hold on to what she actually thought, what her instincts were. Any response different from what he wanted felt impossible, shut down and belittled. As soon as she started to form a response, to tether herself to how she felt, he started up again. It was disorientating. She felt mad.

'I'm just being honest about how I feel,' he said. 'Am I not allowed to do that?'

There was no point in resisting him or trying to change his mind. Jay did what he wanted, always. She either had to leave him completely, walk out of the kitchen, or stay with him on his terms, have him unattached and unaccountable. The former seemed too unbearable. So she agreed. She didn't know how to say no. And to keep pride intact, she began the business of convincing herself it was a good idea, that he was right, though she felt tiny and juvenile, a spare part in his life.

After she had conceded, she wanted very badly for him to not look at her face. She looked down at the kitchen table and he laughed.

'See, I know you, Le,' he said. 'You want things to be simple, right? Labels and that. We're together, there's no one else, we're gunna get married. Can you really do this? The casual thing?' he said.

Leah felt her face flush, reluctant to reveal the truth. She wanted to cry but that would show him she was affected. She knew he wanted her cool, calm, up for it, so she tried to perform that.

'Yeah,' she said instead. 'That's not what I'm saying. It's cool.'

It hurt her physically, somewhere around her ribs, that he was asking this of her without knowing how much pain it would cause. Or perhaps he did know and just didn't care. Part of her wished he would just walk out of her life and never come back so that the choice was taken out of her hands. But he gave her the choice. And she chose him. Love, she told herself, was never straightforward. It was something you had to fight for. It was huge. Jay was just the type of man who needed to be pursued. He still loved her, surely.

He softened, reached over the table and stroked the underside of her wrist. A gesture so tender it made her catch her breath.

Really, Leah is waiting for his love to go back to what it was when they first got together, hoping he will come back to her. He was obsessed with her once, endlessly attentive and affectionate, almost aggressive with his desire. He had come out of nowhere and claimed her as his own and she was dizzy with it, swept up and compliant. She doesn't even really remember what part she played in their getting together, or even deciding to be his girlfriend.

Sometimes she is able to tell herself she doesn't love him anymore. She knows he's childish in the way he is so self-centred. He never offers guests a cup of tea, a habit she finds deplorable. He can't do more than one thing at once or work a washing machine properly. He talks over her a lot and doesn't take an interest in the things she likes. When she's talking about something she's read, a film she's watched, he gets irritated or distracted and changes the subject to talk about himself. It should be unattractive to her that he wants to sleep around but somehow it is not. Somehow all it serves to do is to make her feel dull and paint him as exciting and adventurous and attractive to other women. She knows he's not convinced that she is happy in their situation, but he still carries on with it, which, if she thinks about it for too long, strikes her as plain cruel. But none of this logic matters to Leah anymore. She can't think of a way to untangle herself from him. He's all she's ever known. It's hard to imagine someone else loving her. Sometimes she wonders if it is him she wants or what he represents: that she is, or once was, someone worthy of love, someone he chose.

'Look, it might be good for us,' he said. 'It's just sex, Le, not love. It's because I love you that I want this anyway. Prove we're not jealous. Prove this isn't about possession. You can't own other people, you know.'

'I know that,' Leah said.

'We've been together since we were kids, Le. We've come this far. I just think we should try giving each other some space. I've been so good to you. I think I deserve this. Think what we're limiting ourselves to with all this conventional thinking, if it's just me and you and no one else. Aren't we missing out on all that potential?' He leaned closer. 'It's natural to want to see other people. It's instinctive. We shouldn't repress that. You want me to be happy, right?'

'Of course,' she said. 'Of course I do.'

Since she and Jay cooled things off, she sees him less. He has set the rules and she tries to follow them. He doesn't call her as much, doesn't reply to messages or make plans with her. Sometimes he won't show up to things they've planned with Nathan and Matthew, like he's proving he's keeping things casual. It makes her feel needy, always wanting more and having to distract herself constantly. He finds it unattractive when she expresses an interest to see him, so she has to wait until he contacts her or operate delicately so he won't sense the need in her. She doesn't want to ask after him, in case it gets back to him and she appears affected. She gets the feeling that he puts obstacles between them and when she scales them, when she calls him or knocks on his door, he turns his back, annoyed that she overcame them. Sometimes she tries to play the game too and ignores his calls, but it doesn't work in the same way. She hears through the whispers of Brighton that he is seeing other people. He no longer introduces her as his girlfriend, but his 'best friend', which she can tell he likes and thinks is interesting, pioneering somehow, but it just makes her feel humiliated, like a trivial secret. He tells her she should see other people too but she doesn't want to. The thought of being naked with a stranger frightens her. His reaction when she tells him this makes her feel as though there is a fundamental lack in her, like she's no fun, or somehow unenlightened. When she does see him, he teases her. He says unkind things, like he assumes she has built up some sort of resistance to it. He treats her like a kid and it makes her act differently. When she confronts him, tells him she's had enough, he either walks out, unaffected and unscathed, which makes her want him more, or he tells her he loves her, that he can't do without her. He makes her laugh, he feeds her back the memories they share from school, from when they were children. He tells her she is beautiful. It's exhausting.

Sometimes he doesn't call for over a week. And then he does, out of the blue, wanting something, asking to see her urgently. These moments are so surprising they live vividly within her. Like when she was painting her mum's bathroom recently and her phone rang. She was so stunned to see his name pop up on her screen that she almost fell off the stepladder. When she answered, he was sweet, charming, wanting to take her out. He seems to only seek her when he needs to be reassured about something, when he wants to be loved or mothered. It makes Leah feel pedestrian, boring and domestic and homely. This is how it goes on. She either has to beg for his love or take it in spontaneous surges. She can feel it all unravelling out of her control. As long as there is some proximity to him, though, some brief moments of tenderness when they do see each other, she tolerates it, carries on with it all, so that he is still hers in some way.

In the pub, Leah drains the last of her tea, quickly. Some scale from the kettle catches in her throat.

'I need to go really,' she says, 'I only popped in for a hello before work.' She hates that Nathan probably feels sorry for her, that he knows what Jay has been doing and never explicitly mentions it, in order to protect her.

Nathan nods. He's going to let her go but she wants something now, she realises. She wants more from him. She wants something other than Jay spreading himself all through her head. She wants to be powerful.

'You gunna hug me then or what?' she says.

Nathan obliges, comes round to her side of the bar and wraps his long arms around her. Her cheekbone rests against his collarbone, his chin on the thickness of her hair. With their bodies pressed together, she can smell them both, the chemical tang of his deodorant, her skin sweating off sun cream. She can feel her heartbeat through her body and his too.

They hug for a little too long until his body tightens and hers responds, stiffening, charged, something changed between them.

Leah looks up at him, knowing it's a risk, that she is initiating something. He pinches a piece of her hair that's fallen from her bun, lifts it from her damp forehead, each thin grainy strand. She smells something else now, his actual skin, salty, like earth. He kisses her. She opens her mouth and kisses back and it's warm, so much softer than when Jay kisses her. Less teeth, less pushing. The thought of Jay makes Leah pull away from Nathan, but she already knows it's too late. She's kissed him for long enough to show him she wanted it. She backs away and he holds his empty arms up in surrender, palms facing out.

'Oh my God, Nathan,' Leah says, like the only language for this moment is his name. She shakes her head slightly, looks at him, laughs.

'I'm sorry,' Nathan says. The hugeness of it is written all over his face, his eyes brilliant and awake. He smiles then covers his face with his hands.

'Fuck,' he says.

Leah is dizzy, like she's pumped full of air. Now that it happened, she's more horrified than she thought she would be. They know without words that something is spoiled between them.

'It's cool, it's cool, Nath. I'll see you later, OK? Honestly, don't worry,' Leah says, wanting to get out, to make it go away. She smiles to try and reassure him and to get out quicker. She smooths her hair back, realises a curl is tangled in her hoop earring, tugs at it, backing out of the pub, embarrassed. Nathan opens and closes his mouth like he is going to say something. His hands hang limply by his side.

Leah goes.

In the pub, it sounds more silent than it ever has. A big, gaping absence is left on the stool that Leah sat on. Nathan doesn't know what to do. He touches his lips. They feel hot, full of blood. He walks over to where her mug sits on the bar. He places his palms around it. It's still warm. He calms himself by washing it up, and straightening the chairs, a high ringing in his ears.

Soon, the regulars are pickling on their barstools, swilling lager around dentures and trading crass remarks as currency.

'She looked about seventeen, perfect. Tight.'

Two of them swap stories of battering another. Nathan

pictures a bloody-knuckled Jay, after a fight on the seafront, Nathan pulling him away from a hulking mass of entangled men. He shakes out his shoulders and gets on with the shift.

Sunday

Walking to his car after he has left Mickey's, Jay wonders what he looks like from a bird's eye view and walks with purpose as though he's in a film. He does this a lot, widens his strides, takes ample steps, hopes to look imposing. When he reaches his car, he puts the keys in and starts it up so that he can put music on, loud. He grips the steering wheel tight, pushes his shoulders back. The plastic bag of pills shoved into his boxers feels alive, pulsing. He swears he can feel a heat coming off it. He tries Leah again and is annoyed when she doesn't answer. He drives home, tries not to look paranoid, neutral stance, hands planted firm, chin forward, steady speed, convinced a police car is slowing next to him until it accelerates into the distance. He smiles.

When he gets home, he goes straight to his room and doesn't say hello to his mum. Though he's twenty-three, his room is still the same as it was when he was a kid: sky-blue walls, glow-in-the-dark stars scattered across the ceiling, a dog-eared Star Wars poster. His bed is a cheap single with a metal frame, covered in faded stickers. Endless glasses filled with undrunk water are dotted around and a few dumbbells rest on the carpet in front of a full-length mirror. Jay reaches under his bed and finds an old shoebox with a pair of fluorescent football boots in it. It's been so long since he's seen them that they seem like dead animals, lifeless and dull, disturbed, their brightness faded. On the toe of the left boot is a spot of something rusty-brownish, blood, he thinks, from a time he got a knee to the face and his dad got so wound up he pushed the referee in the chest. Jay notices his arms and hands are shaking a bit and his head is tight like he's had too much coffee.

He looks up to his chest of drawers, to the photo frame with a picture of his father, 'World's Best Dad' in plastic bubble letters on the top. From the angle where Jay stands, he can see it is covered in a thin layer of dust.

In the photo Jerry's huge belly swims over his belt buckle. His shirt gapes between buttons, little open mouths revealing a less white T-shirt below. His nose, red from drinking, bounces the flash of the camera right back. A hefty arm is loafed around Jay's young shoulder and Jerry's eyes are syrupy. His other hand isn't visible in the photo, but Jay knows it was clutching a drink. Ten-year-old Jay holds a toy gun in his hand and points it straight at the camera with one eye squeezed shut. Jay hears his father's laugh in his head, the type of laugh that used to scare the pigeons away from the balcony. He tries Leah again. No answer.

Jay gets up and stares at his reflection in the mirror. He looks like a man. He can't remember when this happened, like it happened overnight, his body took over and grew. He has filled into his bones. His face no longer has any puppy fat. He wears his fair hair short, a number two or three, like his dad told him to. He has a thick neck, big hands. His skin is slightly red in that blond man type of way, rough, less fresh and oil-filled than it used to be. He has lines around his eyes now, even though he is young, and forehead lines too, like his skin is made of something easily creased. He moves his face from side to side. He runs his hands over his head. He says his own name into the mirror.

Sunday

Matthew leaves his room. His grandad is waiting by the door in his cord suit. A handkerchief is folded in his top pocket. There is an umbrella under his arm even though the sky is clear. Matthew feels grotesque in his shorts and vest. He is always so aware of his own body.

Ron seems younger somehow. He seems nervous, more agitated than earlier that morning.

'Is that what you're wearing?' Ron says.

'Yes.'

'God knows what you look like. People won't take you seriously looking like that, son.'

As Matthew gets closer to him, he smells cigarettes and toothpaste.

'People will look,' Ron says.

'It's hot.'

Ron moistens his lips as though to say something, but he doesn't. He holds the door open for Matthew and the two of them step outside.

They walk away from the block, Ron using his umbrella as a walking stick, taking old-fashioned strides; Matthew tall with his hunched shoulders and black hair, his purple vest showing an alarming flash of rib, towering over his grandad like a willow.

Matthew observes the small beads of sweat on his grandad's nose, a gentle dusting of white dandruff on each shoulder. The sunlight stings his back. Heat rises from the pavement. The colours of the town look decadent. Dirty smears of paint make up expansive murals dashed across walls. Matthew and Ron walk in silence along the sea, the smell of salt in the back of their throats. The sun is so bright, Ron's edges seem to blur when Matthew looks sideways at him.

They reach Queens Park, which looks out over the town and its dips and peaks, its cluttered rows of houses, the viaduct, the hills beyond. The sea glints behind it all, undulating and self-aware, almost too beautiful, a scene from something fictional. The town is smeared with summer, like a gauze has been draped over it all.

It is still morning and the park is near empty except for a lady in a fleece and gardening gloves tending to the borders. As Matthew and Ron walk past her, they greet each other with a small nod. In the air there is the sound of insects, a lawnmower, fathers playing with their sons in the gardens beyond. Ron heads towards a bench and Matthew follows.

Ron sits down with a slow lowering motion. Their silence is beginning to burn but Matthew doesn't know what to say. Everything seems futile or wrong. So they sit, they watch the town. A hot, pleasant breeze strokes them both.

'I spoke to your dad on the phone,' Ron says.

'Oh yeah?'

'You need to make sure you keep in touch with him. He

loves you lots, he's just not good at showing it. He's found his happiness out there. But he cares for you.'

'He never seems that fussed.'

'Well some people find it harder to show how they feel. It hurts his feelings when you don't call.'

Matthew makes a noncommittal noise with his throat.

'Life can be harder for some people,' Ron says. He's staring straight ahead like he's talking to himself.

Matthew notices Ron's eyes are becoming wet and full, milky like misty water. He places a hand on Ron's shoulder and considers how long to keep it there. It feels a very intimate gesture. Ron clears his throat and Matthew pulls his hand away.

'It's hard to find people to really talk to, Matthew. You're lucky with Leah. I'm fond of her. You can say anything to her.'

Ron has always liked Leah. He made a fuss of her when she was a child, gave her the odd pound coin as a treat for showing him her favourite books.

'Yeah, she's great.' Matthew wishes he was better at talking and could respond in a more interesting way.

'You know the biggest myth of all?' Ron says gently. 'Life's too short. People say it all the time. It's not short; it's damn long. Especially if you don't have someone to talk to. And it makes you tired. You should keep Leah close, Matthew. I've been wanting to tell you that.' He pauses. 'I've been wanting to tell you a lot of things.' He exhales slowly through his nose. One of his hands holds the other tightly in his lap. His voice holds Matthew still.

'It can make you tired,' Ron says, 'in a way I don't have

the words for, when you can't show people who you really are.'

Matthew senses the subliminal hovering over his grandad's words, something difficult, burning.

'God knows it's hard to say certain things out loud. People can be cruel. More than cruel, they'll kill you. So some people just can't,' Ron says. The light washes his face and make his eyes light grey. He turns to look at Matthew.

'It's different now. I hope. Isn't it? It'll be different for you. Hard, still. Definitely hard. I hope it's not too late for you. I hope it hasn't messed you up,' he says. 'Change is slow. I don't know, Math. People learn how to hate themselves. But I hope to God it changes for you.' Ron considers what to say next. A bird sings in the silence as though it's racing to fill the gaps.

'I think it's too late for me. Growing up, if I wanted to talk about it? Forget it. Well, things were off limits, couldn't talk about most things, least of all this. No way. Secret. Forget secret, illegal. It's not acceptable, as much as people say, to be seen as a weak man, Matthew. I've seen men strung up. I've seen men beaten in the street like sick dogs.'

He carries on, speaking fast like someone has turned a tap on, ran away and left it. His hands are still clasped in his lap.

'At school we were always bruised in one way or another. The things that went on there. Normal, apparently. Beating each other black and blue. Always on the lookout for the weakest. And then the teachers, my God. They had a hand in the game too. But I got on with it. Didn't say anything. Never. Squashed it down. Stamped on it. Drank too much probably, all my life, most people do, kept quiet about what I felt up here.' Ron taps the side of his temple.

'You're a good lad, Matthew. You should be able to live how you want to live in this world. You should be happy. Don't let anyone tell you that you can't,' Ron says.

He talks until it seems he has emptied himself. His body looks tired, slumped. Matthew wants to be able to comfort him, respond with a perfect sentence. Instead, he studies the network of hair-thin veins on the side of his grandad's nose. He seems frail, quivering in the sun.

'I hope you'll take the boxing back up, Matt. You were quick. It's all about being quick. It's not actually about the punch,' Ron says. 'And God knows, a boy like you, you need to be able to run.'

Matthew boxed as a child. His grandad wanted him to learn how to defend himself. He'd been coming home with nasty bruises and lighter burns. They drove to the gym each Wednesday night, silent drives during which Ron listened to Five Live, his big hands on the steering wheel in the ten and two o'clock position.

'Defending yourself is just part of life. It's not the same as violence,' Ron said during the first drive to the gym.

Inside, Ron wrapped up his hands, ready for the gloves, a stampede of fear in Matthew's throat. Punches echoed from outside the changing rooms. Men shouted numbers, feet connected with the sprung floor. The building was cavernous; a high ceiling; metal beams covered in chipped paint, all shades of blue; brownish bloodstains on the floor of the boxing ring and dusty punch bags hanging like carcasses in an abattoir.

The men in the gym frightened Matthew. He feared men

in general, their roughness, what they were capable of. He hated the violence that came naturally to the boys at school, how it was so quickly activated in them, and passed down from their fathers and their grandads like their faces had been. When Leah and Jay got together and Matthew had to watch Jay fighting on the seafront on Friday nights, it turned his tongue to soap.

It wasn't until he met Caleb that he started to enjoy boxing. Caleb trained him, showed him he could be good, that he was light on his feet, that other boys found it hard to hit him, that his slim, tall frame was his advantage. He'd tire them out, leaping around the ring, ducking and weaving until he could jab a punch and catch them off guard. He never liked the feeling of his fist making contact, how the impact shot through the bones in his wrist and arm and made a sound that thudded through the sweat-dense air, but he learnt to tolerate it as long as Caleb was there afterwards to talk to in the changing rooms. Caleb never ran out of questions for Matthew, and Matthew never tired of answering them.

Ron turns to Matthew, waiting for an answer.

'Boxing. Yeah. Maybe,' Matthew lies. Ron smiles a knowing smile then looks down at his hands clasped in his lap, whitening with the grip.

'Look, I want you to have these,' he says, pulling off his two big gold rings.

'My fingers are getting swollen. Arthritis. They told me not to crack my knuckles, who knows if it's a myth but I'm suffering now. They tell you a lot of things you should listen to. Like flossing. That would have saved me a lot of pain.'

Ron slips the rings into Matthew's small palm. Matthew is struck by how soft and pale his hands look compared to his grandad's. Hands that have worked for fifty years. Hands that have held a son and a grandson's head. Hands that are covered in little scars and nicks, one nail half missing from an accident when fixing a car. Hands that can mend and give handshakes that consume another hand.

'I love your dad, Math, but I'm glad I got you.' At this, Ron's voice falters slightly. He clears his throat and gathers himself up.

'Me too,' Matthew manages, looking down at the rings.

'Give yourself a chance,' Ron says.

They look at each other for a second. Matthew feels he should press him, ask him to explain more, to be explicit, but Ron's face is all tight. He tells himself his grandad is being sentimental, dipping into the blue smog of the past and getting weepy in the way old men are sometimes prone to.

'Are you sure about this?' Matthew says instead, slipping the rings onto his pinkie and index fingers. Years ago, he would sit with his grandad in the pub and choose horses from the paper whose names he liked the sound of, and they'd place a bet. He'd slip off his grandad's rings, his sovereign and his wedding band, and put them on each tiny finger. They'd never fit, now they do, loose still, but managing. He knows this moment is significant and already he wants to preserve it.

Ron looks at Matthew's hands, reaches over and takes them in his.

Matthew experiences his love for his grandad physically then;

he feels something in his throat. He wants to speak, to tell his grandad who he really is, about Caleb, about his fear, but he can't. He has so many questions. There are so many decisions to make, so much yet to confront. He is no closer to the adventures he and Leah imagined for themselves as children. It is as though Matthew can see his life rolling down the hill away from him, towards the ocean. But making the wrong choice fills Matthew with fear. It's like the sensation of standing too near the edge of a cliff, knowing you have the power to jump.

So he and Ron sit. All the unsaid things hang like dead ducks, because it is hard to move when you have lived with fear forever. A plane tracks a puffy vapour trail across the impossible blue sky.

And then, Ron turns to his grandson and kisses him, on both cheeks, clumsily. He grasps Matthew's narrow fingers tighter in his large sun-spotted hands, newly absent of his big scratched wedding band and his sovereign. Matthew looks down at Ron's blue veins like mountains seen from a plane. Then Ron gets up and starts walking away.

And though he doesn't know it now, this is the last time Matthew will see his grandad. This is the last day his grandad can manage. The first hot day of the year, another sign that the world keeps spinning. This moment, the warmth of their two hands touching, the feeling of whiskers against Matthew's cheek, a slight wetness left from the kiss, will forever take on the significance of the last time. It will be the moment Matthew will return to, sometimes full of questions, sometimes guilt, sometimes grateful, sometimes resolute with a clarity and peace that time allows. Matthew doesn't know this now, but it doesn't matter. All that matters is the way they sat with old and newish hands clasped together as though each were praying for a different world, as though they already knew about the days to come.

Sunday

Several times, walking towards town, towards the photography shop where he works, Matthew looks down at his hands with their new rings. They feel very far away from his face and not familiar enough to identify them as his own.

He walks along London Road, past St Peter's Church and down towards the sea, turning left to avoid the promenade and instead walking past pink neon bars on the other side of the road. He always makes sure to avoid the seafront. He finds that every time he's near the rusted turquoise railings, he falls knee-deep into a memory of strange men's cars, driving away from light into a darkness so total, then their wide hands on the back of his head pushing him down.

Instead, Matthew looks at Audio, thinks how sad and ordinary nightclubs are without bodies breathing life into them. He can see himself and Leah there years ago, with their questionable fake IDs, the burn of cheap vodka in their chests. He remembers them tumbling down the stairs, the low ceiling dripping with sweat, an occasional weak splutter of dry ice and bright, thin beams of light. The music was loud, and limbs were everywhere, arms whacking torsos, people falling into each other shrieking and laughing and slopping their pints over each other, singing the words to the songs into each other's faces. Matthew's only pair of decent trainers, light-blue suede Adidas, got ruined that night, splattered with fruit cider, sticking to the floor, but he didn't care. Everyone looked free. No one seemed to feel like an imposter, the place stunk of confidence and of people who knew how to use their bodies, dancing and kissing each other's cheeks.

A boy with a soft blonde moustache and small eyes kissed Matthew gently on the humming dance floor like it was the most normal thing in the world. Leah pushed Matthew gently on the back, encouraging him, and turned to dance on her own so Matthew could kiss him some more. Walking home, it had occurred to Matthew that this must be happening in some part of the world every minute of the day. The sun was creeping up over the sea and Matthew felt ethereal, gliding back towards the flats. 'Don't mention anything to anyone, will you?' he said to Leah. She took his hand in hers, swung their arms high like they were kids again, watched their block come into view over the hill.

At work, Matthew looks through people's photos. He knows he shouldn't, but he can't help it when the shop is quiet, and he is the only person working. People develop film much less these days. Sometimes he stares at the fan moving from side to side for hours at a time, hoping for someone interesting to come in. Today, he has a few disposable cameras to develop. He likes these best. People tend to take them on holiday. They make him feel connected to places he has never been.

The photographs provide a good distraction. He thumbs through the stacks of prints, takes them out of their cardboard folders, holds on to the edges with the tips of his fingers and inhales the smell of chemicals. He finds comfort in the pink fuzz of an evening sky with palm trees silhouetted against it, a remote-looking hill, some kind of lagoon with children crouched on rocks, the girls with flowers in their hair in front of flags at festivals, people throwing confetti, groups lined up in front of pubs, posing, kicking their legs and arms out at awkward angles, colourful towels spread on beaches with bodies piled on, the criss-cross of bikinis, the postcard-blue of the sky. All of the photographs are smeared with the faint creamy quality of a disposable camera, lens flares making him nostalgic for moments and places he's not been part of.

He would like to believe in fate, but he doesn't. He'd argued with Nathan about it before, a fire on the beach dying, the last tendrils of smoke.

'How can we know?' Matthew said. 'And do you even want to?'

'Come on, Matthew, you're smarter than that. Surely you at least have to concede that you can't *know* for sure what the fuck's going on up there. There surely is some type of higher power. I don't know, an . . . energy at least? I'm just letting it do its thing. Whatever it is,' Nathan said.

'I just don't think I believe in fate or planets or God or whatever, that's all,' Matthew declared.

'I don't know. It's nice to think there's something looking out for us. Something to talk to,' Leah said.

'Exactly,' Nathan said. 'Honestly, I'm telling you, my mum got my astrology birth chart done when I was a kid, I'm a Taurus with a Libra moon, and it's mad how much it predicted my personality.'

'It's all a load of bollocks. I don't know why you lot are even bothering talking about this. You're just trying to make yourself fit with what it already says about you. It's so general. "He'll have a kind heart." Oh, how profound and specific. It's rocks and dead stars and planets, that's it. You're always talking shit together. It's a nause,' Jay said from across the circle. He burped and chucked the end of his cigarette into the jet-black sea.

But in the photo shop this afternoon, with the smell of old carpet and the fan moving the dust around, it becomes hard not to believe in fate. Matthew picks up a stack of photos at random. It is the usual: misty-looking scenes of bodies crammed into parties, inexpertly used flash, thumbs over the lenses. Matthew flicks through each one routinely until something catches his eye. It is him. Unmistakable. Nearly ten years older, face filled out slightly, hair a little longer, the curls hanging lower over his face, but it is him. It's Caleb. Matthew's fingers weaken and he drops the entire stack.

Sunday

In the pub, Nathan slides a soul compilation into the old CD player and fills up a bucket to mop the floor. The pain in the music is so intimate, it becomes bodily like it's existing in his muscles. He mops carefully until he can feel sweat moving down between his shoulder blades beneath his T-shirt.

Nathan's dad always told him he could be a musician, could do anything he wanted, but Nathan never had any desire for that. He just wants to close his eyes and listen, walk with his headphones in. He loves to watch his dad play guitar, he loves how the music twitches in every sinew, every bone, every strand of his hair, how he comes alive with the music, like someone has plugged him in, like he is playing for no one but himself. Fame or success never mattered to Benny. As long as he can play, he's happy.

It's true that Nathan loves Leah. He's loved her since school and never acted. He doesn't know why. Sometimes he thinks perhaps it's apathy, or perhaps because he never knew how to tell her. Sometimes he thinks it was to do with letting Jay have what he wanted, or maybe because he feared he was no match for Jay. Nathan's not had much luck with girls. He always finds himself comparing them to Leah. They aren't as funny, he thinks. He can't talk to them like he can talk to Leah and he loses interest and has to let them down, which he hates.

Girls like Nathan. They are surprised at his nature, how much he listens to them and is intrigued by their interests and lives. They see him as considerate. He remembers the things that are important to them and brings them up in conversations. He is curious, asks questions in a way that doesn't seem tokenistic and shows genuine enthusiasm when they answer. He is communicative and talks about how he is feeling. He doesn't get angry, he doesn't have it in him. People get the sense with Nathan that they could say exactly what they wanted to him, even criticise him, and he would weigh up what they say fairly. Crucially, he would never do anything unkind to anyone.

'We're all about kindness in this house,' his mum says all the time.

Nathan pours the grey water from the mop bucket down the sink and thinks of Leah's baby hairs gathered around her forehead. The fact that they have kissed seems unreal. He's imagined it so many times and the true version is becoming muddled with his daydreams. Already he can't remember who stepped forward first, or who pulled away.

Though he loves Leah, he has reckoned with the fact that nothing will happen between them. It's become part of his life, some concrete truth. To do anything about it would be strange and disruptive. It would mean he would have to make a change, act. The kiss has altered this constancy, though, and he's unsettled by it, unsure of his next move. Each time he slips his phone out of his jeans, clicks the button on the side, he hopes she has messaged, to give him a steer on the situation. He must have checked it a hundred times but there is nothing. He tries to stop himself but he's started doing it automatically, he can feel it hot in his pocket.

Outside the pub, Benny pulls up in his van, music loud. Nathan gets in and Benny gives him a kiss on the cheek. Nathan receives the kiss without saying anything, reaches behind him for his seatbelt.

In the flat, Elena is on the sofa in her green gardening fleece, painting her nails in bright colours. When Benny and Nathan walk in, she opens her arms.

'My boys.'

The flat smells of something good.

'There's something wrong with him. I can tell,' Benny says to his wife.

Nathan knows he is lucky with his family. He sees himself and his parents as a privileged club. He doesn't worry about making plans and keeping busy because he enjoys his time at home. He knows how much Jay loves being there, how he would trade places with him if he could, and it's easy to understand why.

Nathan's is the type of flat where friends can drop by, day and night, and they'll be fed. They'll be asked to stay, made a fuss of. Nathan's parents express a genuine delight when anyone walks through the door. Elena always has food on the stove, huge vats of curry and rice. Whatever day of the week, the family and their guests eat together, open wine always. There is constantly a record playing and interesting conversations are unfolding. There's pudding after every meal and Elena won't hear anything about people watching their weight. Normal rules don't apply in the flat, it is its own little climate. Time doesn't seem to matter, no one checks their phones or the clock, like nothing important is happening outside of the walls. Nathan's friends never know what might happen after they turn up at Benny and Elena's. It could be a dinner party that lasts into the night. They might end up going for a drive in Benny's van; a last-minute gig; once, a midnight swim in the sea, the cool water up to their necks, their faces picked up by the swollen moon.

Nathan's parents treat his friends as though they are their children. 'We could never have any more,' Elena said to Jay, Leah and Matthew when they were teenagers. 'You're my other sons. Le, you're the daughter I couldn't have.' To be accepted by Benny and Elena made everyone feel exceptional. To be part of that family was to be protected and loved at whatever cost. Watching his friends around his table each time, Nathan is proud to share his parents.

'Most of our dads have fucked off,' Matthew said one Sunday night at the dinner table, a ritual they often indulged in, eating bowls of ice cream and drinking beers that Benny kept fetching from a bucket on the balcony. 'That's why we're all mates.'

'Or popped their clogs,' Jay said.

'Jay!' Leah said.

'What? It's true.' He winked at Elena.

'Jay, you're wicked,' Elena said.

'I do my best, El.'

'That's what dads do. They leave,' Leah said.

'Not always. Look at Ben,' Matthew said.

'To Benny,' Jay said, standing up, raising his beer, knocking over his bowl, 'who hasn't abandoned his family or died of a dodgy heart!'

'Shut up, Jay,' Benny said, laughing. 'It's a pretty low bar to meet.'

'To the absent dad club!' Matthew said. He, Leah and Jay clinked the necks of their bottles together.

When Jay comes round, as he has done since he was a child, Nathan enjoys the version Jay becomes. He is relaxed, not having to fill silences with his voice, not telling jokes at the expense of others, but laughing with Benny and his stories, asking questions, pulling the anecdotes along with enthusiastic reactions. Jay's grateful, eats and says thank you, is full of sparkle, washes up clumsily, asks about Elena's work, doesn't centre himself. The heat and the colours of the flat are a balm to him.

Nathan knows Jay is changing, becoming further and further away from this version of himself. He watches how offhandedly he treats Leah, ignoring her phone calls, berating her in front of others like he's trying to break her down into something else entirely. He hates that when she speaks about a book she is reading, an article that she's got up on her phone, Jay tells her she's showing off. Nathan can see she believes him, and feels embarrassed for sharing her thoughts.

Nathan sees Jay less and less, and when they do spend time together, Jay is distracted, waiting for his turn to speak and complain about some grievance he has had, some unfair way he has been treated. Nathan knows Jay is seeing other girls, that Jay knows he's attractive to women, approaches them easily. He sees how it fills Leah with anxiety. Sometimes he tries to speak to Jay about it, to coax him into releasing her, not because he wants her for himself, but because he wants better for her.

But Jay is good at brushing things off. He tells Nathan that Leah knows what she is doing, she has agreed to this. Instead, Nathan focuses his attention on Leah, making her feel special. He tells her all the time. He hopes, and so do Benny and Elena, that with love, with time, Jay will come back to what he was. But more and more, Nathan sees him inching away, the old Jay fading, the new one striding stronger.

Sometimes Nathan looks at his life and experiences guilt. He sees how Jay is always so reluctant to leave, Leah's constant worry for Raph. He wonders why it is that he has what he has, this safety, the sense he can say anything to his parents.

Benny and Elena are a team, one of those rare couples who are genuinely in love, after thirty years of seeing each other every day. Their names roll off people's tongues like they were always meant to be a pair. Elena loves her husband loudly, 'He's the kindest man I know. A godsend,' she says. Benny looks at her with devotion.

Elena often tells Nathan the story of how they met as she cooks for him, Nathan sitting on a high stool in the small galley kitchen, Elena pausing her chopping to add detail, her eyes crinkled from wine, her smile purpled. She has told him the story so many times that over the years it has taken on the sacred glow of a folk-tale, full of asides and embellishments. Nathan can tell she loves speaking about that part of her life and though he has heard it many times and in many different places, he is always quiet, listens and nods and laughs in the right places.

She tells him how they first crossed paths in the late eighties, how she was a painter back then, driving a knackered VW Beetle that almost touched the floor when she had a car full of passengers. She'd painted each panel a different colour in the wrong type of paint and it'd become patchy from the rain.

She met Benny at a friend of a friend's house on Portobello Road, sitting on a sagging sofa in a council flat. Candles burned in jam jars and wax melted into lids of tins. Speed was the drug of choice for Elena's friends and when her eyes first met Benny's, a group of them were in full foamy-mouthed flow about Thatcher and the need to organise. Elena found amphetamines tedious, preferring instead the subtle high of a good red wine. She grew tired of the conversation, instead focusing her attention on Benny, the most handsome man at the party. He was wearing a leather jacket, cracked at the shoulders and elbows, chasms of nonchalance, and when he turned around she saw he'd painted his name in gold letters on the back.

Nathan has a Polaroid of the two of them wedged into the frame of his bedroom mirror. He's sentimental about it, protective. There is something undeniably romantic about the faded photograph, how it looks like such a relic nowadays, in the age of instant and ubiquitous pictures. It seems to be able to capture a whole era in one small frame. They look so defiant, the two of them, sat wrapped around each other like they will never let go, in some dark room, a dark pub with the remnants of a day spent drinking all around them: an overflowing ashtray, brown bottles, sticky surfaces. Elena's long blonde hair touching the table and her heavily kohled eyes peering out through her thick fringe, Benny throwing his head back laughing with his huge hands, palms up facing the air in celebration of a good joke.

Nathan's mum always tells him how Benny intrigued her the moment she walked into the room, like it was fate that she walked into that flat with the blown speakers and the air velvety from drink and damp bodies. She tells Nathan how she walked up to him quietly like he was an old friend. 'I just knew', she says, 'that this man was who I wanted to tackle it all with.'

The rest happened like sudden rain. They became inseparable, best friends. They travelled, slept in the backs of vans and in friends' studios, Benny playing on small tours, Elena working as a teaching assistant and painting in her spare time. They settled in Brighton. It was never in their plans to have a baby, but Elena tells Nathan how when they found out, they crumbled into each other, each feeling a tug of something they never knew existed, something cosmic and beautiful and terrifying. 'We couldn't wait to love you. Half me, half him,' Elena says. They married at the town hall with a couple they'd met in a café as their witnesses, shared cava and chips on the windy beach afterwards.

Nathan thinks how different his parents' twenties seemed from his. His mum talks of the time with a blissful look in her eyes, her stories ringed with a kind of light, like an old film. There seemed to be more freedom, an impermanence, more room for spontaneity, travel. Relationships seemed more absorbing. His parents seemed to linger more on landlines and dissolve into the walls of pubs, conversations seemed to dig out souls like dirt from fingernails.

Nathan once asked his mum what people did back then, with no mobile phones.

'We just stuck to plans, honey. Meet me in the Morgan Arms at 5 p.m. sort of thing, and you'd just expect them to be there. Can you believe it? Of course, your dad is hopeless at being on time. I can't tell you the number of arguments I've had with that man standing in some shithole phone box that smells of piss, telling him to hurry up.'

'And what about money?' Nathan asked her.

'You didn't need much back then. They looked after people. Dad just made music and played it. I did what I needed to do to get by. You didn't need much to live on. We worked odd jobs to make ends meet and some of us were on the dole; it was a different time.'

Nathan's childhood was full of music, painting with his mum, and living room dens that remained for weeks. She'd wake him up at 3 a.m. to look at the stars. His parents gave him freedom which he never exploited. They respected him. They filled him with compassion for others, gratitude, the value of listening. They were the first he turned to for advice and they figured things out together, the three of them, they shared the burdens of everyday life. In this way they made it work.

It wasn't perfect, growing up. Kids who grew up on the estate were used to the thump of bailiffs at the door, followed by the hurried scurrying of final notices being shoved through letterboxes. Nathan was no different. There were times with no electric, beans on toast every night at the end of the month. Nathan was accustomed to the lines of worry deep on his parent's faces, Benny picking up as much session work as he could, more students, running music clubs at the community centre until it was knocked down for expensive seaside flats, how Elena would crouch over the kitchen table with a roll-up in her mouth moving coins around in piles, adding up sums on the bottoms of bills with red capital letters, the way she could make a vegetable stew last seven days, until it had become so disintegrated, you couldn't tell what it had been.

But people looked out for each other in the flats when things got hard. They took care of each other's children when parents had to work and chucked in extra fish fingers for hungry mouths. They shared food and lent each other money. When Nathan was short on lunch money for school, it wasn't his wealthier friends who stepped in, it was Jay, it was Leah and Matthew.

Nathan has worked since he was fourteen: a paper round, a glass collector at the pub until he was old enough to serve and then eventually become a manager. Elena has worked every job under the sun. She's been a hairdresser, a mini-cab driver, a nanny, a dinner lady at their school. She'd spent some years as an assistant to a flamboyant artist way into his eighties. The job mainly consisted of smoking cigarettes with him and drinking dry martinis at 11 a.m. in his shabby Kemptown studio. At sixteen, Jay and Nathan worked for a catering company that provided luxury dining experiences for Brighton's elite in various marquees and halls, or at the golf club. During an excruciating shift, a sad-looking flamingo was paraded around on a leash for entertainment. Occasionally its handler would wet it with a flick of water from a child's paddling pool kept in the back room where the waiters and bar staff crammed leftover canapés into their faces before heading out to pour more champagne. All the staff were students or actors or writers, waiting for their break, saving for the future. Nathan and Jay didn't want to act or sing or write. They were just glad to help out with the rent.

Nathan's parents have always tried hard to show him that though they don't have money, what they do have is worth more. No matter what, no matter how little money, how little space, Benny and Elena have always had room in their flat for anyone, for Jay when he needed feeding or a safe place, for Leah when Raph was stomping around drunk, for Jenny after Leah's dad had left again.

One night years ago, Matthew knocked round in hot tears. Nathan was at work, but Matthew told Benny and Elena something had happened at the boxing gym. They sat with him and talked it through, made him feel their equal, gave him a fingerful of dark rum.

'You know our door is always open, Math,' they said. When Nathan got home, he and Matthew slept top to toe.

Nathan and Matthew made for good friends. They liked how easy they were in each other's company; conversations felt like a fair exchange. Nathan felt for Matthew, for the way he seemed so hard on himself. It was like he could see the true Matthew, fighting to get free, the way he hesitated before he said anything, backtracked after making a point, afraid of his voice. Nathan tried hard to bring him out of himself. He tried to make him see his virtues, his talents, how he was good at making the world look beautiful through his camera, how he could talk about music and films and art and politics articulately, how he was such good fun on a night out, daft and silly when he let himself go, how when you were with him, it felt like it was the two of you against the world. Nathan would sometimes ask him if he was seeing anyone, a kindness, to try and reassure Matthew. Matthew would shake his head. 'Nothing really,' he'd say. But sometimes, when they'd talk late on a booze-heavy night, walking home from the pub, Matthew would tell Nathan he was lonely and Nathan would say, 'Me too.'

Sitting on the sofa, plate balanced on his knee, Nathan tells his parents about the kiss.

'It was weird. She kissed me. Or I kissed her. I don't know.'

'Maybe you kissed each other,' Benny says.

'Long time coming,' Elena says. 'You're special to each other. Still, it's not a good idea, honey. Leah needs to find her way.'

'Mum's right,' Benny says.

'Say nothing,' Elena says. 'You're still young. Let Leah figure things out.'

'I can't stop thinking about her.'

'I know, Nath. Hey. This may seem huge,' Benny says, 'but it will pass.'

On the balcony, smoking a cigarette after dinner, Nathan surveys their flats and the roads around them, thinking how average it all is but how wonderfully familiar, how comforting. The estate has streaked itself through him, like dirty fingers through Blu Tack. He clocks the ice cream van that sells weed parked up at the corner of the road by the swings with their chains all twisted over the bars, soft pastel chalk drawings on the concrete visible in the half-light, hopscotch and a smiling face. A boy walks past carrying a stack of pizza boxes with a huge spliff in his fist, smoke twisting into the night, a white dog with a heavy-looking collar panting at his feet. Nathan doesn't even notice the seagulls anymore, how they clatter and scream and swoop.

In the evening light, everything is soft and blurred, and dusk is slung over the estate, lavish and gorgeous. Nothing is broken by the edges of anything else. It could be very early morning; it could be a dream. The light makes everything feathery like this. Elena calls it the magic hour. Even the black plastic bin bags of rubbish look as though they have been carefully placed by the side of the road. This is a film set, a time of day suspended like a fly trapped in amber, a time washed in pink and blueish light, where breath can be steady, where Nathan is calm.

He hears people talking about getting out, but it doesn't compel him in any way. His role in the world is already satisfying to him. He enjoys his day-to-day and he is good at it. He doesn't want to prove he is beyond this place. He enjoys waking up to the sea, how it's always there, the fact he can see it from his flat. He enjoys every morning's walk to work, savours the rare weekends he has off. He likes running, sleeping in, record-shopping with Benny in the Laines, conversations with his friends. He's never wanted to be exceptional. He's not fussed if he's the funniest, the loudest.

But the kiss with Leah is still sitting fat on his tongue, nagging at him in a way he is not used to. It has shaken his certainty. He looks over to Leah's flat. Her bedroom light is on.

Sunday

Jay mounts his weight on top of Leah, presses on her ribs, his head buried in the pillow. She moans in a habitual way, keeps her eyes open and surveys the ceiling. There is a damp patch growing. She looks for patterns within its shape. It's been there for years. Smears of grey and mottled black. She makes the little whimpering sounds that Jay likes and hooks her legs around his back, crossing them at the ankle. His hip bones jut into her, it starts to hurt.

Seven years of sleeping together has made these moments practised transactions, so familiar they are second nature. Leah doesn't know anything else. Jay thrusts a few times at a steady tempo. Leah stops her performance after a while, getting the sense he isn't listening. After he finishes, Jay groans and rolls off Leah. He gets straight up off the bed, walks to her desk, reels off a stream of toilet paper and throws it at her.

'Thanks,' she says.

Jay stretches, still naked, and looks down at Leah like he's considering whether to get back into bed. She can't believe how he can stand there naked like that, exposed in the bedroom light, without wanting to cover up. She still finds him so attractive, the golden colour of him, the slight bump of muscles under his belly skin, his thick neck. He is so sturdy. The street lamps outside pour through the half-open blinds and make stripes on Jay's young skin. Sirens howl like they've just realised someone they love is leaving them. Jay leans down towards her, as though he might kiss her but instead, he pinches a roll of her tummy fat between his thumb and index finger.

'My little chubster,' he says.

'I've got to go, Le,' Jay says. He's looking around the room for his clothes. He spots his T-shirt and hooks it with his foot, throws it up and catches it. He makes a little celebration noise as though he's just scored a goal. Leah doesn't smile. She can tell he's messing about to try and minimise the fact that he's leaving. A rooted throb of panic begins its dull announcement. She notices he still has his socks on.

'What?' Jay says, noticing her looking at him. Leah hesitates.

'Are you not staying over?'

'Oh not this again,' Jay says. He puts his T-shirt on. He looks ridiculous in just a top and socks, cock softening, wet at the tip.

'I've barely seen you for weeks,' Leah says, pulling the duvet over her body.

'So what does it matter if I can't stay over? All we'd be doing is sleeping,' Jay says. He's got his back to her now, looking for his trackies.

'I just like having you here in the mornings, that's all.'

'Why?' Leah can feel him losing respect for her, the more she asks him to stay.

'I don't know why.'

'Exactly.' Jay pulls his trousers on, triumphant. His logic always squashes any sentimentality she shows. She looks away.

'Are you upset with me now?'

'No,' Leah says. She hates him for thinking he is always right, his ability to ignore her feelings. She thinks of Nathan pulling her close to him earlier. For a moment, she wonders if it has any currency here.

'I just think you could—' she tries.

He interrupts her, 'Ah, Le. What? What more? You're always needing things. We've talked about this. Relax. It's unattractive.'

Jay leans over and kisses Leah on the cheek. Sometimes, she feels so misunderstood by him that she feels completely insane. Still, she softens slightly at his kiss.

'Fine,' she says. Then she adds, 'I'm sorry.'

She swallows the humiliating arrival of tears, blinks them away rapidly.

She knows it's a bad move to cry in front of Jay. It doesn't work. It makes him angry. He considers it manipulative. It shows him she is badly affected by him, which makes him distant.

She knows there is no point in arguing either. He gets very loud and then he leaves, and he won't call for days if she leaves a bad taste in his mouth. Jay is incapable of compromise. It is impossible to get any more out of him than he is willing to give. He's good at arguing. She suspects he enjoys it, holding his ground until she is exhausted. He thinks it makes him more intelligent than her but really, he is just more indifferent to her than she is to him. Leah learned young a woman's capacity for keeping her feelings to herself.

He carries on getting dressed. He leaves a pile of copper coins on her desk, an empty crisp packet, three scrunched up receipts, the condom, alien-looking and translucent heaped on top of itself, some filter tips.

Her skin is hot and damp and her heart is beating quickly. She considers how else to try and get him to stay. She always wants him more than ever the moment before he leaves because she knows she will be deprived of him now, for as long as it takes him to come back. After he goes, she is always drained, hopeless and exhausted. She hates him when he leaves her there, naked in bed. Jay, the roamer, always something more interesting to do. Her, chained to the flat, feeble and needy of such things as love. Moments before he had been charming, generous, even loving. She'd had her hands on his wide, greedy back and it had felt as though he had wanted her so much, her body had felt small underneath his, she had briefly forgotten the days they had gone without speaking.

She wonders how it is possible to feel lonely even as he stands right there in the room, while she still smells of him, while she lays in a wet patch on her single bed. She wants the after times, the times beyond the fucking. She wants to lay on his chest, waste hours in bed. But Jay is restless, hates lying around, always on the move, wriggling out of her hands. He always has to be doing something, kick-ups, on a mission somewhere, up, twitching, talking, the nucleus that everyone revolves around. Even during the brief moments he lets her lay her head on his chest, it's like it's too heavy there, a big inconvenient lump, arbitrarily tolerated. In sleep, he looks like he is running from something, his eyes flickering behind their closed lids and his hands fidgeting on his chest. When their bodies are next to each other in bed, the gap between them is freezing cold.

Leah thinks about how they haven't kissed at all that night. Just fucked hurriedly, with his eyes closed. He throws his hoody over his head.

'I'll call you in a couple hours, yeah?'

He won't, she thinks, invaded, abandoned but still always hopeful that this time it will be different.

He darts out of her room.

'Bye Jenny,' he shouts to Leah's mum. And then he is gone, slamming Leah's front door – he never considers the volume of things – and running down the balcony with such force Leah hears the echoes long after.

There are photos of Jay and Leah on the wall taken years ago in the photo booth in the shopping centre. Their faces are a bit fatter, Leah's eyebrows badly shaped, both wearing fake Burberry scarves, Leah's baby pink and Jay's blue. There are love letters and hastily scribbled folded notes from Jay in a wooden box on Leah's desk, clunky proclamations of love in blotchy biro.

There's a picture of Leah and Jay as toddlers, fat and pale in a paddling pool in the little garden in front of their block. Their mothers with their stiff perms sprawled out on the grass behind them wearing comically large sunglasses. The women who always told Leah she and Jay were destined for each other.

Jay was popular at school, the first one of the boys to get a footballer-style bleach-tipped mohawk, always fighting boys from the other schools on the football pitch out back. He could have had his pick of the thin blonde netball girls and probably the rich ones from the private school. But Jay chose Leah and she has always wondered why.

At school, she wanted to be the most desirable girl, liked by the boys. She knew she wasn't. It didn't come as naturally to her. Her clothes weren't new or pristine enough. She expelled too much effort and it was obvious, applying makeup in the toilets between lessons. So, when Jay did choose her, keeping up the act was exhausting. It took all she had. She wanted to be wanted more than she wanted to be herself.

She worked hard to be the perfect girlfriend, curating herself as endlessly sexual and easygoing. She would say that she wasn't like other girls, as though all other girls were unreasonable, irritating, barely tolerated. She was unemotional, she said. She didn't mind him flirting with other women. One night, when all the bars were shut and only the strip clubs with late licences still serving, she bought him a private lap dance because she thought he would think her cool and laid-back. Nathan looked uncomfortable but Jay's other friends gave her pats on the back and said she was the best girlfriend in the world as Jay, beaming, walked off to the back room with a beautiful woman. When she thinks back to it now, she cringes.

Leah remembers the two of them as kids, stomping through the town, loud, like they owned it. And in so many ways it felt like they did. Kissing rough, playfighting and watching people buy the things Jay and Leah could never afford from the picturesque shops in the Laines. They could fill weeks in the summer holidays just sitting on benches, holding hands, heading to different corners of the estate, the swings, bumping into people, knocking round at Nathan's, trying to procure a pack of cigs. She still remembers the first sting of his fingers inside of her, not exactly pleasurable, more like an arbitrary marker of their relationship, the unsettling feeling for days afterwards, then recounting the story in the toilets at school the next day, trading lip gloss and eye shadow palettes with ridiculous names. Before Jay there was only ever Mark the Carpet, Raph's carpet-fitter friend who called her 'jailbait', pushed her against the wall in her bathroom and kissed her sloppily, the hardness of his crotch pressed against her thigh.

Being with Jay once made Leah feel distinct, selected. There was a time when it was impossible to feel bored in his company. She felt like she shone, forgot how alienated she often felt among the theatrics of teenage girls, her friends accusing her of padding her bra, the fact they never knew where she really lived, how some of them went skiing and to stables and had fathers who picked them up from school in shiny cars. None of her friends at school knew about Raph, the way he was, how he drank. Jay did. He told her it didn't matter. He told her it was amazing how she coped. Leah forgot about everything at home. The shame she felt was blasted away.

But now his attention is never on her in the same way it used to be. He lacks the spontaneity he once had. They don't go on adventures in his car anymore. She doesn't get the same sense that anything is possible with him. She doesn't feel desirable, formidable or independent like she used to. He finds it tedious when she talks about her life, about Raph and her worries, like she's attention seeking, so she plays it down, not wanting to seem hysterical or damaged. He says he loves her still but to Leah it feels like he is saying it out of some habit, some duty. The further they get from how it used to be, the more Leah doubts it can ever go back, like it's too spoiled. But she keeps going, hoping it will. He brings out a sort of wildness in her in the sense that she would do anything to keep him, at her own expense.

Leah tries to remember the last time she properly held him, and thinks about the day his dad died, how a hush blew around their school, tinged everything blue, how the headteacher sweated in assembly, letting the students know, and how their winter coats rustled like they were not teenagers but a sea of dead leaves. After school that day, Matthew, Nathan and Leah walked home together and knocked on Jay's door. They bought him a bottle of cider and poured some out onto the concrete floor outside his flat like they'd seen done on the telly. Jay let Leah hold him properly that night, he lay his head in her lap until the sun went down and the grass in the park got cold, until the sky was a smoky smudge. Jay never said a word. No one got anything out of Jay on the matter of his father.

After Jay leaves, Leah props herself up in bed, looking at her small room. Still pink and childlike, her old doll's impossibly long plastic legs visible through a transparent storage box in the corner. She used to spend hours alone acting out stories with them, always, without fail, about love, rubbing their smooth crotches against each other.

She surveys her naked body, looks at the way her breasts loll about like big sacks of water, drooping towards her armpits, not perky and sitting on her chest. She looks at the stretch marks like shining tributaries running down the insides of her thighs, the result of a sudden growth spurt in her early teens. She feels too big, too much, blundering in her attempts to be attractive. When she looks at her body, she sees it as fleshy and plump, too mottled and pale, engaged in a constant battle against fat, skin, unwanted hair, blemishes where she's shaved her legs, fat where she doesn't want there to be. The goal of making her body tight and tanned and smooth and desirable seems so far out of reach. For as long as she can remember, she has wanted to be thinner, to have the type of stomach that could be proudly displayed in summer, to have the kind of body hair that could barely be detected, to have the kind of skin that didn't turn red and angry in the sun. She often has the urge to grab great fistfuls of her flesh and throw them away, unzip herself and step out.

To be thin was to be good. She has learnt this. She'd watched her mum doing sit-ups on her carpet every morning, chewing chocolate biscuits for the taste then spitting them into the bin. Leah wants to be so thin, waif-like, easily lifted, flat-chested, androgynous. She wants to be cute, small, miniature. She wonders about the bodies of the girls Jay is seeing.

She cringes, feeling hot, restless, can't locate the source of the feeling, thinks she should have gone on top more with Jay just now, rather than just lying there. Maybe she should have said more, taken charge, been sexy. But she finds it so hard, knowing how much he seems bored of her body. Being naked with him feels like an ordeal, a test.

She picks up her phone instinctively, checks for notifications, for something exciting, but there are just invitations to events she'll never go to and adverts for things she can't afford, clothes worn by beautiful models. She scrolls for a while. All around her there seem to be better women, confident, intelligent, well-travelled, less bored, engaged in a worthy project. She chucks her phone face-down on the bed, walks into the kitchen. Her mum is cutting out coupons from the paper with the radio on low, the familiar theme tune of the Archers.

'What was that all about? Slamming et cetera?' Jenny says. Her face is kind, her eyes bright blue, with little red veins on her cheeks. She doesn't look up from the coupons she is stacking into a tin. Leah sits down opposite her, picks up a roast potato from the bowl of leftovers then puts it back down.

'Nothing, Mum.'

Leah stares straight ahead, her arms on the kitchen table a fortress between her and her mum. She looks at the wicker basket in the shape of a chicken on top of the fridge, full of eggs.

'Why do you do that Mum?'

'What, love?'

'The fucking chicken, Mum. Why don't you just keep them in the box like normal people?'

'Language, now,' Jenny says. 'What's wrong love?'

'It's nothing. It's just Jay. He's been weird lately.'

'Oh.'

'It's like he never wants to see me, he's always got something else on.' Leah hears herself simplifying it.

'I'm sure it's just a phase. Men can get like that,' Jenny says. 'Busy busy, always something to do.'

'Yeah. Maybe. I guess I just feel less like a priority now. Like what's the point?'

'You're good for him,' Jenny says. 'He's lucky to have you, you know. That's the point.'

'Hmm.'

'He's been through a lot, Jay.'

'I know, Mum. It kind of feels like you're taking his side over mine a bit.'

'It's not about sides, Leah,' Jenny says, pressing the lid onto the tin. 'It's a rough patch. It'll get better. He needs you.'

'Yeah,' Leah says, reassuring herself. It's true; Jay calls her his home. He says she knows him better than anyone else in the world. She can't work out whether this is true, and whether being someone's home is wonderful or mundane.

Watching her mum, Leah wonders how on earth this woman could have ever loved a man.

'Mum, do you still love Dad?'

Jenny blows out of her mouth. 'Only the memory of him now, love.'

Jenny leaves to record something on the TV. She gives Leah a kiss on the forehead on the way out, her lips warm. Leah wishes there was a word that could sum up everything she is feeling, transmit it to her mother so she could understand her.

She can't imagine getting up in the morning without knowing Jay is in her life in some capacity, for him to become just a memory. She watches the scene in her flat from outside her body. Two women living in the wake of absent men. Men as heroes. Men as ambitious. Men as dreamers, capable of striding out into the world to do whatever they like. Leah and her mum waiting for them to come back. The slam of the front door still rings in her ears.

And then the tears come. The tears come so fast they hurt Leah's face and make it sting. The tears come so fast she clutches the countertop and crouches down right on the curling lino. The tears come so rapidly, she can't see a thing.

Sunday

The days are so much longer. Matthew notices as he walks home from his shift the tide pulled back, the bumpy sand exposed. He looks down at the rings on his fingers, heavy on his hands. He's felt their presence all day. He keeps working away at them with his thumb, twisting them around. He can still feel his grandad's kiss against his cheek hours later.

He weaves through the town, past a preacher wearing a sandwich board outside a gay bar who tells him cheerfully, 'Hell fire is waiting!' People are on the street, spilling all over the place, claiming little corners and kerbs to sit on and chat in the warm evening air. They drink from six-packs and plastic pint glasses, wringing out the rest of the weekend. The sound of chatter fills the whole road like hundreds of birds beating their wings. Matthew listens to the things people say to one another, anecdotes carefully spun and listened to, girls giving each other advice on what to text back to unavailable men. He floats on the surface of the conversations of others for a while.

Matthew sits on a bench, the sun on his face. There's the smell of donuts cooking, house music from a beach bar. Joyful dogs leap for sticks. The constant sound of water, feet on pebbles, everything totally golden. The sun is low and nothing casts a shadow, like the rules of the world don't exist for a second. Matthew gets his phone out, thinking again of Caleb. He types his name into the search bar on Facebook as he has done periodically over the years. He's never sent a friend request. He pulls up Caleb's profile, careful not to like anything. There's a picture of Caleb, arm around a friend in front of a pub. The caption reads, 'Look who's back in town. Sundays at our new local.'

Matthew recognises the pub, purple-fronted with lots of flowers outside and a big garden; it's in Kemptown. He clicks on the picture, zooms in on Caleb's face and stares at it for a long time. He thinks of the caption, then of the photo he found at work; he knows that Caleb is back in town and wonders how long for, anxious to miss him, worried about seeing him. Looking at Caleb's face, knowing how near he is, Matthew experiences a surge of longing, a keen adolescent giddiness with something brutal hovering beneath it. He is taken back to the boxing gym and the smell of the punchbags, he is yanked back to the nights he and Caleb sat in the changing rooms.

Caleb moved around the gym, Matthew remembers, unaffected by people around him, unlike the other boys who always needed to be the loudest, to have the best endurance, to embarrass their friends. If Caleb didn't want to talk to the other boys or the trainers at the gym, he wouldn't, and he wasn't anxious about how that would affect their opinion of him. It wasn't arrogance. He was oblivious. He didn't seem to care what he looked like, what people thought of him. The way he entered rooms reflected this, entirely on his terms. Though he wasn't liked much, he would smile at everyone regardless, would call people out without fear, would act on his principles. He would correct people. Matthew was struck by this, seeing as he found it hard to even correct the hairdresser when they got his name wrong. Matthew admired it so much in Caleb. He wanted to be around him all the time. He was such a nervous person, low-level flutters always in his gut. But when he was with Caleb, it was like he could absorb some confidence, everything else was insignificant, the world was comprised of just the two of them. Time moved quickly and easily.

The sun is still strong on Matthew's back, sitting on the bench. He closes his eyes for a moment. Before he's really thought it out, he's walking up the seafront, turning off at Sussex Square, past the huge houses with the curved fronts and big windows and railings, and then he's in Kemptown, on the narrow roads weaving through the happy Sunday people.

Matthew buys two cold beers from a corner shop and sits on the steps outside a large house, watching people walk down-hill towards the sea. He drinks one and then the other. The sun starts dipping behind the buildings and the heat recedes slightly. He's overcome with a feeling of foolishness then, drunk now and alone in a part of town where he knows no one. From his step he can see the purple-fronted pub. His head feels light, but he crosses the road, narrowly missing a moped. He walks into the pub, orders a rum and coke, looks around. Inside the pub it is dark and empty. He walks out back. The garden is full, bodies crammed on benches and plenty of people standing. Matthew hovers by the back wall, sipping his drink which is too sweet.

He sees Caleb then, sitting on a bench with three other men, laughing. His stomach contracts. The thought of approaching is too much, so he changes places in the garden, walks nearer to the entrance, hoping Caleb will see him. He feels unwieldly and stupid, like he'll be found out somehow, he looks for something to lean against.

Caleb gets up eventually, says something to his friends which makes them laugh, untangles his legs from the picnic bench, turns and sees Matthew. A tingling starts in his legs.

'Oh my God,' Caleb says. He approaches Matthew, who is leaning against a large barrel.

'Matthew?' Caleb smiles. Matthew thinks it seems genuine.

'Caleb? Shit.' He tries to sound shocked, straightens up. Caleb is taller than he remembers and less perfect. His face and neck is a bit rounder and he has grown a short beard.

'Oh my God, it is you!' Caleb pulls Matthew into an embrace. Matthew smells the deep spice of expensive cologne, the sting of soap and laundry powder. His cleanliness makes him somehow more attractive.

'How long's it been? Since, well . . . you know.' Caleb is playful, confident like Matthew remembers, smiles a smile which seems to indicate their past, manoeuvres himself into a position of intimacy.

'Six . . . no, like eight years?!' Matthew assembles his face into a face trying to recall something. They are both a bit breathless now. Their smiles are too large and it makes them both start to laugh. For a while they stand wide-eyed, surveying each other, quietly laughing and shaking their heads.

'God. Do you want to have a drink?' Matthew asks. 'Have you got some time?' He gestures to his own near-empty glass.

Caleb hesitates slightly.

'You don't have to. Just thought I'd offer. I don't make a habit of it, you know, drinking alone. I just, well, it was a nice evening and I fancied it.'

Caleb laughs. Matthew continues.

'Not that I'm always drinking, I don't do it all the time, you know, I just . . .'

He lets the hand that is gesturing to the empty drink fall at his side.

'Mate,' Matthew winces slightly at the platonic term, 'it's fine, I've already had a couple myself.'

Matthew marvels at his coolness, how he doesn't seem flustered.

'I should get back to my friends really. I've not caught up with them properly yet, only been back a few days.' He points to the group of men who are assembled on the bench. The men look over. Matthew feels himself going red.

'Join us, if you want?' The thought of introducing himself to all these men makes Matthew weak with nerves.

'It's OK. I've got to get off soon.'

'OK. I can stop and chat for a bit before you do. I'm desperate for a piss though. Wait there. I'll do that and then I'll grab my beer.'

Matthew nods. He waits for Caleb to return, fidgeting with his hands.

'I'm back.' Caleb waves his hands out at the side like an old-school entertainer. It's a bit geeky and Matthew laughs. A small slither of bench has become available and Caleb nods at it, a gesture for them to sit down. They do, shoulders touching.

'How've you been then? I haven't seen you since . . . thingy,' Matthew says.

'Yeah. We moved. To London for a bit. Well, I say London, it was Croydon really.'

'Yeah, not the same,' Matthew laughs.

'I know. I remember my dad telling me we were going to London and me having this image of townhouses and Big Ben and the river and all that and then we turned up to this pebble-dash bungalow.'

'The glamour.' Matthew notices their ankles touching but doesn't move his foot, hopes that Caleb won't either. The feeling of being in such proximity to Caleb is like a current running through him. He's reminded of his old desire to be totally in Caleb's orbit. Being near him again, he can feel a glow beginning inside of him.

'Are you still in the same place?' Caleb says.

'Yeah, yeah, still in the flat. With Grandad.'

'Oh that's right, how's he doing?'

'Same old same old.' The mention of Ron makes him uneasy.

'Your dad still away?'

'You remember.'

Caleb makes a face as though it's no big deal.

'He is, yeah.'

'Ah, shit. That must be tough.'

'Honestly, it's not.'

'Well that's all right then, mate.'

Matthew wishes he would stop calling him mate. He wonders why Caleb isn't as nervous as he is and if this is significant, if their encounter means less to him. Matthew can't think straight, can't really listen, always preparing the next thing to say or ask to keep the conversation going, scrabbling around for questions that will keep Caleb rooted to the spot. He's overcome with an unfamiliar urge to rub his face against him, to be as near to him as possible. He pictures scenarios of the two of them together beyond that moment, Caleb in bed in the morning, Caleb walking with Matthew by the sea, Caleb turning towards Matthew from some bar and asking him if he wants the usual. Matthew has never wanted to be close to someone so much. I want to make him laugh, he thinks, then can't think of a single way to do it.

'So what do you do now?'

'I work at a camera shop. A printing shop. In the Laines. I fix cameras, develop film for people. Artists and amateur stuff too. But I take photos as well. Never sold one or anything like that though,' he adds, wanting to make this clear.

'I hear you,' Caleb says. 'I do a bit of that myself. Did you do the whole uni thing?'

'Yeah. I mean no, I didn't. Sorry. Don't know why I said yeah.' His words won't come out easily.

Caleb is talking, Matthew notices he's not been listening. He catches the tail end of the sentence.

'And that's basically how I got into it. It ended up being quite fortunate living in London, for the design stuff.'

'Design. That's amazing.'

'Sounds cooler than it is. It's a lot of corporate stuff. Shit logos for companies with questionable ethics, if I'm really honest with you.'

Caleb crosses his leg, lifting his foot so it is no longer skin on skin with Matthew's. Matthew's heart drops a bit.

'I travelled for a bit, South East Asia, all that, but have been working pretty solidly,' Caleb says.

The notion of this seems so far away from Matthew's life, he hopes Caleb doesn't ask him if he ever travelled.

'So that's why you never came back. To the gym?' Matthew says. 'London, uni, travelling, the dream.' He hopes Caleb understands the humour in this, and worries it has come off as scathing.

'Well, partly the move to London. And life, yeah,' Caleb finishes his pint. 'But my dad wouldn't let me back in the gym after what happened with me and you.'

A jolt of shame pulls Matthew's navel.

'I joined a gym in Croydon but I gave up after a while.'

The light fuzz of drink seeps from the centre of Matthew's forehead and spreads around his body.

'I wondered why you didn't say goodbye,' he says, quietly.

'I figured you'd assume,' Caleb says, turning to Matthew.

Matthew can see the sweat collecting by Caleb's hairline, little beads. They look briefly into each other's eyes. Matthew still thinks about the way Caleb's hands felt when they linked with his when they were kids, exploring each other's bodies at the gym. How his hands felt thin and incomplete in the grip of Caleb's, how Caleb's hands were fuller, heavier.

He had always known, really, that he'd played some part in Caleb leaving. All his life he had felt his whole body singing with guilt, but none such as when Caleb's father found them.

They used to kiss after practice when there was no one else in the changing rooms, while waiting for Caleb's dad to collect them. It started with how Caleb would hold him in the aftermath of a punch, Matthew's body slumped between Caleb's arms in the ring, recovering. The first time he kissed Caleb, it was a release, the hiss of steam escaping from something. It made sense. At first, they didn't know what they were doing, they thought they were just messing around, springing apart at the slightest noise then not speaking for a week. At first, they were all teeth and closed eyes. As time went on, they grew to expect it, drew their bodies close to each other as soon as the last boys had left the gym, and it was just their coach left in the office on the other side of the building, waiting to lock up. They'd kiss slower with mouths open, they would inhale the scent of each other, Caleb's Lynx mixed with the smell of hours of hitting other men, Matthew's cigarette smoke in his hair, the soft fuzz of his upper lip against Caleb's neck. They would talk between kisses, would do more than kiss, reach for the parts of each other no one had ever touched before. Matthew's young body plain and pale, untattooed back then, his narrow ribs, Caleb's body bigger, wider, Matthew overtaken by him. They never talked about what they were doing, the facts of their situation, that they were two boys touching, kissing and holding each other. It was an agreement made without words, just the two of them, existing solely behind the doors of the changing room.

There was only a small window of time for them to lock their bodies together, a blade of light, a freedom, half an hour of waiting for Caleb's dad to come in his car, to regard Matthew suspiciously, say nothing, grind his teeth. The boys learned how to fill those thirty minutes with each other, to feed on enough affection to last them until the next time.

Those times, those snatched, hurried hot minutes, had been some of the best of Matthew's life. To be liked so much by someone like Caleb, to be investigated by his curiosity, to be held, was so profound to Matthew; another boy felt the way he felt.

When Caleb spoke, he was always tender. He was so much

gentler than the other men Matthew knew. A voice in direct opposition with his height, his width, his skill for punching jaws.

'What's your favourite colour?' Caleb said one night when the air in the gym was so cold that their breath bloomed like spirits in front of them, leaning against the lockers, their bodies exposed to the air, sweat cooling, panting slightly in the aftermath of fucking.

Before Matthew could answer, Caleb stopped him.

'No. Don't answer. I can guess.'

The thought that someone knew him enough to guess anything about him was the most grounding moment of Matthew's life. He turned and kissed Caleb on the shoulder, felt the warmth of his skin and the muscle twitch slightly at his touch. He held his lips there, sucked slightly, tasted him. Caleb placed a hand on Matthew's chest and they sat like that for a while, connected again.

His whole life, Matthew had felt like a shadow, like he was barely there, flitting, hovering, somehow partial. Caleb's hands on his body, his kisses, his gentle questions were a claiming of the fact he was physical, he was a creature worthy of desire, worthy of knowing. Caleb made him feel as though he wasn't disappearing day by day. Before Caleb, Matthew had learnt that to be invisible was to be safe. But Caleb saw Matthew in a way he had never been seen before, it made Matthew feel real.

Matthew had always been able to tell that Caleb's dad didn't like him. He made it plain. The car journeys home were tense and the one time he had gone for dinner at Caleb's house, Caleb's dad had been unkind and cold, making jokes about how Matthew was thin and clapping him on the shoulders too hard.

The evening Caleb's dad discovered them, he pulled them apart like they were two fighting dogs. Matthew smacked the back of his head on a metal peg and the moment fractured. Matthew's entire body was lit up with humiliation, his body coiled to protect itself, blood rushing to his face, an explosion in his head. He knew what they were doing was secret and that the worst person to witness it was Caleb's dad. Caleb was gone in seconds, Matthew left with the echo of the door slamming, and the sound of his heart in his ears.

'My dad kicked me out after a year. When I was eighteen. When I came out properly,' Caleb says. 'I mean, he knew. But it wasn't until I told him, officially, that he actually kicked me out. Luckily, I'd got a place at uni and I could get a student loan.'

Matthew wants to say so much, but instead just says, 'Shit.'

'Did you tell your grandad?' Caleb asks with confidence Matthew can only imagine. He makes the question seem matter-of-fact, as if he is just asking what Matthew has eaten for lunch. Matthew says nothing.

Caleb nods an understanding nod.

'Listen, I've got to go, I better get back to this lot.' Matthew feels like someone has just clubbed him around the head with something blunt, he's dazed and drunk now.

'But can I have your number? Maybe let's catch up after. Late dinner or something? This is wild!' Caleb stands up.

Matthew looks up at him, blinking. Caleb is holding out his phone. He enters his number, stunned, trying to stop his hands from shaking, checking to see that he's typed it in correctly. Caleb walks back to his table.

Walking home, Matthew notices he is smiling stupidly. It was over so quickly, he wishes he'd said more, offered up more of himself. He goes over it again in his head to relive it, squeeze some more joy from it. His palm still holds the heat of Caleb's phone. He notices the chill in the air but his skin is hot and sensitive.

When he makes it to his block, the edges of night are just starting to curl around the city. Lights fuzz from behind the curtains of all the flats but when he reaches his, it's dark, the door is double locked. Matthew lets himself in, closes the door behind him lightly.

The flat is empty. The room smells of old jumpers, the stale mustiness of a cluttered space. The living room is full of books, roughly stacked in dark wood cases. There's a small old sofa; Ron's armchair, a mammoth open palm that he always looks so small sitting in; and a coffee table piled with last night's dinner plates and two whisky tumblers, cloudy from finger-prints. On the walls there are Hockney posters, framed cheaply, colourful and bold – Ron's favourite. The clock on the wood-effect mantel ticks faintly. 9 p.m. and Ron isn't home.

Sunday

Jay sits in his car with the engine running, takes a swig of energy drink from a can. It's late and he's up by the racecourse, pulled into a lay-by. A quilt of orange streetlights stretches out below him and beyond that the sea sighs a night-time breath. He's just sold twenty pills to a kid in a Vauxhall Corsa and the cash sits in a sandwich bag in his glove compartment along with some empty crisp packets. He pulls out his phone to send Mickey a message, sees a text from Leah.

Come back later tonight if you're free. No worries if not xx

Jay chucks his phone onto the passenger seat. He can tell she's trying to sound casual, but he can hear the need in her voice.

Most of the time, Leah's devotion is convenient for Jay. When he doesn't want to see her, though, he wishes she was more indifferent. He chips away at her to get her to do what he wants, then is annoyed with her on the occasions when she acts hurt or disappointed, like it's a weakness, or she's deliberately trying to make him feel guilty and do what she wants.

99

He hates that he has any responsibility for her feelings, wants to do whatever he chooses to without consequence. He's not convinced that she is OK with their situation, but he tells himself it's not his fault if she's unhappy, he's told her his conditions and she has agreed to them. It's her choice.

He starts the engine and drives too fast towards home, his block rising up from the darkness.

Jay lets himself into his flat, heads towards the living room, which is dark apart from the white glow of the TV. His mum is curled like a cat on the sofa, her legs tucked underneath her and her cheek resting on the arm. She's still in her nurse's uniform, an empty ready-meal pasta dish on the carpet.

'Hey Mum.'

'Hi love.' She doesn't look up.

She's watching the programme she loves in which a woman with platinum blonde hair visits packed-out theatres in regional towns and speaks to the audiences about messages she receives from the dead.

'Not this shit again Mum.'

'Don't start. I've just done a twelve-hour shift,' Pauline says and chucks a pillow across the room at Jay.

He catches it, gives her the finger, sticks his tongue out between his teeth.

Pauline rolls her eyes. She rests her cheek back against the arm of the sofa.

'How was work today?'

'Fine,' Jay says.

'Make any sales?'

Pauline thinks Jay works at a call centre slightly up the coast, selling insurance plans.

'Some.'

Jay sits down in the armchair opposite his mum. It's still dented by the weight of his father, there's a dark round patch on the fabric where his bald head used to rest and slowly excrete its grease. As a kid, Jay would stick his fingers in the creases collecting at the back of his dad's head, that thin pale grimace dotted with stubble, and would be smacked around the ear afterwards. His father's hands were rough, large, the type of hands that looked like the skin couldn't contain them. His wedding band cut into his ring finger splitting it in two. Jay remembers those huge hands, wrapped around a kebab like a giant holding a body in a carpet, or wide and splayed and held above his mum's face. When this happened, they'd pack a small bag, leave and go to Elena, who took them into the comforting fiasco of her kitchen, fed them. There, Jay found the safety of video games with Nathan, untroubled sleep in Nathan's bed, the easy love of Nathan's family; Benny stood sentry at the window. There was music, noise, food, walls crowded with pictures Nathan's family had painted themselves, the things they had coloured beautiful.

'Your dad's so cool,' Jay said to Nathan in bed one night, looking up at the ceiling. 'I wish he was my dad.'

There is nothing else left in the flat that belongs to Jerry apart from the furniture, which Pauline said would be too expensive to replace. It is quieter without him. Jay and his mum's voices lower to match the faint rumbling of the voices on the telly. Everything is clean and ordered, pristine kitchen counters, the only sign of life visible is a neat white loaf in its blue plastic packaging sat by the toaster. Jay has never seen his mum cry over his dad. He knows they are both relieved but it's too complicated to say it. The two of them move around each other in the flat like colleagues squeezing past each other on a staircase. This is how the years have fallen away.

Jay watches TV without taking any of it in. He looks over at his mum, who's fallen asleep. He gets his phone out. Leah has texted him a question mark because he's not responded. When she does this, he is compelled to keep ignoring her. He reads a message from a girl he's been seeing. She's keen and thinks he's exciting, and it's been keeping him entertained but he's too tired now and locks his phone.

He covers his mum's feet with a blanket and kisses her fresh-smelling hair, walks to his room. A shiver moves through him. On his bed, he falls straight asleep.

Sunday

Matthew sits on the edge of his bed, waiting to hear the scrape of keys against the lock. The air is dead. The fridge hums, low. His phone buzzes against his thigh and makes him jump. It's Caleb.

I'm done with this lot – drink?? CXx

He clenches and unclenches his fists. He waits a while. He walks from room to room as if his grandad might be hiding somewhere or asleep in his bed. He isn't. The flat has the chill homes get when no bodies move around inside for a while. Matthew stands by the front door, looking out of the window, waiting to see Ron. His phone goes again. A single question mark. Then, a few minutes later:

Don't worry if you're busy x

Matthew panics and types something back hastily:

No on my way will be 20. Bench outside the Royal? xx

He looks down at the two kisses and they seem stupid now he's sent them. Before he can change his mind, he leaves the flat, sees a bus in the distance gliding down the hill, knows he can make it if he sprints so he legs it down the stairs. On the bus he can't stop thinking about Ron, worried then irritated. He spends the bus ride looking out the window at people, trying to see if any of them are his grandad. The bus drives too fast and their faces blur into smears.

When he gets off the bus, the scruffy town shimmers with a dreamlike quality. Matthew experiences the surreal sensation that arrives when something unlikely suddenly jumps happily into your lap. He considers his entrance, how he will walk. He decides to keep his head down until the last moment to avoid prolonged eye contact. He glances at himself in car windows and shopfronts, hating the way he looks, lanky and awkward, head too big, shoulders too stooped, wishing he'd worn something nicer. His outfit seems tired and uninteresting. He's convinced his clothes fit all wrong, jeans too short, T-shirt hanging off him, wishes he had a comb in his bag or some deodorant. He feels dirty and hot and uncomfortable, burdened with himself.

His stomach knots anxiously. Twice he reaches for his phone to cancel but the thought of seeing Caleb in the flesh again, of feeling that everything else in the world is peripheral, sucks him into the belly of town.

Caleb is waiting as Matthew arrives, sat on the long wooden benches by the theatre, legs crossed, white T-shirt, sunglasses on his head, hands resting on his knees, observing the people walking past. It's dark now and the streetlights are on, one beam shining down on Caleb, picking him out like he's special.

Matthew approaches him, thinks again how assured Caleb looks, set comfortably in the world, chest open. He's just looking, not at the ground, not hiding behind a phone. He turns and sees Matthew walking towards him, rises and pulls him into an easy hug. He smells of something minty, chewing gum masking ale, and that cologne again.

'Hey,' Caleb says with a smile. He tries to pull his sunglasses off his head but they tangle in his hair.

'Shit,' he says. Matthew hopes Caleb is nervous too.

'So . . .' Caleb says.

'So . . .' For a minute it's awkward, they stand in silence.

'You hungry?' Caleb says. 'I know a really nice place?' He phrases it as a question and seems a bit unsure. Matthew exhales.

'Yeah, wherever, I'm easy,' he says, grateful to be able to reassure Caleb.

Caleb looks slightly relieved.

'Oh good,' he says. 'I came the other night and it's all right.'

They start walking, the town seems busy and it's not easy to avoid bumping into people. For a while they don't talk as they weave through the bodies. Matthew is still a bit sticky, hoping for some cool air.

'Sorry I didn't message you earlier. My mate was chewing my ear off,' Caleb says.

'Oh don't worry. I haven't been waiting by the phone.'

It's meant as a joke, but it comes out wrong. Stiff, cold, prickly.

'Oh. No, I didn't think you would have been. Sorry.'

'No don't be sorry!' Matthew tries to laugh to ease some tension but it sounds painful, a bark. He can't think of any small talk.

They reach the restaurant and join a small queue outside the door. Once they are seated, Matthew looks around. He considers the place a perfect choice, a standard-looking Italian in the Laines that he's never been to. The walls are panelled in light-coloured wood, the floor an uneven stone. Tables of different sizes are crowded in, each with a red tablecloth, a candle in a beer bottle, paper napkins folded into triangles. On the walls there are black and white photos of the rotund owner with various celebrities who have presumably eaten at the restaurant. Caleb points to a picture with David Seaman and they both laugh. Matthew starts to feel relaxed among the noise and the people. The atmosphere is warm and friendly, the lighting low, there is music on and couples chatting and laughing. The whole place seems unpretentious, built entirely on the basic principles of simple times and good food. Matthew and Caleb's table is in a corner, with a pillar obscuring them slightly from the view of the other diners and Matthew feels safe, private.

'It doesn't look much, but the pasta is sensational,' Caleb says, smiling and gesturing around the place. Matthew wonders what sort of a person you have to be to know if pasta is sensational or not. A waiter in a black shirt waves at Caleb like an old friend, which Matthew finds impressive. Another comes over and wipes their table roughly with a cloth, puts some paper menus down in front of them. They order wine and bread. Caleb looks straight into Matthew's eyes for the first time since they met that evening. Matthew fights the urge to look down.

He takes a sip of his wine. An almost instant calm comes over him, seeping through his body like morning mist over a wet lawn. He's careful not to drink too quickly, noticing Caleb hasn't touched his yet.

'I was thinking about you. While I was with my mates just now,' Caleb says after a while, picking off little bits of crust and nibbling them. Now they're sitting still, Matthew notices Caleb seems a little drunk. He's in charge though, directing the mood towards something intimate.

'Really?' Pathetic answer, he thinks.

'Yes, really. Don't you think it's wild? Bumping into each other after all this time.'

Matthew wants to stand on the table and declare it the single most exciting thing that's ever happened to him, but instead he says, 'Yeah. It's nuts.' He keeps his Facebook stalking to himself.

Caleb smiles his massive smile again and holds Matthew's gaze. Matthew worries his lips have gone purple from wine.

'So, tell me about your job?' he says to break the silence. 'D'you enjoy it then?' Asking about work makes him bored of himself but it's the only thing he can think of.

'Yeah.' Caleb takes a sip of his wine, finally. 'I mean, I get to travel a fair bit, but the works pretty dry. Pays well.'

Matthew pictures Caleb in a different country, Copenhagen, maybe. Meetings somewhere exotic. Caleb in a clean shirt with a laptop under his arm, smiling at clients, making people laugh, shaking hands firmly, showing them complicated designs.

Again, he hopes Caleb won't ask him much about his life, where he's been, what he's seen. He doesn't want to have to reveal that the most travel he's done is on budget airlines to Spain every so often to see his mum, where she lives in an apartment block with mostly other English people. Travel beyond that has never been affordable, there was always a reason not to. Matthew's worked since he was in year ten. He and Leah sometimes make lists of places they will go one day but beyond that he doesn't let himself think too much about it.

'How'd you get into it?' Matthew says.

'I was miserable at school. Liked art, had this teacher who thought I was good at drawing, used to go to her at lunch. It was her that got me into the idea of going to uni really, helped me with all the forms and stuff. And it was amazing. When I got there. I actually met people I liked, who liked me. I got into a grad scheme that got me the job I do now. And now I don't have to live with my dad.'

'Cheers to that,' Matthew knocks his glass against Caleb's, feeling like he's made progress in the conversation. Caleb laughs.

'Yeah, school was shit,' Matthew says.

They share a sympathetic look. To Matthew's surprise, Caleb reaches over and gives Matthew's hand a squeeze, then stays holding it. Matthew wonders, not for the first time, if Caleb sees this as a date.

'Do you talk to your dad much?' Caleb says.

'A bit. On the phone,' Matthew says.

The waiter comes over holding their starters and breaks the spell.

'All right, lads!'

Caleb pulls his hand away to make room for the plates and Matthew is glad, he was starting to feel his palm becoming clammy. After the waiter is gone, Caleb reaches beneath the table and strokes Matthew's knee, which seems like such a radical move, he can't believe it.

The food is good and Matthew manages at least some though his mouth is dry. After a bottle of wine, his face is flushed and when he thinks back to his empty flat and his grandad, he seems able to tell himself that Ron is home now, sleeping in front of the TV. Being away from his block makes everything up there feel abstract.

The conversations flow better and Caleb orders a second bottle of wine. They respond quickly, fluidly, to each other's anecdotes about music, films, times they have drunk too much.

Caleb is handsome but he has a sort of goofy, uneven quality that becomes more apparent the more they talk. He uses his hands a lot, he's loud. It's easy to make him laugh, a gulping, deep laugh that he indulges in without covering his mouth, even when he is chewing his food.

After the restaurant and the second bottle, the evening becomes soupy, slow motion. They split the bill and leave, the lights strung between lampposts in the Laines blur and twinkle. Already Matthew knows that when he's trying to retell this, the wonder of it won't translate. He can't believe it is happening to him, that Caleb still wants his company.

They find a bar nearby, walking arm in arm this time, bodies close enough to feel the heat coming off each other. The night unspools, easy now, a clear warm sky, no queuing for the bar that they happen upon, which they both agree is utterly appropriate, the atmosphere ideal, cosy and not too busy. They talk about the characters from the boxing gym, wonder what they are up to now, make up wildly unrealistic stories about them.

'What if Keith was a fag all this time, just like us?' Caleb says.

Just like us, Matthew thinks. Caleb makes it feel like he and Matthew are floating above everyone else, in possession of something protected that others can only gesture at, look upon from the outside.

In the bar, Matthew talks about the photos he takes in his spare time. Caleb asks questions. 'What got you started?'

'I don't know, it just makes me feel good. Being able to tilt the way the world looks. Zoom in on things that are unnoticed. Make people see bits differently. Feels like I'm doing something positive. Something I get.'

They laugh and drink black sambuca, the liquorice lingering on their breath. After a sweet orange cocktail in the low-ceilinged bar, tealight candles in jam jars spluttering out as the hours draw on, Matthew says what he's wanted to say to Caleb for so long.

'I missed you. Which is crazy. We were just kids.'

'Yeah, I missed you too.'

Matthew's heart is beating fast. There is something about the way Caleb holds his gaze that makes him want to take the leap and speak plainly like they used to.

'I'd never missed anyone like that. I missed you so much, I wanted to . . .'

Matthew trails off.

'Go on.'

'I wanted to die. I know that sounds dramatic, but I felt like that for a while.' Matthew folds his cocktail napkin into a neat triangle. 'Sorry, this is morbid.'

'Don't apologise,' Caleb says. He squeezes the place on Matthew's forearm that he's holding. Looking at the hand on his arm, Matthew's shame is drawn out of him, disappears like water on a sun-hot stone. He is defiant, believing Caleb. Why should he care if Caleb is the same, if they are here together?

'I never speak about this. I'm usually a cold fish. That's what Leah calls me.'

Caleb laughs. Matthew feels a shot of pride that Caleb is laughing with him. He is aware, very palpably, that he is letting Caleb in again. He can almost feel himself opening, like there is a door in his chest, exposing his lumpy heart to the wooden table.

'I struggled,' Matthew says, 'with myself. With what I am. I used to not cope very well.'

He thinks about the Railways Lands. Warm strong lagers in the day and cutting crescent moons and names into himself, filling them with ink.

'And what about now?' Caleb asks.

'Sometimes it's hard. Less. Nowadays I just sort of ignore it. I wait until it doesn't hurt anymore. I pretended what happened with us wasn't real. For ages. I had to, to survive.'

'When did you know . . . that you were?' Caleb says. He is still holding Matthew's arm. Matthew has relaxed it slightly and is enjoying the warmth.

'About six, I guess. Yeah, six or seven. You?'

'Yeah, around that time. And you never came out?'

'I guess I haven't really, yeah, A few people know. My best mate. Her boyfriend, but only because she told him. A couple others. My friend Nath. I always found it hard to say it.'

Sitting there, considering this, Matthew remembers in primary school when he and Leah watched a sweet-faced pop star, fresh from talent show victory, give an interview on some modern-looking sofa in a television studio. He came out as the nation watched, uttering the words simply. 'It won't surprise you to hear,' he smiled. Matthew wanted to be sucked right into the television, to sit next to him, to say 'me too'. The next day, the playground was hell, and Matthew kept his feelings about it to himself.

'And how long have you been single?' Caleb asks him.

'Always,' he says and pulls his hand away. He starts to feel himself closing off, embarrassed. The conversations of the drinkers around them become less charming, more braying.

'But you've been with other men, right?' Caleb says, taking a sip of his bright drink. Matthew notices again how fluidly he talks about relationships, the implication of sex, his voice loud, shoulders relaxed. Matthew doesn't want to talk about the times he's bent his body underneath the touch of someone whose face is cast in shadow. He nods, sweeping some wax off the table and into the palm of his hand.

'Never been in love?' Caleb says.

They look at each other, smile at the same time. Matthew unstiffens.

'Not yet.'

They go home together. Matthew is grateful when Caleb suggests the flat where he's staying in the centre of town. Caleb's clothes are folded over the back of a chair. There's some nice leather luggage neatly in the corner, his chrome-coloured laptop charging next to a smart notebook, cologne and an electric razor on the windowsill. An adult's room. Matthew can't imagine a life where he could welcome someone spontaneously into his bedroom.

He checks his phone but the battery has died. He thinks of calling Leah to check if the lights are on in his flat, but Caleb takes his arm and pulls him into his chest. The air condenses around Matthew and they kiss. Matthew closes his eyes, his body rushes, bright colours moving behind his eyelids and any thoughts beyond the four walls that surround him are sent hurtling out of his head.

Monday

The sun rises above the sea and floods each little box with light. Jay stands on his balcony, watching items on the washing line form shadows against his skin. The day is his, his mum left early for a shift. He watches the estate come to life. People jog out of their houses, lock up quick and make a dash for the bus or to their cars, call things behind them like 'I'll do it after work' or 'hurry up' to children who clatter behind them with square lunch boxes and book bags. The old lady who lives on the ground floor stands behind her red metal gate and tells whoever she can that she's worried about the smell of skunk in the corridors and that people have been feeding the gulls. People carry bin bags around the back of the building in their dressing-gown and slippers, a fat toddler plays in a red and yellow plastic car. Everything happens as it normally does, except Ron doesn't walk back from the shop.

The sun makes the tarmac smell. A father lifts his young son onto his shoulders in the basketball court beneath to let him pass the ball through the netless hoop. Jay's dad is in his head again, thundering around up there with other sore memories. Drinking too much at Jay's tenth birthday party while Jay's mother looked pale in the corner. Or on the sidelines of Jay's football matches, screaming himself red, the sound of his fist smacking the ice-packed grass when Jay conceded a goal. Standing at the shoreline, the water racing to his boots, skimming a stone into the horizon, turning around to a young Jay, 'Come on then. Beat that.'

Music leaks from Nathan's house as it always does. The windows are open and Elena is laughing. Jay wants to be near her, to be a little boy again and to be fed a sandwich without a crust and ripe nectarine wrapped in a bit of kitchen roll. He wants to be set up at the kitchen table with scrap paper and felt-tips and told he is good at something, humming his tunes as he concentrates on drawing footballs, big juicy suns, seagulls and the perfect line of blue sky swiped across the top of the page. He wants to be held against her chest while the smoke from her incense curls around her kitchen.

Jay's spent so many hours in that flat, sitting on Elena's fluffy purple rug, cross-legged with Nathan, playing Nintendo, eating lentil soup and heavy homemade bread. Elena would take them swimming after school at the tired Prince Albert pool with its faded colours and wet tiles covered in hairs, bring them home for tea, their skin wrinkled and smelling of chlorine, goggle-marked eyes. He had his own pyjama set in their airing cupboard, the paintings he made at primary school are still behind a magnet on the fridge in a thick wedge.

Elena protected him and Nathan, she stood up for all the children on the estate. When a mother from their primary school had called Jay and Nathan feral on account of where they lived and that they were allowed to walk home from school alone, Elena marched into the playground and told her to mind her own business. The woman held her raincoat around her chest as though Elena could make it dirty by standing two feet away.

Jay and Nathan didn't get invited to birthday parties after that. They didn't mind. They were once invited to tea at a house in Montpelier Gardens, the sort of house that's detached with security cameras, huge windows and ornate lamps, where the parents have a dressing room attached to their bedroom and a fridge that spits out ice at the touch of a button. On the wall along the staircase were large prints of holiday photos, the gleaming blonde family playing with tired-looking monkeys in Sri Lanka. Nathan and Jay were glad to get back to their block where everything was familiar, where they were allowed to touch what they wanted and they didn't feel small.

'Are we allowed to be happy if we live here?' they asked Elena when they got home. She laughed.

'Of course we are, boys,' she replied.

'And why has the school across the road got a climbing wall?' Nathan said.

'Our Jenga has blocks missing. And someone's drawn cocks on them,' Jay added.

'Well. Some people's parents pay for them to go to school, so they can have nicer things,' Elena told them. She crouched down so she was eye to eye with them both.

'Don't you ever apologise for who you are. Or where you came from,' she said.

Jay stared down at his unfashionable shoes, two thick black blocks on his feet with the Velcro barely managing. He surveyed his second-hand school jumper, shiny from too much ironing and chewed around the sleeves. He dreaded the register the next day when his teacher would ask the free school meal kids to put their hands up.

Jay always told himself he'd be rich when he was older, although Elena told him it didn't matter. But he wanted it. He wanted a better car, a better life, the freedom money allowed. He wanted to buy his mum a house and tell her to give up work. He'd not done well in school. He was bright but he couldn't pass tests, got distracted easily despite the nights Elena would sit with him at her kitchen table and try to break it down for him. He could figure things out if he spoke them out loud, but with his eyes on the page, numbers and letters swam, moved and grew new parts, switched places. He didn't know how to say this, got frustrated and lost focus. Teachers always asked him to leave the room. He relied on making people laugh instead, was chalked down as a lost cause, too disruptive. When his dad died, he pretty much stopped showing up.

Nathan emerges from his flat, clocks Jay, pulls on a T-shirt and walks towards Jay's front door. Jay thinks he looks a bit nervous, uneasy in his company.

'You good?' he says to Nathan.

'All good. Yeah.'

'Working?'

'Not today, worked all weekend. What you doing? Not at the call centre?'

Jay leans over the balcony. He thinks for a moment about lying but wants to test, to dip his toe in the water for a reaction.

'I've been selling a bit. For Mickey Hallahan.' He addresses the flats in front of him rather than Nathan, hoping to sound casual.

'For Mickey Hallahan? I thought you were flogging insurance things or whatever?'

Jay shrugs.

'Shite money. Shite hours. Full of cunts.'

'Mickey Hallahan? You're a melt, Jay. He battered that kid not long ago at the Pavilion Tavern for literally nothing. He's a nutter.'

'He's all right.'

'Is he?'

Jay gets aggravated, stops enjoying Nathan's attention. 'Yeah, well this is why I didn't say anything. It sounds more serious than it is. He's got loads of people in Brighton doing it, even kids from the college and that.'

'Right.'

'It's all very simple and easy and I'm not moving enough to get into trouble or anything.'

'If you say so.'

'Don't give me the holier than thou shit, Nath.'

'I'm not,' Nathan says calmly. He pauses. 'I just think it's dumb. And, well, unethical.'

'Oh here we go. High horse. Knew you'd be like this.'

Jay's shoulders bunch around his ears and tense like a bull behind a fence. He kicks at the brick wall with the tip of his plastic slider.

'My mum needs the money, as well.'

Nathan gives him a sympathetic smile.

'If you need money, mate—'

Jay cuts him off.

'I've got money.'

'OK.'

'Don't tell your mum, Nath. She'll go mad at me.'

'You're right about that.' Nathan reaches into his pocket for his tin of tobacco, pinches what he needs between his fingers and then passes it to Jay.

They watch Matthew walking fast up the hill, towards the flats with his head down. He looks up, sees Nathan and Jay and heads for their side of the block. He looks pale and tired.

'What the fuck's up with you then, you miserable twat?' Jay says. He means it to sound affectionate but Matthew looks at him blankly. Though Jay and Matthew have grown up together, Jay doesn't understand him. He can't communicate with him in his usual way, with his jokes and physicality. They have never felt easy in each other's company when left alone.

'I can't find my grandad. He never came home last night.' Matthew tugs at the skin of his throat like it's a scarf.

Some instinct within Jay springs into life, he turns to face Matthew, alert.

'What? Are you sure?'

'He wasn't home last night and when I got home this morning, he'd not been back. Bed not slept in.'

'Well have you gone and looked for him?'

Matthew looks at Jay with contempt. 'Yes. Just now.'

'Shit.' Jay puts his hands on his head to help him breathe a bit better. 'One of his walks?'

'All night?'

'Have you tried calling?' Nathan offers.

'He hasn't got a phone. Never has. Hates them,' Jay says, remembering how many times Ron complained about how intrusive mobiles are.

119

Jay presses his head against the rough brick wall. He exhales. 'This isn't right. What are you going to do?'

'I don't know. I actually don't know.' Matthew looks panicked.

'Call the police?' Nathan suggests.

'No, that's dumb,' Jay responds, leaning over the balcony, looking.

'Is it?' Nathan shrugs.

'Isn't that a bit premature?' Matthew says. 'I don't want to overreact.'

'Yeah but, this is fucking weird.'

Jay looks over to Matthew's empty flat.

Monday

Before the police arrive with the news that evening, everyone is sitting in Elena's living room. Jay stands by the window with his back to the room, Matthew is hunched on the arm of the sofa, Benny on the floor, Nathan and Elena share the small sofa, legs touching.

After the boys had driven around town checking the places where Ron might be, the betting shop, his favourite park, the pub he liked best, the only place they wanted to be was with Benny and Elena. Benny put his arms around Matthew and Jay, poured them a little glass of rum without asking. Then the sun started to dip. They called the police and waited, everyone quiet and still.

Matthew hates how close they all are together. He wants space. People keep looking at him. The windows are sweating, the flat humid.

'Can you turn the fucking music off, I can't think straight.' Jay is irritable now, a hulking mass illuminated around the edges by the light coming through the window. The door goes. Three gentle knocks.

'That'll be Leah.' Matthew gets up to answer.

He opens the door. She reaches up and puts her arms around him.

'I left work as soon as they'd let me,' she says. 'Math, it's going to be OK.'

Matthew nods, not taking any of it in. Everything seems to have accelerated too quickly. They bend through the chaos of the hallway, boxes of odd shoes, too many shelves on the walls stacked with books.

When Leah gets into the living room, Jay doesn't look away from the window or acknowledge she's there. Nathan looks straight at her. They've not spoken since the kiss and he's done nothing but think of her. She walks to Jay, who's got his back to the room, and puts a hand on him. He jumps slightly, looks down at her.

'Oh. Hey.'

'You all right?'

'Fine.' He goes back to looking out the window. He manages to give the impression that it is odd that she's arrived, that she is not part of this. Leah feels silly standing near him while he's not talking to her and turns to face the people in the room. Nathan keeps giving her quick little glances, then pretending he's not.

'So when did you last see him, Math?' Leah says to fill the silence. 'Yesterday afternoon?'

'Yeah. At the park.'

'What time, babe?' Elena asks.

'I dunno. Two-ish. I can't remember. Actually, yeah, it must have been earlier because I went to work for two.'

'And what did you do there?' Elena says.

'We just . . . sort of sat.'

Matthew thinks of Ron's hands, his rings.

'Sort of sat?' Jay turns from the window to face Matthew.

'Jay, honey,' Elena warns.

Jay turns back around.

'Yeah, we sat. We talked.'

'What about?' Elena says.

Matthew feels some instinct to protect his grandad.

'Um. The usual stuff.' Everyone watches him, wanting more. 'It was strange,' he says reluctantly.

'Strange how?' Jay talks to the window.

'Did I say strange?' When Matthew talks, his voice sounds very far away. 'I guess he was emotional. He gave me things. His rings.'

Jay looks at Matthew's hands.

'He gave you his rings?' Jay says.

Matthew doesn't answer. The furniture in the room seems to shift all around him.

'Jay, you're not helping,' Leah says. Jay gives her a look, narrowing his eyes.

'What the fuck?' he mouths at her.

'So he just never came back then? Wasn't there when you got back from work? Did you wait up for him?' Leah ignores Jay and looks straight at Matthew.

'I went out. After I got home from work.' Matthew can't look at anyone. He pictures him and Caleb on the floor, the feeling of carpet beneath his knees, Caleb tracing a finger over each of Matthew's tattoos, his skin hardening with goose bumps, Matthew feeling beautiful, fluid, the heat of Caleb's room, the white curtains with the honeyed sunlight sponged over them, Caleb sleeping beside him, the sound of his breathing. The memory splinters and warps in Matthew's head into something ugly.

'You got home and he wasn't there and then you went out again?' Elena pushes.

'I thought he'd be home by the time I got back. By the morning.'

'Where did you go?' Leah asks gently.

'A friend's.'

Jay sighs.

In the silence that follows, the reality of what is happening dawns on Matthew. It's like he's not there, watching from somewhere outside the room. He pinches the skin on his hands to stop himself from feeling faint, presses his shoulders into the wall behind him.

'Do you think he's hurt himself?' Matthew says. 'He wouldn't do that, would he?'

They see the police car arrive through the gauze curtains, and Matthew hopes that they have arrived for someone else in the building, some weed-smoking teenager. He hopes this even as he watches the two officers approach the flat, holding their hats to their chests.

Leah hears Matthew's sharp intake of breath; she sees the moment something rises out of him; some part of him leaves and hovers, ghostly for a moment above them before his knees give way. She holds on to him and lowers him to the ground.

The truth arrives like bones being set; it stops being hypothetical and solidifies. Words are said in temperate voices, things they won't remember the specifics of after. It's very quiet, almost awkward as the police speak. They place Ron's soft brown leather wallet, his brogues and lastly his big square glasses down on the table, a soft sad beat dispatches as the weight of the items lands on the surface.

Matthew sits on the floor, his body light and wasted, like he is vibrating, like his muscles have no strength. He stares at the items, suddenly lifeless. Glasses with no nose to rest on. Shoes with no foot to place inside them. Wallet with no thick finger to reach inside and withdraw a coin for a pint of milk and a paper. He can only listen to the far-off voices of the officers. They say some things about witnesses and next steps. Matthew thanks the police for coming. He tries to get them to leave quicker by offering platitudes. 'At least he's in peace,' he hears himself say, but it means nothing.

Jay slaps the door frame with his open hand and leaves. Nathan stands with his mouth slightly open until his mother pulls him towards her and holds him. Benny walks out after Jay, shouting his name, comes back shrugging. Then the sound of Jay's car driving too fast, away from the block. Matthew can feel something touching his head, realises it's Leah's hands stroking his hair. The police officers' radios crackle and other voices enter the room. He closes his eyes and everything slows down. The sounds around him rounded and distant as though he is underwater.

Tuesday

None of them sleep after the police have left. They stay up until Tuesday's sun rises and brings a glow to the sea. They stay in Nathan's front room, blinking and shaking, a shape of bodies clustered together in the dark. Candles burn and diffuse their sweet scent. Elena makes Matthew drink some warm, sweet milk with cinnamon stirred through it, followed by a huge glass of gin with no ice. People say things and repeat them but to Matthew, they are just sounds.

Leah tries Jay's phone throughout the night. In the morning, she knocks on his front door and no one answers. She tells Matthew he needs some sleep. Under his eyes the skin has gone slightly purple. Leah takes him by the arm and guides him into her flat where her mother is sat peeling an orange at the kitchen table with Raph, the smell of coffee, the radio on low and the light an early-morning grey. When Leah tells her mother, her face crumples, and she shakes her head once. 'No' is all she says. Raph's face twists into a knot. He gets up and takes a beer from the fridge, opens it with his teeth.

'Raph, don't,' Leah says. Jenny purses her lips. Raph leaves the kitchen and his bedroom door slams.

126

Leah puts Matthew to bed, where he sleeps for the whole day, curled like a fossil. She keeps walking in and looking at him, at the comma his body makes under the duvet. When night comes, she makes a bed for herself on the floor and stares up at the ceiling for hours, thinking of Ron.

When she was young, he'd helped her ride her bike properly for the first time. It was winter. She'd fallen off twice and she was scared, hesitant to get back on, gravel imprinting the pads of her hands. Her mum ran alongside her, holding her hands out to catch her if she fell. Ron had been watching from his window and came out onto the tarmac. He had a deep red scarf that he took from his neck and looped around her waist, holding on to the ends like reins. He ran behind her, holding on to the scarf until she wasn't afraid anymore, riding up and down the path in the middle of the block until, without her knowing, he slipped it away and she rode on her own. When she was older, he taught her how to change the inner tube on her tyre and he was so patient, the sleeves of his checked shirt rolled up to his elbows. It was Ron who made the rope swing for the kids on the block, a thick blue knot holding in place a smoothed-off plank of wood, hanging from the large tree on the corner of the estate. Ron knew Leah loved books. He got her into Dylan Thomas with a mildewed volume of poems. He read her the beginning lines, leaning against her kitchen door frame, snapping it shut, winking at her and passing it over. 'You'll want to read the rest.' He gave her cassette tapes of *Under Milk Wood* that she played to get her to sleep at night. Often he'd leave her books on the windowsill outside her flat, a lot of crime novels, war poets, Dickens, and non-fiction which she didn't like as much, but she read them anyway. She liked the challenge of wading through their density. The best he'd given her was a slim volume of Emily Dickinson poems with a rough, red cover.

'You're a star, Leah. I can feel it.'

Imagining the smell of those books, the feeling of the rough wool scarf tight across her belly, of his slightly stained smile, it breaks her.

Wednesday

When Matthew wakes up, he forgets for a moment where he is. Light is coming from behind Leah's blinds. The open window sucks them in and out as though breathing. He can't recognise the shapes in the room. His bones are heavy. He sits up partially, trying to get his bearings. When he remembers it all, he lets his body fall back onto the bed.

That's when the chaos in his head begins, grappling with the logistics of the truth. The fact that Ron is no longer here, the shock of it. That there was once a body, a man walking around inside it and now there is not, feels too abstract a thing to believe. Then there is the question of why, but that feels too huge. And then the guilt. The deep sense that there was something wrong, something that Matthew couldn't solve. There is embarrassment for some reason. There is fear of all the attention this will bring. It makes his body feel as though it is shrivelling up. There is a terror, a dread, a fear of the sinister sadness like a root burrowing down through him. There is sheer fury. There are tiny moments of peace, relief even. And then there is tiredness like Matthew has never known.

He closes his eyes again. The light interrogates him, bores

down on his eyelids and shows him the red-pink colour of his body, makes him feel he should be doing something, should be thinking, not sleeping, finding the words for this, but he can't move; he is too tired. He watches the sun disappear, hours later, changing all the colours in the room.

Thursday

Matthew doesn't know what day it is. It feels like the timeless, liminal days between Christmas and January, pointless, strange and bloated. The days pass like this, a surreal wash. Like oil seeping from the bottom of a car. They merge into one homogenous shape, everything blank, suspended.

No one knows what to do with themselves; they make it all up as they go along. There is heat and sitting and nothing else. It feels obscene to go to work, so Matthew and Leah sit on the sofa in her hot living room. They watch the news each morning; he doesn't get dressed. Grey-faced politicians still trudge into parliament.

Visitors come by with dishes of food covered in cling film. Mothers fuss over Matthew, heat up the food and try to feed him. The guests are a welcome distraction. They provide a kind of temporary structure to the day but everyone clamps what they really want to say right under their tongues. Matthew feels sorry for their obvious discomfort. People keep asking him if he's OK and he just keeps smiling and saying he's coping, wanting to be normal and to reassure them. He can't find any words to say how he's feeling, it's all too expansive, a massive endless sky. He wants to be in the dark, indoors, with the television playing comforting programmes, not to have to think or talk to anyone or explain.

Then life carries on. Leah has to go back to work. Her boss shows little interest in her bereavement. Nathan goes back to the pub but stops by in the mornings with food, candles, bundles of dry sage to burn from Elena.

Matthew sleeps late. Several times in the night, he wakes, his body flings him upright and he grasps at his own breath, uncertain where he is, running his palms along the walls to try and locate himself.

When he dreams, he dreams he is talking to Caleb, who laughs and sneers at him, turns his back when Matthew tries to explain what has happened. He reaches forward to touch Caleb's cheek but Caleb treats him like a stranger. He dreams his grandad walks through the estate as though nothing has happened and it has all been a mistake, a misunderstanding. His face is blue and bloated. He's trying to pull his trousers on. Matthew knows it's his grandad though he doesn't look the same, a changed vision. Matthew feels, very strongly, that he shouldn't be back. He tries to ask his grandad why he is there, what happened but he doesn't make a sound.

He drinks tea. He drinks so much tea, his mouth is constantly coated. The tea gives him tight painful headaches and does the opposite of waking him up; rather, he feels like he is floating. He only eats when his body sends him a physical reminder to eat and even then, all he can manage is an omelette. The eggs take on a strange taste, like grief has shocked his tongue into tasting something else.

The gulls are still relentless. The windows are always open;

132

it's hot and getting hotter. The heat isn't a good backdrop for grieving. Matthew wishes for grey and rain, black umbrellas and miserable people. The heat is so loud. The sounds of the street, tyres and reversing trucks and wind and voices, all pour on top of him. There is no pause, no respite. He still has to piss, his body still sweats, and he takes long hot showers.

Eventually, he takes some walks alone, hovering spectral into town with his skull feeling as though it is made of polystyrene. As he leaves the block, some people raise their hands in greeting, some keep their heads firmly down and ignore him. The block of flats, usually so alive and thriving with bodies and shouting and music, is silent. Death stinks it up. Everyone has got the memo; mourning is in progress. The sea looks sad behind it all.

In town he watches people on the street nipping into shops or meeting friends at cafés like nothing terrible has ever happened. Matthew wonders if he will feel like that again. The kids still smoke under the pier, the starlings still swarm in formation and make patterns in the sky, inexplicably coordinated. The pubs are still full. Matthew watches men, fathers and uncles and sons, drinking too much until they are bawling in the street about football scores and old pain. The town is alive with the sound of subliminal music coming from somewhere. Everywhere people spend money, there is too much traffic. The city is full to the neck with summer tourists spilling out of shorts with sunburnt shoulders, the benches on the seafront groaning with the weight of lager, grim-faced teenagers saving for the summer carrying huge round trays and having their arses pinched. Men walk around with their tops off and their dogs on shoelace leads. The white hippies with dreads and battered guitars litter the grass of the Level like empty crisp packets. The whole place reeks of bins and the sting of the sea.

Matthew wades through the deluge of Facebook messages each day as word spreads. People post generic statuses about mental health awareness and reaching out to others. After three days, the condolences stop. People seem less interested in writing long captions about suicide prevention and kindness. Other people die in the town. A boy from school who Leah remembers used to smear Vaseline on his acne drives his moped around a bend too quickly and hits a tree. Memorial graffiti tributes are daubed onto the sides of buildings and washed off by the council the next day. Crews of red-eyed boys tie trainers together by the laces and throw them over the telephone wires in the Laines.

People will move on soon, Matthew thinks. This will become a story. The details and truth of it all will become some distant little memory, further and further away, like when you're trying to recall a dream to someone, and it keeps slipping and tumbling. That's the thing about memory. It's unruly. Some mornings Matthew wakes up and tests himself on how much he can remember about Ron. He swears it's getting harder.

Matthew has to go to the police station twice. Benny drives him. They sit in a comfortable silence with the radio on. Benny gives Matthew a few heavy affectionate pats on the shoulders that put Matthew at ease without having to talk. Benny always seems to know exactly what to do. It is Benny who offers to make the call to the oil rig and tell Matthew's father. Matthew is weak with gratitude.

The funeral is somehow arranged and all the logistics following a death are considered. Notes and shopping lists and phone calls are made, mostly by Leah. Meanwhile, Matthew is hollow. He nods and says yes to things, hating that the decision lies with him. He wants to be far away from it all.

Leah washes Matthew's boxers and T-shirt in the sink and leaves them to dry outside in the heat each day. She makes him sandwiches and lets him sleep. She feels that everything is too small for this level of sadness. Her bed is too small for him, the tealight candles she burns in the flat throughout the day are meant to be a symbol of respect, but they are too tiny. She wants to transport Matthew into a clean, sparse mansion where he can grieve in luxury. Instead, they sit together among the dust and the sun showing the smears on the windows and the telly and she ticks things off lists. She is good in a crisis. She enjoys how it focuses her. Sometimes she wonders if she almost enjoys a tragedy, the permission to feel and how it pulls her into action.

Raph leaves one morning and doesn't come back at night. Leah knows enough about her brother to know he's on a bender, that he'll come home days later promising not to do it again. She stays up listening for him, hoping he will come home. She listens to Matthew's breathing, wondering where Raph is, staring at the white square of ceiling, waiting for the sound of the door, the heaviness of Raph's boots, the sound of a metal lid scraping the neck of a glass bottle, a card racking up on the countertop, the click of a lighter, the springs of the sofa, the TV on low—his particular cacophony of sounds.

Matthew feels awkward in Leah's house, aware it is not his. He is conscious about how tall he is, another body in the kitchen, another person on the sofa, another dirty plate or cup. He tries to wash up twice and Jenny stops him.

Sometimes he stands outside Leah's flat and watches his own front door. He keeps expecting his grandad to come home. He keeps expecting to hear his snores in the room next door. Sometimes he thinks he sees him in town, on one of his walks, or his profile on a bus driving past.

The truth of his grandad's pain starts to become overwhelming, a constant physical presence in his body, like someone is pulling something sharp through him internally. He can't watch anything on TV about anyone unhappy. He can't listen to the radio station Ron liked. The smell of Drum tobacco kills him.

There is the time they sit eating curry in Elena's living room and Benny plays the Johnny Cash record Ron had liked on the record player. Benny looks over at Matthew's face and pushes the needle off the vinyl.

There is the time Matthew sits next to an older man on the bus and wants to bury his head into his shoulders and shriek.

There is the time he smells Ron's soap on someone and feels as though someone has spun him around until he can't stand straight.

But he carries on.

Caleb calls twice and sends some messages. Some are just question marks. Matthew knows he's probably seen it on Facebook, other people from the estate posting about it, the local paper running a headline, but can't bring himself to tell him first-hand what has happened. He turns his phone off because seeing Caleb again seems impossible.

Monday

Matthew stands, arms goose-pimpled and shivering in the cold air of the expensive supermarket in town, waiting in a queue to hire wine glasses. It has been a week since they found out. Leah is by his side with a red cardboard folder in her arms. She is saying something but he isn't listening. Something about saving money by asking Jenny to make the sandwiches.

'Math? Are you listening? She's going to do them all. Meat and veggie.'

'That's great, Le,' he says, thinking how expensive it is to host a funeral and how this isn't something he has ever considered. At the undertaker's, they had opted for a cardboard coffin to save on costs. Leah had taken charge of that too, made sure they got a nice colour. They reach the front of the queue. Leah begins.

'They're for a funeral.'

'I'm very sorry for your loss.' Matthew is sick of this phrase. It's all people say to him. The man behind the desk speaks quietly like they're discussing something secret. 'Were you wanting red or white? Or flutes?'

'What's the difference?' Leah says.

'Well, reds are typically larger. Taller with more room in the glass. As the wine is generally fuller-bodied.'

Matthew sighs. 'Can we just have like fifty average wine glasses, please? They don't have to be either, I really don't care.'

'They come in crates of twelve, sir. I can do sixty?'

The glasses chime inside their crates as the sales assistant places them down on the counter. His fringe is combed and gelled upwards in an old-fashioned way. His eyes are small behind transition lenses which make the skin around them look grey and make Matthew uneasy.

'Will you be needing champagne flutes in addition?' He writes something on a form on the desk in front of him.

Matthew can't bear to be around anyone. Everyone irritates him. He has a headache.

'No.'

He feels Leah fidgeting beside him.

'Just the wine glasses, please. Matthew, I'll fill this out.' She gestures to the form. 'Just meet me outside.' He recognises her trying to avoid a confrontation, smoothing out the exchange in the way she always resorts to.

Matthew takes the lift up to the exit. Out in the heat of the day he feels exhausted from the effort of being in the world. Everything makes him tired lately. Sleep is the only relief, he just wants to sleep all the time.

Away from the cool dimness of the supermarket, the car park appears strange. Matthew is giddy. People move around him like cartoons. He is struck by how fragile their bodies are, at the mercy of a car coming too quickly around a corner, an undercurrent while swimming, a tumour blossoming undetected. Standing still, he is very aware of the sounds in his stomach, his food digesting.

Years ago at a fairground in a village nearby, Jay convinced him to go on a particular ride. It was a huge wooden barrel with a door in the side. You were told to press your body against the walls and the whole thing started spinning. The force of the spin pinned your body to the wall and then the floor came away. There was no way to stop until it was over. Matthew hated every second, knowing he was trapped. He came out drenched in sweat and threw his guts up on the floor, couldn't walk straight. Jay laughed, bent over, hands on his thighs.

Leah calls his name and Matthew turns around, disorientated. Everything is a shock. He can't shake the sensation that he has been thrown a ball, reached out to catch it, only for the ball to vanish.

'You look thin,' she says, 'and that top is filthy around the collar.'

Matthew plucks at the fabric of his T-shirt.

'I think we need to go back. To your flat. You need some clothes.'

Matthew nods, dreading this. Leah links his arm. She smells of her, of her flat, of laundry and the cheap apple perfume she wears.

Walking up the steps to Matthew's front door, they can see flowers in garish plastic wrapping piled up on the doorstep beginning to rot and curl.

The flat is silent and dark. Leah turns on the light, illuminating the furniture, which looks startled. The light that the lamp casts is anaemic, pale yellow. Everything is just there, as it was days before. There are reminders of the once-living everywhere. The dent of buttocks in the armchair, the smell of Ron which Matthew can't help feeling has faded, smoke and mustiness. Leah tries to open the windows, but Matthew asks her not to. He wants to sit and breathe it all in, he can't stand the thought of the salty wind coming through and cleansing it all out.

There are half-drunk coffees. There is washing in the laundry bin, balled-up socks and several handkerchiefs. There are crosswords half finished, the wastepaper basket is full. There are books partly read with the pages folded at the corners or laid open, face-down. Everywhere are things that suggested to Matthew that there would be a tomorrow.

Matthew picks up a book and reads a few lines from the folded page that is holding the place. He wants to read what Ron had last read. It is something about famous bridges of the world. He notices a tiny little bloodstain on the corner of one of the pages, imagines his grandad reading late into the night and getting stung by a paper cut.

On the doormat is a folded piece of notepaper, ripped at the bottom.

Leah picks it up, unfolds it. She scratches her head roughly and scrunches it in her hand.

'What is it?'

'Don't worry.'

'Leah.' Matthew reaches out his hand.

Leah passes him the paper and he reads:

Sorry for your loss. Would love to talk to you further about your grandad's suicide, get your angle, give me a bell.

There is a name, the name of the local paper and a number written hurriedly at the bottom of the note.

It occurs to Matthew that no one has said the word suicide yet. The sight of it written sends a shooting feeling through the bottom of his feet.

Leah looks down at the note in Matthew's hands.

'Why do they want to talk to me?'

'You know what they're like. The drama. Chuck it.'

Matthew's body's feels wrung out like an old towel. The fact that someone knows who he is and what has happened fills him with dread, as though he is being watched.

His legs feel unattached to his body, he sits down in his grandad's chair and runs his flat hands all over the surface of it, feeling the fabric underneath. The absence is so glaring, so huge now he is in the place Ron used to live, sleep, shit, shave, drink his coffee.

Leah gathers Matthew's things quickly and shoves them in a Tesco bag with a snowman on it.

'I can't believe it,' he says.

Leah stops. She kneels by Matthew's legs on the floor.

'He never said anything. He never said he was going.'

Leah holds on to his legs.

'What would he have said?'

'I don't know. Something. Asked for help.'

'What if he couldn't?'

Matthew finds it hard to focus on anything in the room. His eyes fill and the objects around him swim and swell.

'Yeah, I dunno. I just never even asked to see if he was OK.' Matthew says.

'You did,' Leah says. 'You loved him so much.'

Her head bends towards Matthew, eyes pleading and wet.

'This isn't on you, Matthew. This is so much bigger. It's not your fault. It's not.'

'I miss him so much.'

'I know. Hey. Look at me. I promise you it will get better.'

'Le. You're so wise.' Matthew kisses her on top of her head. Her hair smells a bit dirty with a hint of coconut. 'Why can't you be this nice to yourself?' His lips move against her hair.

'What do you mean?'

'Jay's not been about. Since we found out. It's been a week.'

Leah's stands up and brushes dust from her knees.

'You know what Jay's like. He's not good at this stuff. He sent a message.'

'A message?'

'Yeah. A text.'

'Where is he?'

'Does it matter?' Leah says, too quickly. 'It's fine.'

She turns her back on Matthew and picks up the bag again. Matthew knows she is trying to stop herself from crying.

'Let's go,' he says, rising from the chair, plumes of dust expanding in the air as he does.

On the way to the door, Matthew catches sight of a soft maroon sweater, folded neatly and draped over the back of a wooden chair. He can see Ron wearing it, the wool slightly bobbled on the forearms and under the armpits, how the fabric stretched over Ron's soft paunch, how a moth-hole by the collar had been darned in a cotton slightly the wrong colour.

He picks it up and holds its gentle weight in his hands, rubbing his fingers over its softness, limp and lifeless. He lifts it to his face and buries his nose in it, inhaling deeply. Coffee, cigarettes, sage soap and, very faintly, cologne.

Matthew slips it over his T-shirt, despite the heat. It's a little too short for him.

Tuesday

Leah is walking to work. Her phone goes off in her hand. A text from Jay, devoid of sentiment.

I'm fine. See u soon.

The happy sounds of a seaside morning are all around her. Music plays from a car waiting in traffic. She can smell bread and chip fryers on the strong wind that whips her hair around her face. It is early and the day is still cold and colourless. She has left Matthew sleeping. She watched him earlier, in the pale blue part of morning, watched his eyes moving behind his lids, cheek twitching mid-dream, wished she could kiss his forehead and inhale every bad feeling swilling around inside him.

A voice calls after her.

'Oi.' At first, Leah doesn't realise the 'oi' is for her. Like most women, she has trained herself not to hear them anymore.

'Le.'

It is a voice she has known all her life, her name so familiar sounding.

'Le.'

Leah looks up. Raph is sprawled out on the grass. He's not been home in days, and he is wearing the fact on him, the stubble on his face, sore-looking somehow, like it's attacking his cheeks. The skin around his eyes droops but the pupils inside are huge and roving. Leah stops where she is but doesn't approach. Raph's shirt looks dirty and is unbuttoned right down to his belly. He doesn't seem to feel the cold. A lazy, intoxicated smile plays all over his lips and when he speaks, it's drawling and sluggish.

'What's up, sis? You don't want a drink?'

He holds up a huge blue plastic bottle, its label gone, its contents frothy. She can smell the acid of cheap cider from where she stands. Today, he is feeling like being unkind, she can tell. She has experienced every one of Raph's moods. This is the worst, the least movable.

'It's nine a.m., Raph. I'm on my way to work.'

'Oh it's Little Miss Perfect, is it? Judging me for enjoying a drink.'

Leah looks at Raph's companions. A thin girl with a low, greasy ponytail and a dirty hoody, a tooth missing from the front of her mouth, rolling a meaty-looking joint. Her cheeks are pale and she looks young. A man with fuzzy ginger hair and beard wearing a World of Warcraft hoodie and giant denim flares ripped around his laceless skate shoes. He seems to be unconscious, lying on his back on the grass, a smile of pink belly poking out of the bottom of his jumper.

'Where've you been?' Leah says. 'I've been worried.'

'Chill, Le. When did you become so boring?' Raph looks at his friends and laughs. This is typical of Raph. He is never fazed by genuine concern for his welfare.

'Can you come home tonight, please?' Leah says. She tries not to shout or sound angry. She doesn't want to blow the chances of getting him back to the flat. Bargaining with Raph is a delicate operation. Leah has a variety of tactics she's learnt over the years. Taking him to the pub is usually successful, getting drunk to get him on her side, but this is not the morning for that. This morning she decides to appeal to his human qualities, the role of older brother, the blood bond.

'Please. I miss you.'

Raph leans his head back with his eyes closed, enjoying the dangerous velvety feeling of being wasted in the daytime.

'Yeah, maybe.'

Leah looks at him a little longer, considering whether to say more. He takes a lengthy sip of the cider, his lips clamped around the bottle neck.

'I'll see you at home, yeah? I've got to go to work.'

Raph makes a noncommittal sound from his throat with his mouth full of drink and Leah waves to his friends, who don't notice. She looks at her older brother's blood-bright face, his eyes shut, chin to the sun.

It's true that growing up with Raph was fun. He was unafraid in a way Leah admired. He would steal things for Leah from the shops. Sweets when they were younger and then, when they were older, makeup sets from Boots, CDs from Woolworths, T-shirts. He threw things off the balconies to watch them splinter into a million pieces. He'd set fireworks off the roof of the block, not caring if he burnt his hands, worth it to see the gold against the orange-brown sky over the sea.

He told her all the time that she was beautiful, that she was smart. He had the wildest imagination. When she was a kid, he'd tell her stories that would turn her small dull bedroom into other worlds entirely; rainbows brushed wide overhead, jungles, deep forests and the bottom of oceans.

'Le, we're fish. Come on, let's swim over here and get your pyjamas on! Quick, or the stingray will get you!'

He'd scoop her from the bath and tell her she was a sausage roll, ready for some flour and a pastry case, sprinkle talc on her fat belly and wrap her in a towel.

He took her up to where an abandoned car sat on the hill with its rusty mouth open and they would pretend to drive it. He taught her how to aim and throw, wedged a stick into the pebble beach and made her practise hitting it with a stone. He made up songs, did little voices, impressions of their teachers, he was weird and she loved him for it. He made trips to the launderette fun, pretending to throw her in the huge belly of the drum while she laughed and kicked, throwing her over his shoulder, spinning her around, not caring about the noise they made, how people looked at them.

And then when they were older, he bought fags and drink for her and her friends, let her enjoy the status it afforded her, he took her with him to the pub and bought her scampi, let her have sips of his Guinness, made her laugh with different accents, with his broad and sunny charm. He was a good brother.

But he drank. More and more, the older he got. Leah watched his stomach pumped twice in one year, rode with him in the back of ambulances, holding his hand. He couldn't keep friends, was always fighting. He got into drugs. He changed who he was so often, the things he liked, the clothes he wore, the way he spoke, like he couldn't keep track of himself. He tried a northern accent for a few months once. He'd be in tracksuits one week, a hat with a feather in the side the next. He couldn't hold down a job. He often lost his temper. Raph felt things somewhere deeper within him. Things seemed to cause him more pain. Some days he didn't get out of bed. Some days the same song would thud from his room on repeat for hours.

Jenny couldn't see what was happening to Raph. She was incapable of hearing the truth about her son. Leah paid for some counselling sessions until she'd run out of savings, put him on waiting lists for doctors. She tried to hide his drink. She cleaned up after him when he was sick. She sat on the edge of his bed when he was grey-faced and hungover, trying to cheer him up. When he went missing, she knew the flats where she might find him. For as long as she can remember, thoughts of Raph have always been in her head, wondering where he is, hoping he is safe.

She doesn't know what will happen if she leaves him there, leaves their flat and their life. There are things Leah would like to do, things she always thought she would. She worries sometimes that her life is unravelling like a ball of wool. The years have passed quickly since school and Leah hasn't been anywhere really. She watches other people posting online about their long trips to foreign cities with large rucksacks, swimming in wide rivers in remote places with distinctive-looking trees. It seems totally idealistic, reserved for a different type of person. She reads long statuses about people's work, people she knows from school, the impact they are having, their sharp and fully formed opinions that they feel confident enough to share with the masses. She swings from caring deeply about how deficient her life feels, to telling herself it doesn't really matter, that everyone's life is different, that she can find value here, with Nathan, with Matthew and Jay, that her wants are trivial in the grand scheme of things.

At work, Leah sits behind the reception desk with her shoes off and one leg tucked underneath her. She tries not to think of Raph. The computer hums loudly and happy presenters chat on the radio in between pop music that Leah secretly loves. She reads her book under the desk.

'Tell me what matters,' the man in her book asks his wife. 'Nothing,' she replies. Leah reads the line over and over again.

When the shift ends and she is shutting down her computer, her phone goes off. Nathan. She puts it on the desk, screen side down, ignores it. She cringes at the thought of the kiss. It keeps ringing though. Eventually, he texts.

Leah, you need to come now. It's Raph. xx

Leah's bare feet rub against her trainers as she runs down the hill. She hasn't had any time to put socks back on and she can feel her skin loosening on her big toes with each stride. She makes it to the beach. The sea has spat fat pebbles all over the promenade during a storm. The sky has darkened and is low and furious over the grey ocean. She sees them from far off, Raph and Nathan sat in a wooden fishing boat by the closed-up shrimp hut, Nathan sat upright with his hand on Raph's back. Raph is hunched over with his head between his legs. Leah speeds up. Nathan turns when he hears her approaching. Leah clambers ungracefully into the belly of the boat, tumbling in then gathering her body up beneath her. She crouches in front of Raph. He spits between his dirty feet.

'Raph. Where are your shoes?'

She kisses the top of his head, feels sand against her mouth. His eyes are glassy, roaming, wine-blackened dry lips.

'He came into the pub earlier. In a bad way,' Nathan says. 'I followed him around till he slowed down. Shall we get him home? He's chilled out a bit. Was saying all sorts earlier.'

Nathan is calm as ever, though his eyes are drooping at each edge with tiredness. He is covered in mud and there are scratches on his cheeks.

They shoulder Raph, a side each, and manage to get him out of the boat, his chin flopping on his chest. He's wearing tracksuit bottoms that slip down, doesn't seem to be wearing any boxers underneath. Nathan flags a taxi on West Street as Leah holds on to her brother. Nathan whispers something to the driver, Leah sees him stuff some extra money into his hand and then Nathan helps Leah bundle Raph into the car. The drive is long and bumpy. Leah reaches across her brother's lap for Nathan's hand, which he takes in his warm palm, links his fingers with hers.

At home, the flat is dark. Leah runs a shallow bath and with Nathan's help peels off Raph's clothes and lowers him into it. Nathan and Leah wash Raph in silence, the only sound is the water running down his skin. Raph keeps twitching, startling her, like he's is having a series of electric shocks. Leah watches Raph scratch his scalp, his fingernails filthy, recognises her own hands in his.

The bath gives Raph a little more colour in his cheeks but his face still clings onto a grimace. They get him to his bed where he collapses straight away, wrapped in the towel. Leah covers him with his duvet and puts a pint of water on the bedside table. She pulls the curtains and leaves his door ajar.

The bathroom smells of salt and piss and drink, the metallic smell of cocaine sweat. Nathan pulls the plug and rinses away the ring of black mud, scrubbing at it with his bare hands without protest. He gathers up Raph's filthy clothes. The movement expels a faint waft of tobacco. He puts them in the wash.

After he is done, he exhales and leans against the bathroom door.

'I'm gunna head. Get a shower.'

'You can stay?' He looks like he will say yes. His eyes move over Leah's face.

'It's cool. I'm only round the corner, aren't I.'

'OK.'

Her legs ache. She imagines asking him not to leave, more forceful this time, but it's complicated and humiliating.

'Thanks so much, Nath. I'm really sorry,' she manages. She wants him to take charge, walk forward and kiss her again.

'Anytime, Le.' He turns and leaves.

The door slams. Then the silence of the flat again.

Raph wakes at 1 a.m. Leah is lying on the sofa, half watching a programme in which minor celebrities with impossibly white teeth have to undertake humiliating challenges like eating spaghetti with their hands tied behind their backs. She hears the click of the kettle from the kitchen. Raph is standing with his back to her, turns when she enters, his face grey in the kitchen's bright lights.

'All right?'

'All right.'

There's a silence during which the kettle boils.

'I'll have one if you're making one,' Leah says, cautiously.

Raph doesn't respond but he pulls another mug from the drying rack with a shaking hand.

'How you feeling?'

'I'm fine. Bit tired.'

Leah feels nerves in her belly. A hot feeling up her neck like a fever. It would be easy to ignore last night and just be grateful he's safe. But she pushes on.

'Raph?'

'Please, Le, don't start.' His voice is small.

'I'm just worried about you.'

'I'm fine.'

'OK. But you're clearly not.' Leah reaches out to put a hand on his back. He winces at the touch.

'I'm a grown man, Le.'

'Well yeah. It's all fun and games until you're fucking about like a lunatic in one of those boats with no shoes on though, Raph.' Leah tries a laugh.

Raph smiles weakly.

'I was drunk.'

'I know.'

'I just took it a bit far.'

'A bit far?!' Leah's voice rises. She sees Raph react. Tries to bring it back, like coaxing a nervous dog.

'Why did you get so fucked? You muppet.'

Raph shrugs.

'You won't do it again, will you?'

'Of course not.'

'You say that every time.'

'I know. I mean it this time. I actually do.'

'Are you not happy? At the moment?'

Raph laughs.

'I'm fine, Leah. Honestly. Just all this stuff lately. I needed to blow off some steam. I'm allowed to have a drink.'

'*A* drink?'

Raph doesn't respond.

'It's OK to be struggling. There are things, people that can help.' Leah can hear herself being tepid and general.

'Oh sure.'

'There are. I can help sort something,' Leah says, though it seems like a reach.

'What even is happiness, Le? Do you really believe in all of that?' She can hear the scorn in his voice. 'That you're just going to get happy one day and stay like that?'

'Well, yeah.'

Raph smiles coldly.

'You're naive.'

'OK, well, what then? Happiness doesn't exist so you're just gunna do this to yourself. Is that it?'

'No.'

'What then? You could have a good life, Raph.'

'Ah,' Raph says, 'wondered how long it would take for this shit.'

'Well, you're thirty. Still here with us.'

'So? So are you?'

'You know what I mean,' Leah says. 'A job, some routine maybe, some purpose, might help.'

'What like you're doing now? Sign me up.'

'Don't be mean. You're funny and smart. You could do something you love.'

'I will,' Raph says.

'And get out there. Meet someone. You're handsome.'

Raph grunts. 'Meet someone, yeah? Settle down. Pop a kid out? Get a shit flat I can't afford? Work all my life for someone else? I can't think of anything worse. Who'd want to bring a kid into this shithole?'

'You're being deliberately cynical.'

Raph gives her a pitying look.

He surveys his mug of tea. He picks it up and puts it back down. He searches in his dressing-gown pockets and retrieves a squashed packet of fags. He takes a sip of his tea and then puts the tip of a cigarette to his mouth.

'I do feel grim. I'm gunna quit. I am,' he says.

'What, fags? Or the lot?'

'The lot, Leah. I'm done. I'm tired.'

He takes a long, rasping pull of the cigarette.

'Mum will kill you. Smoking in here,' Leah says.

'She won't,' Raph says as he exhales a long, concentrated stream of grey smoke. He demolishes the fag in three tokes, the cherry on the end becoming long and dangerous like lava.

'I love you mate,' she says. 'You're the only brother I've got.'

'I love you too.' Raph modifies his face into something resembling sincerity. Leah reaches towards him and gives him a hug. She rubs his towelling clad back, relaxing a little.

'I mean, it's just dumb, Raph. Doing this to yourself all the time,' she says into his shoulder.

'All right Le, I get it. You've made your point.' Raph pulls away from the hug.

'Do you? Really though?'

'Oh fucking hell, Le. Don't lecture me. You get fucked all the time. What's your life saying? Your job? What are you doing? And Jay?'

'All right, Raph. Jesus. You don't have to be like that,' Leah says.

'Look at your boyfriend. Or is he that?' Raph says, stubbing his fag out on a teabag on the counter. It hisses. 'One minute you're sat in my room crying because you've heard he's shagged some bird, the next you two are out for a bloody panini together.'

'Well, we're still very important to each other.'

'He's an idiot.'

'Yeah, he can be a dick, I know.'

'For God's sake. I picked up off Jay last night, Le!' Raph laughs.

'What do you mean?'

'Jay. As in, your "soul mate" is shifting pills all round Brighton,' Raph says, pushing past Leah and walking through to the living room, laying down on the sofa with a drawn-out sigh like a blow-up mattress deflating.

'You've bought pills off Jay?'

'Last night, yeah.'

'Like what?'

'Some Valium. Some E. Saw him last night down by the Volks selling to a load of kids.' He sighs it out of his mouth as though it's tedious, eyes closed.

'You saw him last night?'

'Yeah, with a group. Lads and girls,' Raph says. Leah feels a hot flash inside her at the mention of the women.

The voices on the TV seem to get louder.

'Since when has he been doing that?'

'I don't know. What does it matter anyway?' Raph has lost interest and is flicking through the channels on the TV too quickly, making Leah's head hurt. He settles on a cartoon, shuffles deeper into the sofa, his breathing heavy.

Leah is frozen to the spot, not sure what to do, looking around her mum's flat at the old familiar sofa cushions, the worn blue lino. The nasty, jolting shock of it has seemed to skew the room around her. She stands among the clutter of their lives. Her, Raph, her mother. The chipped mugs draining on a tea towel by the sink, week-old newspapers in piles, pictures hung on the walls that she's seen every day for years. It all seems mundane, depressing, suddenly a prison, mocking her life.

She feels a total stranger to herself and, worse, Jay is more like a stranger to her than ever, crueller than she thought, or just stupider. She thinks of him, prowling around Brighton with other friends, other women, without a single thought of her, getting on with his life, acting like she is completely irrelevant to him. She imagines him talking to Raph, handing him the drugs, taking the folded warm cash from his hand, without feeling any duty.

She wants to speak to him but she knows she can never do this on her terms. He is uncontactable. Besides, speaking to him would involve the process of hearing it all from his mouth, making it into no big deal. She hates him so intensely in that moment while a terrifying question also enters her head: *How am I going to get through this without having to leave him?*

Raph has fallen back asleep. She knows he will sleep on and

off for days. She stands in the doorway of the living room, watching his chest lift up and down steadily. She approximates how many hours in her life she has spent checking to see if Raph is breathing, watching his ribs expand and contract.

She begins to hear Nathan's name in her head. It feels as though it is coming from somewhere remote, like church bells on the other side of a valley. Then, it is pushing to the front, becoming urgent, squashing all other thoughts, thoughts of Jay, Nathan's name is barging them out of the way. She wants to see Nathan and no one else.

She is putting on her shoes, thinking about his eyelashes like a baby giraffe, his stillness, his broad back behind the bar in a worn-out T-shirt. How he listens and the spit collects in the corners of his mouth when he is considering something, rolling his tongue over his teeth, teeth that overlap slightly at the front. She is thinking of the way he had sat in the boat with Raph against his chest, stinking and lurching and swearing and throwing weak punches. She is thinking of Nathan's hands cleaning the bath. That slow, languid gait. Ears like little antenna sticking out, flooded red when light shines behind him.

Leah puts on her coat, looks at herself in the hallway mirror as though to confirm she is capable of making this decision. She knows what she is doing before it has even happened, something about it makes sense, is inevitable. She heads out of the front door and crosses to Nathan's flat.

His front door is unlocked when Leah arrives. The lights are low inside, the darkness almost violet. She pushes the door into the dim and calls out Nathan's name. The coats on the hook in the hallway sigh as she brushes past them. Nathan opens his bedroom door and comes out.

'Le,' he says.

She sees that he knows why she is there; something about it has transcended language.

'Is it just you here?' she says.

He nods. She pushes the front door shut behind her with a click and slides the bolt across.

It happens in reverse. Before they have even touched she sees it. The pile of damp clothes. The feeling of skin on skin. The sweat, the breath, the texture of the floor beneath her. That smell of powdery deodorant. Her pale neck. Hands suddenly boiling hot. The grabbing of flesh and fat. She knows that afterwards Nathan will let her lie on his chest with his fingers in her hair, she knows he will hold her and not want to let her leave, she knows he will kiss each finger, her palms, love her so hard. She knows she will think of Jay, convince herself she wants this more than him but she knows, already, that afterwards she will be disgusted by it, that she is doing this to try and free herself from Jay.

She walks to him, puts her arm around his neck, kisses him and is weightless suddenly. Leah pulls back and looks at Nathan. They look at each other, knowing they are being or about to be transformed, a few inches between their faces. They are only a few inches before the true transgression. She thinks how easy it is to close this gap, how it is so available to her and how good it will feel to be so wanted. She can see in his eyes how happy he is that she is there. The feeling of being desired hurtles her from somewhere limp and low, a feeling like her skin does not belong to her, like hot rain is rushing all over.

They kiss again. A small tentative kiss at first then both mouths open, warm, then the blending of two bodies, two faces rubbing against each other, the fumbling for the bedroom door behind them, the undoing of zips and buttons.

It is gentler than with Jay and it lasts longer. Nathan's skin feels softer and his body slimmer. Leah doesn't touch him much but he kisses between her legs and she lets him. At times it feels strange, alien.

Afterwards, laying on Nathan, she cries. She cries because she feels too many things at once. She cries at how willingly Nathan loves her, how obvious it is. She cries because she knows on some level how much this will hurt him, how long he has wanted it and how she has exploited it, how she thought she might be redeemed by it but just feels emptied out. She cries at how she only has her body to give him, because she doesn't love him the same, because she loves Jay and can't stop. She cries because she thinks of Raph. She wipes her face, doesn't want him to see.

Nathan is the first to speak.

'Fuck,' he says. They look at each other and laugh. Leah reaches across to Nathan, traces a finger around the circumference of his long face, the bridge of his nose, the tips of his ears, lips, chin.

Nathan kisses her again but for Leah it's too probing. She pulls her face away. Now that it's done, whatever flirtation they had all these years feels like it's been stamped out. She is very aware that she has no trousers on. She spots them lying a couple of feet away, pulls them towards her. Nathan seems to take her lead and pull his T-shirt over his head. He hooks his jeans up from around his knees, zips and buttons them, looks awkward now that they are getting dressed, like he's been caught out. For a minute they look at each other. Then Nathan turns away, puts his face in his hands.

'What have we done?' he says.

Leah looks at his back, can see a muscle move beneath his skin, a little cluster of dark brown freckles between his shoulder blades.

'It's OK,' she says. 'I won't say anything. Promise.'

'That's not what I mean,' he says. He pauses. He takes in her face. 'You're so beautiful, Leah.' He touches her cheek.

She looks away. He is not usually so direct, she's not sure it suits him though she is flattered. She shrugs it off, doesn't want to encourage more intimacy between them.

Nathan sits down next to her, leaning against the bed, fully clothed now.

'How's Raph doing?'

'He's fine. He woke up. About an hour ago. He always does.'

'Good.'

'I'm sorry. I'm embarrassed. About him.'

'Stop it.'

'Were you scared?'

'Not scared. Sad. I couldn't stop thinking of his face, all evening.'

'Mm.'

'You know you don't have to be responsible for him? If you're not there to look after him? He'll cope.'

'Maybe, yeah.'

'You can't be there forever.'

'I know.'

'You ever gunna leave?'

Leah laughs, pictures Raph's head bobbing semiconscious against his chest like a sea-worn buoy.

'And go where? And what about Raph. Jay? You lot?'

Nathan pauses.

'We'd live.'

He looks at the carpet.

'Are you really OK though, Le?'

'Yeah. I am. I think. I will be.'

'You've looked so sad. Even before Ron,' Nathan says.

'When?'

'We were here, you, me and Jay. A month or so ago. The football.'

'Oh, that. I was fine. Just thinking.'

Leah remembers the afternoon. It had been a particularly bad one. Raph was missing again after a violent row. Jay, in one of his moods had been acting strange about her coming to watch the football, implying her presence was a sign of her need for him, being hostile and saying he wanted to spend time apart.

'You don't even like football,' he said. 'It's so obvious why you're coming.'

It strikes Leah as incredibly moving that Nathan notices her moods in this way and stores up questions, ready to ask. He can tell when anything happens between her or Jay. Or when something bad happens with Raph, even though Leah often feels the need to keep Raph's drinking to herself.

Most of the time, Leah feels her thoughts are light, flimsy things, spiralling away from her like sycamore seeds, changeable things to be doubted. Every time she thinks she has herself figured out, she questions its validity, if it is a true feeling, if it is legitimate. Often, Jay tells her she is over-reacting, that she is choosing to feel sad, which derails her completely and makes her wonder if any of her instincts are to be trusted. Having Nathan validate her sadness feels so good, so unusual.

'What are we going to do?' Nathan says after a while. 'About us.'

Leah knows the answer.

'Nothing,' she says, standing up. 'We can't. Because of Jay.' This is true but it's not the only reason. Leah is grateful for the excuse.

Nathan doesn't argue. Everything feels totally immovable.

Leah waits for him to say something. She wills him to do something cruel or embarrassing so that she knows she is right not to truly love him. The lamp light catches the sweat on his forehead.

'Whatever you need,' he says.

'Did you know? About what he's doing? Jay?' she asks.

Nathan frowns.

'Selling drugs. To my brother.'

'To Raph?'

'And whoever else will buy off him, I suppose.'

Leah pictures Jay, his swagger, long strides, greetings, hand-shakes, oozing confidence like rotten figs in a bowl.

'Shit,' Nathan says.

Leah nods, wanting more outrage from Nathan.

'I knew he was working for Mickey. But Raph? He knows what he's like.'

'Mm. Well he did,' Leah says.

Nathan looks caught.

'How did it all get to this?' he says.

'I should talk to him. Call him, see where he is. I should check on Raph too. And Matthew.' Leah gets up. With Nathan, she feels in control, like she can do what she wants, leave whenever and not worry about it.

'Can I do anything?' he says.

'Just don't say anything,' she says.

Nathan looks wounded. 'I wouldn't. You know that.'

They smile at each other again. She leans over and hugs him but not as tight as she might have. She hopes he won't kiss her again and he doesn't. The moment for kissing seems to have vanished completely. They are Nathan and Leah again. He lets her leave, sits plainly on the floor and watches her go.

Walking back to her flat, Leah pauses for a moment, looks out at the town, feels the night on her cheeks. The wind whistles through the block, up the staircases, along the balcony. She's not sure whether she's doing this because she wants to or because she feels she should stop, take a moment, consider the last hour. She goes over it in her head, both ashamed and indifferent. She is both wild from the deceit and terrified of what it could do.

Every light in the town below seems to hold a memory of her and Jay right in its fist. Nowhere is safe from the stink of him, it's like he owns all of what should be hers. Wherever she is, she expects him to bowl around each corner, he's so sewn into the city. Every place triggers thoughts of a time they have spent together and the corresponding emotion, whether he was kind or cruel, whether she was happy or desperately sad.

Visions of the two of them together play out brightly. The 1A bus glides past below her and it all comes into sharp focus, then a deep ache. He kissed her first on the top of that bus. His breath was milky. There's where she climbed up a lamp post to impress him. Other girls were doing it, he was egging them on, thriving off their daring. She did it too, couldn't stand to be any less fun, fell, grazed her knee and arms. He laughed. But later, back in his flat, he cupped warm water in his hands, the tender side of his hands fleshy and pink, and washed the grazes that she couldn't reach. Roughly, haphazardly, but he washed them without being asked to and something about this touched her.

There's the warehouse, beyond the viaduct where they stumbled across a rave on the way home, looked at each other with spontaneous eyes and darted in. There were polystyrene ceiling tiles, ancient-looking fire escapes, breezeblock walls tagged in thick pen, wires, blue plastic barrels, rubble and plastic sheeting everywhere. They danced among shirtless boys in bucket hats, tall speakers rigged high, the writhing mass of skin, learning each other's rhythm, kissing with sore mouths, being part of something enormous, but so obsessed with each other, everyone there for the same purpose, to forget themselves or what they thought they were, and to dance.

There's the park where they fucked against a tree, Jay rolled in piss and Leah had to put on a late-night load of laundry, stoned and giggling. There's Kensington's café where she'd order chips and cheese and gravy and he would tease her, say it was disgusting, all congealed and greasy but he'd still pay at the end.

She remembers waking him up with kisses, how he used to turn over and take them, how lately he always has his back to her, trying to clutch more sleep, stiffly lying like a low wall. She thinks of his shoulders, his belly, his knees. It kills her.

The thought of forgetting the good things feels like some kind of grief. But they are so many years ago now they seem so distant. She can't remember the last time they went to a park and lay down on a blanket, the last time they shared a meal somewhere that wasn't a living room. What did they talk about back then? How did they fill the hours? Was it just each other's bodies? Until he got bored of hers? The thought that he was ever yielding and obvious in his affection seems like something she might have made up in her head.

Despite all this, it's still him she wants. There is no logic to it. She wants to know how he is, where he is, who he is with. She still can't relax until he arrives when they're waiting for him to join at the pub, still wants to impress him, to be wanted by him. Though between her legs is still damp and Nathan's smell is still on her skin, she reaches for her phone and calls him. No answer.

Wednesday

Jay comes round with a metallic taste in his mouth, a low humming in his ears and a headache. It takes him a while to realise where he is. He looks around, blinking, trying to focus. MDF boards, painted blue and graffitied over. A curled-up link fence. Tufts of dry-looking grass and sand. A few lone cars, including his. Something on his face is making it stiff, dry and clay-like in its consistency. His nose is blocked. He reaches up to touch his face and a flake of the substance adheres itself to his fingers. Dry blood. And then it comes back to him.

Walking along by Black Rock, drunk, music in his headphones, distracted, he felt them before he saw them, something changed, the air became coarse somehow, the skin on his back felt sensitive, he felt an instinct to cover his neck. And then they were there. Five of them, obscured by the night, just outlines, dark clothes. No weapons, no need. He was alone. Blows came and thudded against him. He couldn't hear, the music in his headphones still going until they were ripped out so he could hear the final punch. Then the wet feeling in his sinuses, the bubbling of liquid in his mouth, winded and trying to suck in the air, a pain rippling out from his core, the burn of the backpack strap being ripped from his bare shoulders and the sound of feet walking away with over two hundred pills that technically still belonged to Mickey Hallahan.

Jay puts his head in hands. He tries to do the maths, thinks through his headache, to work out what he owes. He groans, his split lip opens with the movement of his mouth. He reckons close to two thousand pounds has vanished into the night like smoke. He admires how simple it was for them to take everything he had. He leans against the fence, letting the shock vibrate through him, the truth of how rapidly you can become indebted. His lip oozes something watery. He can't see, the total dark pulses around him.

He starts laughing. This makes his lip sting, so he stops. Besides, he feels stupid laughing alone on the floor. Then useless, then angry. He gets up. For a moment he wonders if this is some form of retribution, some punishment. But he soon shakes this idea off. Things are not predestined, he tells himself. Life is a series of mistakes, coincidences and hurdles and you push on and get on with it. He has been unlucky. The bigger question is the question of Mickey and how he will react. There is something about him that seems coiled up, eyes dark and wild. Jay gets into his car.

He can already hear Leah's voice in his ears when she sees his face, the bruises. Even her hypothetical reaction annoys him. He hoists himself up and takes a look in the rear-view mirror. It's not as bad as he thought but there's a mark on his cheekbone and his lip is swollen and cut. It's his ribs that hurt the most, bruised and also experiencing a sickly tingling, arriving in surges. It's the earliest part of morning and Jay can see the sun beginning to illuminate the line of the horizon like a hot wire.

On the drive home, he feels a wave of nausea. Hungover and battered, he pulls his car into a lay-by as his mouth fills up with spit. He opens the door and swings his legs out, vomits between them onto the grey gravel floor. The acid tang coats his mouth and he can't get rid of it. It feels like it is clinging to each tooth. He puts two pieces of chewing gum in his mouth and chews until his eyes stop streaming from the menthol. He feels grim and sore but it's entirely appropriate, even enjoyable. He wants something solid, some tangible symptom of his emotional pain, to help him forget that when he gets home Ron won't be there to talk to. His hands shake slightly as he puts them back on the steering wheel. Somewhere low down in his throat he can taste tar. He turns the key, fights the urge to bash his head into the steering wheel. It's time to go home. Back to the flats, to Leah, to the truth of it all.

Wednesday

Leah is on her balcony. Down below, Matthew lays on the grass in the middle of the block with Nathan. She watches them from above. They look peaceful with the sun on them, lying, not talking, like they could be sleeping.

She recognises Jay's car in the car park then. He's home. The ground falls from underneath her and makes her stomach drop out. She takes a deep breath but can't get enough air, like two big male hands are squeezing her ribs in at the side. She turns her attention to the door of his flat. As if on cue, he comes out, looks over in her direction. She's aware how hot she is, how she possibly smells and how her lips feel tight from the sun. She needs lip balm, a shower, things that will make her more attractive.

Jay glances towards Nathan and Matthew but walks towards Leah first. She can't help but be glad that he wants to see her before them. For days, she has imagined everything she will say to him when he finally shows up, how calm she will be, how she'll get her point across, but the moment she sees his big face looking down, his shoulders drooping like an old tulip, she's just relieved that he has come back. She throws her arms around his long neck as though in worship, pulls him close. She doesn't know why she moves her morals with him so much so that even the most unreasonable things seem normal. Ron's death seems to have made her want him even more, to forgive him everything and get through it together. She still wants to kiss him, wipe away the memory of Nathan.

He lets her breathe him in for a few seconds before pulling away.

When they speak, it's awkward, like they're strangers.

'Well hello,' she says, grinning. He looks a little embarrassed, childlike in the shadow of the balcony above.

'Hey, Le.'

'Are you OK?'

He nods quickly at the floor. 'I'm fine.' He looks beyond her, down onto the grass where Matthew and Nathan are.

'Why are you being weird?' she says.

'What? I'm not.'

'You can't look at me.'

He looks at her, briefly, defiant for a second.

'Don't be dumb. I can.' He flicks his car key in and out of its plastic case like a blade.

'Where've you been? What's happened to your face?'

'Yeah. I needed some time. It was all a bit much. Ignore the face. It's dumb. Looks worse than it is.'

'OK.' Another pause. Jay sort of shrugs at her and indicates for them to go inside.

'I could have done with you around, Jay.'

'Yeah. Sorry.' Jay runs his hands over his head as though Leah is being tedious. She notices he smells a bit unwashed.

'It's been really shit,' she says.

'It's been pretty shit for me too.'

'Where've you been?'

'With mates.'

'Which mates?'

'I knew you'd be like this. People deal with things in different ways. You have to respect that.' He employs his skill of positioning himself as the reasonable one in the conversation. Leah is disarmed.

'I know, I am respecting that I just . . . I don't know. I think you should have been with your friends. With your girlfriend.'

Jay raises his eyebrows.

'Leah we've talked about this. I'm not your boyfriend. I'm not always going to be around to do whatever you want me to do.'

'That's literally not what I'm asking.'

'It is. You want me around to comfort you. You need to learn to do that yourself.'

'What? That's not what I'm saying,' she says. Everything has vanished out of her head, she can't grab on to any of the reason she had before he arrived. It's like she is in sand when she talks to him, sinking up to her neck. She worries that any minute he will turn and get back in his car.

'I just—' It's easy for him to stop her. She's not got the force she needs to carry on.

'Please Le, don't.'

'Don't what?'

'Don't be on my case.'

'I'm hardly on your case.'

'Things are hard for me too.'

'Things are hard for me! And I don't go around doing exactly what I want to,' Leah says.

'Well maybe you should. Also I haven't really done anything wrong, if you think about it. You're the one who's having a go at me about our relationship after Ron's literally just died. I mean, what am I getting out of this? Me and you?' He looks right at her. His eyelashes are made golden by the sun, there is a tic in his jaw. He's becoming irritated. 'Where's your support for me?'

Leah's cheeks get hot. She wants leverage. She knows she's starting something enormous but it's the only thing she can think to say.

'I know you let Raph pick up off you. The other night.'

'What?' Jay looks up and his eyes flash.

'Raph told me.'

Jay rolls his eyes.

'How could you do that? What's wrong with you?' Leah says. Her voice gets a bit louder, she feels she has a grip on something. It feels good.

'What do you mean, what's wrong with me?'

'How could you do that? You know what he's like. Did you know me and Nathan had to drag him home the other night?'

An image of her thighs on top of Nathan briefly enters Leah's mind, her hands in his hair.

'And . . . How's Raph now?' Jay raises his eyebrows, infuriatingly calm.

'He's OK. Now. But it was bad.'

'Exactly. Raph's fine. He's always fine in the end, Leah, he's just a wreck head. Takes it too far sometimes. You're not helping him by being all dramatic about it.'

'He's more than that, you prick.'

'Don't call me a prick, Leah.'

She stands her ground.

'How long have you been selling drugs? It's actually pathetic.'

Jay rolls his eyes again. He is so sure that he is right. Leah can't remember a time when she ever felt so sure of anything.

'I'm not a drug dealer.' His eyes are sea-glass blue.

'Oh OK. You're not. What have you been doing for work then?'

'I told you. Just bits. That bit of work helping out that man with a van. Some sales.'

'Sales?'

'Yeah, this isn't the time.' He tries to push past her and into the flat.

'When's the time then?'

'I don't know, but can we not?'

'No. I want to know why. Why did you do it?'

'Why not? He'd have got it somewhere else if not from me. If anything, it's better this way.'

'Better?'

'You know what I mean.'

'I honestly don't.'

'Leah, listen to me, hear this loud and clear. Raph is a drug addict. He's always going to take drugs. Wouldn't you rather you knew where his stuff was coming from?'

'That's a fucked logic.'

Jay shrugs.

'He's not an addict,' she says.

Jay laughs. 'OK,' he says in a stupid voice.

'Why can't you just say sorry?' she says. Her voice sounds strangled, high pitched. She can feel she's losing control, becoming emotional.

'Stop shouting. Let's go inside.' Jay looks over his shoulder. A woman is smoking on her front step. Jay looks at Matthew and Nathan down on the lawn.

'Don't tell me to stop shouting. You shout all the time.'

'Shh,' Jay says. He's half laughing.

'And where have you been? I've been here. Alone. Sorting all this shit out. I've been with Matthew. Sorting the funeral.'

Jay looks angry then.

'Oh good for you, Leah. What do you want a medal for sorting out the funeral? What was I supposed to do exactly? You and Matthew are always together anyway, it's not like I could have helped him. You, him and Nathan in your weird little club.'

'Oh don't start this.'

'Start what?'

'This thing you have with Matthew.'

Jay turns away.

'You should have been there for me. Forget Matthew.'

'Why should I? I had to get my head straight.'

'You're selfish.'

'How am I?'

'Why do you always need an explanation for things that are obvious? You're always asking me why I'm upset. What you've done wrong. Why I feel the way I feel.'

'That's because you're *always* upset about something or other.'

'I'm not.' She can feel him wrenching the argument, turning it on her. It makes her manic.

'Oh, no, you're right. You're an "easy girl".' Jay makes quotation marks with his hands in the air. 'A walk in the fucking park. It's hard for me to be with you, you know. There's always something. Always some problem you have with Raph or something. Do you know how stressful that is for me?'

'For you?'

'Yes.'

'Oh my brother is hard for you? The only person you care about is yourself. Do you even give a shit about this? About Ron? Matthew? You're a dick to him all the time, Jay.'

'Of course I care, are you dumb?'

'I'm not dumb, you're dumb.' She feels childish, throwing his insult back weakly at him but her head is a mess, she can't think of anything else to make him see her point, can't believe how it has spiralled.

'I knew him more than you did anyway,' Jay says. 'I'm just as fucking sad about it.'

'What does that even mean?'

'I'm just saying it's actually probably worse for me.'

'Yeah, you keep telling yourself that,' Leah says. She's scared of arguing and how she can't take what she has said back, but she wants him to be fair, to love her, to say sorry. Every time they argue like this, Leah feels there is something between them that changes, that it's getting worse and she'll never be able to get the stain of it out.

'I just wanted you here. With me,' Leah says.

'Well, you're not that easy to be with. You *need* so much from me all the time. You expect things. It's pressure. Turning up at my house when we don't have plans, expecting me to stay the night when I'm at yours. It's the expectation. Constant expectation. You make me act like this, Leah. You're so insecure and I can tell. You used to be so much more confident. What happened to Leah from school?'

He is so intense, staring right into her face. Leah is humiliated. She notices how big he is, what a force, how the veins in his throat are standing out. You could kill me if you wanted to, she thinks, remembers him smashing his Xbox controller at the wall.

It's true that being with him makes her feel like she is losing small pieces of herself each day. And the more insecure she gets, the less attractive he finds her, despite him being the architect of it. She knows she shouldn't believe him when he says unkind things, but she can't help but accept it. Recently he asked if they could talk about the sex he has with other women, for an experiment, to test their strength, he said. She saw the thrill in his face when he approached it.

'I'm sorry if that's how you feel about us,' she says. 'Honestly, you're making me feel like shit.'

'I'm not making you feel anything. You started this. You're choosing to be the victim here.' His eyes shine. 'You're acting weak, Le.'

Leah says nothing, stands there, picking at the skin around her nails.

'Let's get in the house.' He looks at her. 'Please, babe,' he says.

She takes one step into the flat and it's enough, Jay pushes her inside and shuts the door behind them. In the dark of the corridor they are suddenly very close. He has his hands on her shoulders. 'Stop this,' he says. He guides her backwards. 'It's me,' he says. She backs down into the narrow hallway, legs buckling at the pressure of his touch, his wide palms. She tells him to get off and tries to hit out at him. He holds her by both wrists.

'Don't do this. It's me. I love you,' he says. And then he is kissing her. It is that easy for him. He can change and say it just like that and she kisses back because it is so urgent, he wants her so intensely for the first time in such a long time, because she wants so badly to be touched.

She wants him to be the good Jay, the one for whom she is enough, the kind Jay, not this Jay, the angry and the dissatisfied stranger who occasionally turns up on her doorstep. She wants it so badly that she doesn't say anything when his kisses start to feel rough. He lifts her up like she isn't at all heavy and carries her into her room and lays her down on the single bed. She tries to ignore the fact that he smells so much like another woman, all sweet and powdery around his collar, tries to forget the fact he has been missing for days now and all the girls' names that she sees flash on his phone while he's sleeping. He is inside her quickly, and it stings a little, and he doesn't pause to put a condom on. He doesn't kiss her much, and she thinks he might be gentle in the wake of all this sadness, but he's not. He's quick and it hurts more with each time he pushes into her. She turns her head to bite the pillow, her eyes start to sting with wetness. She feels limp beneath him. She doesn't know how to tell him to stop. She tries to pretend that because he is on top of her right now, he might be back to what he once was to her.

After a while, she feels herself disconnect, the pain is still there but it becomes numb, like her own body is dulling it, trying to make it bearable. Her head starts to empty as he pushes in and pulls out. He finishes with a twitch and gets up quick, clears his throat. He leans down to kiss her, but she turns her cheek away. His kiss seems to indicate he knows he has done something wrong, that something has changed between them. For a moment he looks as though he might say he is sorry before he turns from her. She notices how the light catches his hair, tries to remember the parts of him that are soft and beautiful.

'I'm getting water,' he says, pulls his white boxers up. She notices a small smear of blood. A pain is still present between her legs, and there is now a sort of dull pulse inside her, roaring like the sound of a river far away.

Wednesday

Jay pulls his clothes on while Leah lays in bed. She seems different, distracted. She didn't try to hold him after. She pulls the duvet over her body entirely and rolls away from him as he buttons his jeans. He looks at how soft the shape of her is and he has the urge to run his hand over her side, over the dip at her waist. He swallows the instinct to sit back down on the bed, tells himself she is being unfair, rolling over like that. He tells her he needs to go and she barely reacts. He leaves her room, pops his head into the kitchen and drinks from the milk bottle next to the kettle, shoves a handful of cornflakes in his mouth, straight from the box.

Outside Leah's flat, he ignores his phone buzzing in his pocket. It's Mickey again. He turns his phone off. He can't think of anything he wants to do, he's inert, has nowhere to go, nothing to do but think. This feels like torture, a long dry desert stretching out, waves of heat hovering.

Some kids kick a football against the fence and it rattles the metal poles that hold it. Jay watches them for a moment and remembers when it was him and Nathan, when all he cared about was school ending so they could walk home with their jumpers tied around their waists and their hands in crisp packets and pen marks all over their arms and cheeks. Or a few years on from that, hiding behind the bins smoking Benny's flavoured tobacco. Or the first time his mum asked Ron to watch him. Jay sat in his quiet living room while Ron read to him from a choose your own adventure book and the loud hours vanished. It hurts so much to think of this that it starts to make Jay feel unwell, his eyeballs heavy in their sockets. His head is like an elastic band pulled too taut. The sound of the ball on the fence becomes unbearable. He gets in his car, decides to go for a drive. It's hot and he winds all four windows down. On Lewes Road, he notices the turning for the cemetery. He doesn't know when he decides to, or why, but he indicates right.

He parks his car and walks with his head down, worried someone might be watching him. Some muscle memory lodged within him tells him where the grave is, and he finds it easily, which is underwhelming. He hasn't been to his dad's grave since the day he was buried, that strange day where Jay felt indifferent and frozen, more concerned with the logistics of the burial than the fact it was his dad they were lowering into the ground. It was all much more boring than on TV. No one broke down. No one asked him to throw a rose on the coffin. It was still and mundane, a lot of waiting around. He wondered about the purpose of the piece of green cloth that lines the grave and didn't pay attention to what the vicar was saying. In the church hall afterwards, he found it annoying when anyone spoke to him, found it hard to stop himself getting angry. He took himself into a corner, pulled out and shredded every tissue from a peach-coloured box.

The grave is a simple black rectangle, shiny stone like a dark lake, perfect except for a small blob of bird shit on the right-hand corner. There is a dried-up bunch of roses placed on top, which Jay picks up and puts in a bin by the path so he has something to do. He can't help feeling as though he is at a gallery, standing by a great masterpiece that deserves his time, wondering how long to admire it, knowing he should be in awe but actually feeling bored and stiff. Each second aches in the heat. He can hear the buzzing of insects and somewhere beyond, men shouting at each other. The grass has been cut and the smell bleeds everywhere, the fresh wet sharpness of it. Jay starts finding other words within the words on the grave, to pass the time, waiting to feel something.

Standing there, slices of memory arrive. His dad, arms in the air at a Seagulls match, swooping down on Jay and grasping him by the shoulders, shaking him in celebration of a goal, lifting him up as the crowd moved around them, elated. Jay feigning embarrassment when his dad told him he was handsome, when he would spoil him and take him out for steak. Jerry getting excited when Jay cracked his nose during a football game but still scored, coming right up close to Jay and kissing him on the mouth, Jay watching him through the blood and streaming eyes. The easy comfort of Jerry passing him a pint, the long and loud afternoons at the pub with him, how he always had crisp notes in his wallet, was always charming to cab drivers and sang Sinatra in the shower.

The first time his dad took him to the pub Jay was sick from too much drink. It happened very quickly, one minute he was enjoying the weightless feeling of drunkenness, his hot face and the sense that he could say whatever he wanted, the next minute, he couldn't stand straight. He felt as though some huge, heavy force was knocking into his sides, throwing him off balance. Then spit started to collect in his mouth and he knew he would throw up. He remembered the look on his dad's face, mocking and tinged with the beginnings of anger, so he took himself outside, his limbs haphazard and disobedient, and he threw up on the patch of grass across the road from the pub. He felt better, reached his hands into his jeans, found some change and bought a huge bottle of water from the off-licence next door which he downed in long sustained gulps. He went back into the pub and started drinking again, taking his flat pint from the edge of the bar and smiling at his father.

The pictures tumble and roll over each other in Jay's head like refracted light. He thinks fondly of his dad, then pictures his mum jumping at the sound of the doorbell. He wants someone to take these thoughts away, tell him they're no longer relevant, that he's fine, fixed.

Instead of his father, he wants to remember Ron. He closes his eyes in the heat. He thinks of Ron, only Ron, wants Ron as sharp as possible. Ron reading to him as a kid. Him and Ron drawing a map together. Newspaper ink stains on Ron's fingers. How Jay would google crossword clues on his phone for Ron and taunt him with the answers. How Jay once cut the straight white hairs at the base of Ron's neck and they fell like snow into little heaps. How Ron once made up a milky bowl of Dettol and soaked Jay's hand after he had got angry and punched a wall. How he'd patted it dry with a clean-smelling towel and dabbed bubblegum-pink antiseptic on the grazes. The time Ron made Jay darn a woollen sock for him, asked him to thread a needle with his young eyes and then showed him how to stitch. Jay thinks of Ron's veiny hands clasped together with his chin resting on them, sitting across from Jay in his small kitchen.

'You don't have to talk, son. If you don't want to. You can just sit. Everyone's so loud all the time,' Ron said. Jay's dad had just died. Ron had invited Jay round for his tea. 'To give your mum a break,' he said. He opened a tin of treacle cake. He sat opposite Jay, reading the paper. Jay was calmer, more at ease than he had ever been. They spent more afternoons together after that. And they did talk. They talked about the things they both liked, easily, quietly, conversations as satisfying as sitting indoors during heavy rain, Ron's stories pooling like moonlight on the kitchen table. Ron told Jay things about his life he hadn't told anyone else, showed him photographs creased from age. There was a richness in the afternoons they had spent together, a weight to them, a secrecy.

Sometimes they drove to Ron's allotment. 'Come on,' Ron said. 'There's always things that need fixing.'

They seemed to be able to talk best side by side with their hands busy, knuckle deep in soil, or Jay pushing a wheelbarrow full of old fence posts, Ron walking by his side.

When Jay was angry, Ron told him to be gentler, to sit and to breathe and to busy his hands and for once, it hadn't sounded like a useless annoying cliché. They talked about Jay's dad in a way Jay did with no one else.

'There are lots of different types of fathers in the world,' Ron said. 'There are men whose language is violence. You can't help which one you get. And you've been unlucky. I was unlucky too,' he said.

'I still miss him sometimes, you know,' Jay said.

'Well, life's not straightforward,' Ron said. 'People are many different things at once. Your dad had his qualities.'

'I'm annoyed sometimes, like I'm supposed to hate him. Sometimes I'm angry with my mum.'

'You don't have to hate him, Jay. I don't imagine she'd ever expect that from you. But you do have to make sure you do nice things for her. She works too hard, that one. She's got a sadness inside her.'

'I'm just angry all the time,' Jay said.

'It's OK to be angry. People fear anger. It's a very natural emotion, so long as you don't let it rule you. You feel it, you let it go. You move on,' Ron said.

'What if I'm like him. My dad.'

'Well, you've got to admit to yourself that you may be. Then ask yourself if you want that for yourself. And if the answer if no, you have to change. You've got to believe that you can be better. That you're made of different stuff,' Ron said. 'There's no easy answers.'

Jay knows he can be cruel. He sees bursts of his father in himself, they emerge from him quickly and with heat. But he doesn't know how to stop. He tells himself he is misunderstood, that he has been given a raw deal, worse than Matthew and Leah. Certainly worse than Nathan.

'I don't think anyone gets me,' Jay said.

'That's life, son,' Ron said. 'That's what they call living. No one's going to hold your hand. You've got to figure out a way.'

Everything Ron shared was balanced, matter of fact and unsentimental. He seemed to be able to respond to everything with a single, measured sentence. And because he wasn't talkative, would never say something for the sake of it or even ask many questions, when he spoke, it was weighted with a significance.

Jay got the sense there was no judgement with Ron, which made him feel forgiven of himself. He needed Ron's moderate face when he was feeling particularly wretched.

'Try me,' Ron said when Jay had started trying to tell him about quitting his job at the call centre, arguments with Leah, about the women he'd been seeing. Ron listened and nodded.

'I'm not one to judge,' he said. 'A man needs to be the ultimate judge of himself.'

As much as Jay loved Ron as a man, he also loved the attention. Ron made Jay feel like he was special, singled out. Sometimes he envied his friends. He envied Leah, how she could talk so easily about the things she enjoyed, how she could watch a film and have an angle on it or a criticism. He'd read some of her writing once in an old notebook, reflections about a weekend they had spent at the beach with Nathan and Matthew and it was so accurate and beautiful, it was like he was back there. It irritated him. She talked with Nathan about what they read in the papers, they followed the same people on Twitter and would discuss it at the pub, homelessness on the rise in Brighton, the community centre shutting down, male celebrities accused of sexual assault. Jay would half listen, not getting involved. With Ron, the virtues of his friends, of Leah, disappeared and he was the focus. Ron's eyes were on him, interested in what he had to say. He didn't have to share.

Already Jay can't remember the intricacies of the conversations they once had. They are like sand running through his hands and the harder he tries to grip on, the more grains slip out from the cracks between his fingers.

Jay opens his eyes, looks down at the grave again.

'Hi Dad,' he says.

He stares down at the soil, fidgety. Something feels as though it is about to burst in some abstract part of him, a balloon in the sun, too hot. He makes to walk up the hill but then turns around, overtaken with a sudden compulsion. He gathers his saliva in his mouth and spits, one long thick streak of spit down onto where his father lays beneath the earth. He enjoys it.

Jay walks up the path to his car, the sparse summer clouds breaking apart in shapes overhead. He notices Matthew then, stood by the gate, shimmering in the sun. Jay swallows. He feels a tug of dread, has no idea how to act or what to say. He's not seen Matthew since the news. He doesn't want to share his pain right now. He wants it for himself.

'Hi,' Jay says.

'Hey.'

'What you doing here?'

'Needed to get out,' Matthew says. 'This all feels a bit like going mad. The flats. They're so hot. So small.'

Jay smiles. 'I hear you.'

There is at least ten foot between them. They don't step any closer to each other. Jay squints with the sun in his eyes, body full of tension.

'I've come to see where he's going to be buried,' Matthew says. 'Where he chose.'

Jay nods.

'Fuck, Matthew, this is so shit,' Jay says. 'Sorry,' he adds, regretting his choice of words.

'No, don't be,' Matthew says. 'It's better than people just saying "sorry for your loss" all the time.'

Jay suddenly wants very badly to cry, the unfamiliar feeling of hot tears forming unsettling him. He rubs his face with his hands roughly instead, like a kid overwhelmed with something unfair.

'I'm really sorry, Matthew. He was a decent man. Your grandad.'

'So everyone says,' Matthew says.

'He had a way, this way', Jay continues, 'of making you feel like what you were saying, was . . .' he searches for the right word, 'important.'

Jay kicks a tuft of grass with his foot.

'I'm finding it hard to remember what his voice was like,' Jay says, half laughing, realising now that he wants a piece of comfort from Matthew, his grief to be acknowledged.

'I know what you mean,' Matthew says. 'I spent fifteen minutes just staring at his toothbrush the other day.'

Jay sniffs loudly.

'I miss having him around,' Matthew says. 'I can't believe he's just not here.'

'Yeah.' Jay looks up to the sky, trying to make tears retreat back into his face.

'Hey, I better go, Matthew,' he says briskly. He can't stand being there with him in the tight heat.

'How do you do it, Jay?' Matthew says.

'What?'

'Just get on with everything?'

'I don't know. I just do,' Jay says. 'Try not to think about it too much.'

'Easier said than done,' Matthew says. 'I wish I was as fearless.'

A long silence hisses between them like tinnitus. Jay shifts from one foot to another.

'Do you think he meant it? Meant to do himself in?' Jay says.

Matthew digs at the wooden fence with his fingernails.

'I have no idea,' he says. 'I don't think we ever can know. If he wasn't happy, he was keeping it quiet.'

Jay thinks of the first time Ron told him the story of Billy. He remembers Billy and Ron's faces in a blotchy photograph, Billy's hand on Ron's chest. He wonders if Matthew knows, then feels a little possessive over the secret.

'Do you think you can ever really know someone?' Matthew says.

Jay can't help it then. Tears stream from the corners of each eye. He looks down, as boys learn to do when they cry. The sun is bright, and he is metres away from Matthew. He half hopes Matthew can't see, half hopes he knows.

Wednesday

The lights in the clinic are too bright, toxic strip lights overhead. The walls are brilliant white. Everything is plastic. On the coffee table there are out-of-date magazines with cover stories about celebrities on holiday showing cellulite. On the walls are posters advertising Botox and veneers; before-and-after shots of fat tummies sucked free of their wobble; sunspots blasted away by lasers. Leah has looked at these things so many times, they all seem like a TV set now. She's worked here for longer than she would have liked, but the pay is decent, and she doesn't have to do much.

Leah is on the afternoon shift. She's not had time to shower since Jay came over and she feels dirty and sore. A man is shouting at her. Leah looks back at him, wanting get back to reading her book.

'No, what I'm saying is, you only get the discount when you buy in packages of five,' she says.

'Yes, love, I heard you the first time. But you're missing my point.' He is a square man with small teeth. His fists are balled tight on the reception desk. Small flecks of spit land on the open diary in front of Leah and make the ink swim.

Leah sighs and rolls her eyes.

'Would you like to speak to the clinic manager? He's in today.'

'Oh, finally. Now she wants me to speak to the manager. After all that.' The man looks around the empty waiting room like he's trying to gather outrage from others. His wife is sat on a plastic chair by the door flicking spiritlessly through an out-of-date magazine. She doesn't look up.

'I'll just call him for you,' Leah says. 'You can go upstairs and wait.'

'Thank you, Leah.' The man regards Leah's name on her small rectangular badge.

'Wait here,' he says to his wife.

'Fucking moron,' Leah says under her breath. The tingly sensation of adrenaline retreats, her face flushed.

'He is, isn't he?'

Leah looks up. The man's wife is in front of Leah, red nails clasped around the lip of the reception desk. Up close, she's beautiful but she looks tired. The makeup on her face has settled into the lines around her eyes. Her blonde hair is tied in a small neat bun at the nape of her neck. On the third finger of her left hand is a wedding ring stuffed with diamonds and an engagement ring with a huge rock. Leah thinks how rich she is, but how she is still a human, at the mercy of sweat and spots and wrinkles, just like the rest of us. She has a zip on her skirt just like everyone else, and, Leah noticed, a tiny speck of something between her teeth. She looks so small up close, smaller than she'd looked on the other side of the waiting room.

'I got up to say I'm sorry about him,' she says quietly. 'I just came up to say that, to apologise. He does it all the time. Who gets so upset about teeth whitening?' She smiles. Her own teeth look expensive.

'No! God, I'm sorry. I really didn't think you'd hear that. I'm a dick,' Leah says.

The lady laughs. Her laugh is naughty, knowing. She smells of something heady, the richness of good perfume.

'It's OK, sweetheart. God, it's good to have someone who thinks it too. He is a moron,' she says.

Leah laughs then, nervously.

'I'm thinking of leaving him, if truth be told. Fat bald idiot. If it wasn't for Sebastian.'

There's something inherently fun and glamorous about her, conspiratorial, which draws Leah in. Despite her life seeming so far away from Leah's, she feels attached to her somehow. She wants to go on a shopping trip with her, or brunch.

'Our son,' the lady explains. She waves her phone in front of Leah's face. On the screen, Leah catches a brief glimpse of a pale-looking boy with a side parting, smiling in a maroon school uniform, grey socks pulled up to his delicate knees.

'I love this little boy,' the woman says. She pauses for what feels like a long time and looks like she might cry.

'Have you got kids?' she asks.

'Me? No.' Leah shakes her head.

'Do you want them?'

'I haven't decided. I don't know.'

'Got a boyfriend?'

Leah hesitates.

'Yeah. Kind of.' She's too humiliated to answer this question with the truth.

'Is he kind, sweetheart?' the woman says.

'He is. Yeah,' Leah says. She tries to make her answer sound convincing.

'Oh. Well then. That's good. That's the most important thing.'

Leah feels like she has betrayed some part of herself. She wants to reach over the desk and hug the woman. She wants to talk more, ask for her advice, tell her the truth about Jay, have the woman tell her it would be OK to run away, that she is strong enough. She wants to know about her life, what it's like to be married to the angry man upstairs, what it's like to grow a child and love it so much. She imagines this woman at her age, in her twenties, on a beach in a different country with a man who she doesn't love too much and a bottle of beer and no idea where she might end up. She is sad for her, scared for herself.

Leah hears raised voices from upstairs. She notices the woman's eyes are wet. Her neck is wrinkled and soft. She puts her phone back in her expensive-looking handbag.

There is the sound of feet from the stairs.

Her husband comes bursting through the door into the waiting room.

'Fuck this, we're out of here, COME,' he says. The woman gives Leah a maternal wink. Then they leave.

Walking home after the shift that night, Leah passes the cafés on London Road. In the daytime, they are always full to the brim with mothers, alone, shaking prams, drinking coffees. To her, they all look lonely.

A group of young girls with pushchairs are up ahead, a tangle of shopping bags, unwashed hair scraped back, out the way of grabbing hands. Some are holding their babies to their chests casually, letting their little limbs bob like buoys, holding them fearlessly and naturally. Leah recognises two of them from school. She's watched their lives unfold on Facebook these last years. Young girls but girls who know how to hold a baby confidently.

On the bus, she glances at passengers and looks for their wedding rings, wonders how many people are happy, how many are in the middle of a disaster, if the husbands are on their way to fuck someone else while their wives wait at home. Someone's phone rings and they answer it sounding thrilled. Leah imagines the person on the other end, wherever they are, loving them so much, ringing to check up on the progress of their journey. People perform the simple evening rituals of asking if anything needs fetching from the shop, requesting things from the take-away, getting off the bus to fetch hot heavy damp paper bags smelling of spices. Some people love each other and it's that easy, she thinks.

The bus is warm and crowded. Leah gets off a few stops early and walks the rest of the way home. The air is cooler than it was in town. The evening is daubed in pools of orange light from streetlamps. The lightbulbs on the pier flash like angry teeth. She walks along the beach, through the widening night. The tide is out and the wet stretch of sand is twinkling under the strong moon, the sky darkening quickly like a nasty bruise, yellow and light blue and inky black. She takes her shoes off and walks along the soft wetness of the sand, the gentle expanse that the low tide reveals. It feels good beneath her feet. She picks up some sea glass, smoothed by the ocean's tongue and holds it in her palm as it glitters in the dying light. She tosses it back onto the ground and it makes no sound.

The balls of muscle boys zoom past on their scooters doing

wheelies, racing each other, looking for a thrill, gaffer tape on their mudguards. She thinks of Raph again and the weight of his body against hers, trying to carry him home, then the weight of Jay pushing her down onto her bed. She thinks of the man shouting at her at work. She checks her phone, nothing. No message of comfort from him, no apology. She wants to smash it against the floor. She swears the seagulls are looking at her funny. Things seem unfriendly, she's on edge, jumping at things in her peripheral, the night taking on a sinister mood. The whole town seems in pain, all the trauma of what's happened is woven into everything. It starts to expose her to the truth of her unhappiness.

For the first time, her town makes her feel sad. Her life seems little and ordinary. It seems to always be Monday morning, she is always tired. Lately, she finds it hard to be enthusiastic about anything. Another lifestyle, another job, another town, another country, seems the only key to happiness.

She sees how she has stayed for so long, paralysed by the weight of a town she's known since birth, afraid to leave the only certainties she has: Brighton, Jay, the flats. She sees that she has been afraid to leave Raph. But now, the idea of waking up each morning and doing exactly what she wants, without thinking of them, gives her a sturdy longing. She puts some music in her ears, some whimsical guitar, imagines she is a slender girl from a film, that she is walking through a new city.

She watches her block come into view. The little boxes of light, blinking. She thinks of all the lives contained within that one building; the joy and the devastation. She imagines what everyone is doing in their flats. Someone is probably having sex, someone is frying onions, someone is definitely crying or hoovering or staring at the ceiling. She wonders how many nights Ron lay awake in bed contemplating how long to keep on living, how many people in there feel like she does, how many people want to get out but don't know how, or can't. How many people never will.

Though it is still hot outside, the air close and sticky, when Leah gets home she takes a long bath, a thing she only does when she really needs to pass the cruel long hours that snail along when she's sad. In the too hot soapy water, she runs her hands over her body and loves the feeling of it for a brief moment. She puts her hands between her legs, thinking of Jay, then thinking how he wouldn't call that night, or for however many more nights. And then she thinks how nothing feels quite as good as when she touches herself alone.

The water drains out of the bath, leaving strands of her hair behind in strange shapes. Leah hears noises from Raph's room. She jolts up with instinctive panic. It's a whirring sound, something mechanical. She wraps a towel around her and pushes the door of Raph's bedroom open, in the way you learn to when you don't know what will be on the other side.

Raph is inside, sat on an exercise bike, spine hunched in his dressing-gown with his back to the door, pedalling furiously and looking out to the sea through the window. A small patch of sweat is spreading out across his lower back, Leah can see it seeping through his dressing-gown. She notices he is wearing a large set of headphones, the faint thud of muffled music.

She shouts his name. He doesn't hear at first so she walks round to where he can see her. He is startled, loses his balance and falls from the saddle.

Leah laughs, helps him back up, hoping he'll laugh too. He does.

'Jesus, Le, you scared the shit out of me,' Raph says. He's still smiling, wipes his forehead with his sleeve.

'What's all this?' she says. 'When did you get it? How did you get it up the stairs?'

'I got it from Argos. I'm on a health kick aren't I, babes?' Raph's a bit manic but dripping with charisma.

'How much?' Leah said.

'Three hundred quid.'

'Three hundred quid?!'

'Yeah, but it's worth it. An investment.' Raph looks at Leah, serious now.

'And I'm off it all now, Le. The booze, the gear. The fags even. I can't do it anymore. I don't want to end up in the fucking ground. I even had a green tea today.'

'Oh Christ, a green tea?!' Leah smiles, the relief of the conversation is physical, her shoulder blades drop down her back.

'I went to my first meeting, Le. The one at the church. The one you got a leaflet for.' Raph is slightly breathless.

Leah tries to respond calmly, encourage Raph without applying pressure. Her heart beats fast.

'You did? Oh yeah, how was it?'

'I mean, a bit lame. Obviously. A lot of very watered-down squash. The biscuits tasted of empty cupboard. And there's some really rough blokes there. Have you ever seen that dude walking round by the Level who's got a snake tattooed on his forehead? He was there.'

'Is that what it is? A snake?'

'Yeah. Saw it close up and everything,' Raph says, laughing.

She laughs with him. It feels like their secret club from when they were kids, when they'd laugh at their mum's friends and the vicar, when Raph protected Leah in the playground.

'It's a bit sad, Le. The stories you hear. A bit depressing if you ask me.'

'It's good, Raph. It's a start.'

'I saw the doctor as well. She's given me something.'

'What did you tell her?'

'Just that I get in my head sometimes. Find it hard to sleep. Drink too much, probably. And the rest.'

'What's she given you?'

Raph slips his hand into his dressing-gown pocket.

'These little beauties.' He waves a pill packet in her face.

Leah reads the word 'DIAZEPAM' on the front of the cardboard box, warnings in small letters, a green pharmaceutical cross. She feels briefly emptied of something, a pang of fear, then a burst of heat to her head. She rips a bit of dry skin from her lip with her front teeth.

'Sedatives? You gunna take them?'

'Yeah. Course, why wouldn't I?' Raph gets back onto the bike. 'She's given me them until I can see someone professionally. I'm on a list.' He starts pedalling.

Leah tastes the iron of blood. She licks her lip.

'Don't take too many of them, will you? I know what you're like.'

Raph rolls his eyes.

'I got them from the doctor, Le. It's not like I'm doing a load of cheap whizz.'

'Hmm.'

'Proud of me then, yeah?'

'I am. I'm really proud of you, Raph.' Leah puts both of her palms around his face and kisses his cheeks.

'Get off! I'm all sweaty.'

'Yeah, you reek.' Leah steps back, looks at him, feels something good swell in her chest.

Leah sleeps with the window open that night. She always does in the summer. She's never scared, not in her block. She loves the sound of other voices in the building, the opening and closing of doors, people chatting over a cig on their balconies, or shouting things across. In the distance, the sea breathes. Lying in bed, she hears it, the sea, thinks of how they all take it for granted, this huge heaving mass of water right on their doorstep. This terrifying, endless thing. Huge, omnipotent, unknowable. The backdrop to their whole lives. The thing that will always be significant because she grew up beside it. That night it sings her to sleep and she imagines a different future for herself. One where Raph is happy and she is free, having left the sea behind for something else.

She wakes up in the early hours with a feeling of dread. She glances up at Matthew sleeping in her bed, his thin frame. She hears the exercise bike through her bedroom wall, looks at her clock. It's 3 a.m.

Wednesday

Jay stands outside the soft glow of Nathan's flat. He can hear low music, Benny saying something and the comforting way Elena responds.

It's late but Jay's never noticed or cared about things like that. He knocks again. Elena answers. He wants to throw himself into her arms.

'Jay, love. I haven't seen you in a while.'

'Hey, Elena, yeah. I've been busy.'

'Too busy for us now?' Elena says, but she's being playful, tilting her head and smiling.

'Now now,' Jay says. It's easy to fall back into how it is between them, familiar and warm.

'I'll behave.' Elena pulls the door open as wide as it will go. 'Well come in, honey, come in. You know you're always welcome.' She makes way for him and he squeezes his body through the narrow landing and into the living room.

Jay is hit by the smell of fig candles and incense, the heat of the place.

'Sorry it's hot, you know these windows are tiny.'

Elena's hands are covered in soil.

'I've been working late. Nathan was just running me a bath. He's nipped to the chippy if you want some food?'

In the living room, Elena lights a roll-up. Jay feels a rush of warmth towards her. She throws herself backwards onto the sofa, puts her bare feet up on a large drum that acts as a coffee table and gestures for Jay to sit. He stays standing, hunched slightly under the low ceilings, a tendril of hanging plant knocking against his head.

'So what's been going on, honey? You taking care of yourself? It's a tough time for everyone.'

'Yeah, El. I'm doing fine.'

'You working? I've seen Leah but not you. She's been round with Matthew. Poor sod. Didn't see it coming.' Jay avoids this.

'Yeah, yeah. Working at that call centre, you know, out of town, Shoreham way. It's good. It's all right.'

The lie tumbles easily from Jay's mouth. He can feel Elena's eyes homing in on him.

'It's just that? You've just been busy then, yeah?' she says, passing him the lit fag, brushing her fringe away from her face and staring intently. Blood floods the expanse of Jay's cheeks. He bites down hard.

'Yeah.' Jay takes a drag, avoids her eyes.

'Jay, is that a bruise? Have you been fighting?' Elena says, standing up. She is tiny but as she walks towards Jay, he is rooted to the spot.

'It's just some kiddies trying it, El, it's honestly fine. The usual.'

Elena takes Jay's face in her hands and moves it this way and that.

'El, stop.' He tries to laugh it off.

'Jay, what are you not telling me?' Elena says.

She reaches up and put her palms on Jay's shoulders, manoeuvring her face into his eye line.

'Go on, honey. It's me,' she says. 'Look at me.'

He can't hold her off.

'I'm in some serious shit, El.'

'Come here,' Elena says, and pulls him close to her. He weakly responds, arms limp around her.

'Jay honey, hug me properly. You know I don't trust people who don't give proper hugs!'

Jay lets his body relax and wraps his arms around her. In her grip, he feels loose, like he's been holding his body tight for months and has just released it.

Elena strokes the back of his head. Jay lets himself enjoy it for a minute before he starts to regret saying anything. He pulls away and smooths his jumper down, pulling at it with pinched fingers.

The front door shuts and Nathan walks in, holding oil-soaked parcels of chips.

'Nath,' Jay says, grateful for the interruption. Watching Nathan with the food in his hands, walking into the flat, how his mother smiles at him, Jay can't place his feelings; whether it's love he feels, or jealousy.

Nathan is confused, a little panicked at the sight of Jay, sure he's come to confront him about Leah.

'Jay. Hi mate. What are you doing here?' he says.

Jay doesn't know. He only knows that he wants some comfort and this flat is the first place he thinks of when seeking that out.

'Fancy a tea. In the court?' Jay says. 'Too hot in here.' He doesn't know how to tell Elena all the things he needs to say. He's certain if he stays she will employ her unsettling talent of reading his mind.

'Yes, mate. I'll stick the kettle on,' Nathan says.

'Jay, stay here,' Elena says. 'I need to talk to you.'

'You're all right El, I'll give Nathan a hand.'

In the small kitchen, Nathan can't look at Jay. He washes some pans while the water heats slowly in the kettle.

'I've only got goats milk. It's all Mum buys. She says we shouldn't consume anything from an animal bigger than a goat,' he says, trying to gauge from Jay's reaction if he is angry, if he knows yet about Leah. He makes the tea, puts three sugars in Jay's, like he's always had it.

'Don't bloody leave my mugs down in the court again for the birds to shit in,' Elena says as they leave through the front door.

'Jay, this isn't over!' she shouts behind them.

'What's that supposed to mean?' Nathan says to Jay as they walk down the steps.

'Fuck knows. She's got a bee in her bonnet about something. As per.'

They sit with their backs to the metal fencing, rolling cigarettes between their fingers, their mugs beside them.

'I need to talk to you about something,' Jay says.

Something darts through Nathan's stomach. He looks sideways at Jay and feels like he might throw up.

'Go for it,' his voice flickers.

'You know I've been selling a bit. For Mickey.'

Jay touches the bruise on his cheek. He looks around for the lighter on the tarmac to relight his cigarette. Nathan passes it to him, easy as breathing, their rituals. Jay cradles the flame in his palm, protects it from the wind, illuminates the bump on the bridge of his nose.

'I lost some of the pills.' Jay explores the inside of his mouth with his tongue. Worries at a tooth, winces.

Nathan exhales, relieved.

'And what does that mean?'

'It means I owe Mickey Hallahan over two grand and I have no idea where I'm going to get it.'

'How did it happen?'

'I think I just wasn't very discreet. I got pissed. One night when I was out selling.'

'Is that what's up with your lip?'

'Yeah. It's not too bad.'

'Shit.' Nathan pauses. 'Don't tell Leah. She's got enough to worry about.' He says it without thinking.

'What do you mean she's got enough to worry about? I'm the one who's just been robbed.'

'Right, yeah. No. You're right,' Nathan backtracks. He chucks his fag as far as it'll go, sees if he can hit the bins.

'Are you not scared?'

Jay downs the rest of his tea and burps with his mouth closed.

'What's the point in being scared? I'll sort it. Just need to figure out how.'

'If you say so,' Nathan says, not knowing whether he is convinced by Jay or if Jay himself is convinced. Nathan blows a smoke ring into the night, a jagged chalky circle. Jay swipes at the black air in front of him, punches the smoke away.

They sit in silence for a while. Jay smokes laconically.

'I love sitting here,' Nathan says.

'Why?' Jay exhales. 'It's a shit hole.'

'It's our shit hole.'

'That's what your mum always says.'

'Remember racing me down the corridors?' Nathan says. 'Every day after school.'

'I always won,' says Jay.

Nathan's partly saying it because he's taken with a surge of their childhood, sitting here smoking with Jay, remembering the days when they'd all twos on a fag. Jay and Leah would share and then Nathan would get the end. Matthew never got a look in. But he's more saying it because he wants Jay to say something, prove he's the same friend Nathan knew as a kid. It was easy then. The four of them, knocking for each other on weekends, heading for the beach, winter or summer. Nathan, Jay and Leah, dragging Matthew along, clustered together, damp from sweat or rain, chucking chips at pigeons, Jay farting and protesting it wasn't him, punching Nathan and Matthew in the arm by way of saying sorry each time he went too far, passing time doing nothing but playing music off their phones, never wanting the night to come with its cold and force them back home.

They took E together for the first time, provided by Raph. 'Don't go taking a whole thing at once, yeah, and if it doesn't work, chances are it's a dodgy one so don't shove a load in your mouth!' They took it in turns to nibble crumbly chemical texture from a pill shaped like a dollar bill. The local kebab shop sold stolen fags under the counter and they

bought forty and sat on the roof of their flats chaining cigarettes, staring out into the city, rushing and stroking each
other, speaking about how it felt important that they were
from this place, that they were true Brighton kiddies, they
belonged to the city and to each other, they knew the real
town and that made them special. It was easy to be friends
when everything was new, when they were younger. Jay
seemed different then, excited by life. He took care of Leah.
He brought out the good in Nathan, coaxed him out of his
moderate self.

Now, the profile of Jay's brow is strong against the blushed
evening. He frowns deep. His lips are full and strained into a
tight position. He seems thinner, cheekbones jutting out like
a protest. It's hard to connect this man with the younger Jay,
Nathan's perfect companion during the gormless summers they
spent together year on year, playing basketball in the court
until Elena called them both in from the balcony, penalty
shoot-outs just the two of them, horror films until four in the
morning, recording music off the radio and onto cassettes
because they couldn't afford the CDs. Nathan wonders if they
have a friendship anymore or just a habit, a hangover from
being kids on the same estate. *You're lost, mate*, Nathan thinks.
Completely lost.

'What have you been up to?' Nathan says, staring ahead.
'Since we found out about Ron?'

'I've been about, mate. I've been about.'

'Leah said she's not seen you much.'

'Why you talking to Leah about that?'

'I'm not. She just said.'

'Yeah well, you know what she's like.'

Nathan remembers the smell of Leah's breath close to his face and wants to shove Jay hard in the chest. Sometimes he is tired of restraining himself.

Thursday

'We need a night,' Matthew says to Leah.

It's the middle of the afternoon. Pavilion Gardens, chicken wings and a bottle of wine, like they used to. Together, in this town, they've accumulated so much past, so many summers spent together when the other kids from school went abroad with their families. They could make a couple of quid last three days in a town filled with tourists spending money, giddy drunk on the penny falls on the pier. They'd make up dance routines by the bins on the estate, invented a pop group called MaLeah, a hybrid of their names. They blasted songs by boy bands out of their open windows and the tinny music snaked, metallic, around the estate, their young voices singing along. They danced in Leah's mother's dresses in secret. They lay on their bellies and drew together in thick felt-tip, bigger houses, beautiful people. They watched *Robot Wars*, *Fresh Prince* and *Buffy* on Leah's tiny telly and lusted after Spike the vampire. The little squares of grass between the flats felt to them like wide, vast plains to be conquered and known. They rode down the seafront on their second-hand bikes, down to Morocco's the pizzeria that sold the best ice cream in town, where they would share

207

one scoop. They got drunk and went in the sea, the water foaming around their legs, jeans rolled up in the shallows, salt drying chalky on their skin. They smoked paper together because they couldn't find fags. They drank in the streets and danced to Britney playing off their phones during the Pride march. They dared each other to shoplift. They would assess their loot, sprawled out on the grass in the Pavilion Gardens, two little prawns in the sun. Those were fuzzy afternoons, chain-smoking in quick little puffs, watching the sky above them turn mackerel, dizzy feelings rushing out of them.

Leah looks at Matthew and sees him as the thirteen-year-old he was, and remembers the thin little boy with eczema scabs on his arms, telling her in a quiet voice how he liked boys, how he wasn't like Jay or Nathan. He sobbed into the grass afterwards while she ran her hands up and down his back and felt the bumps of his spine. He is still an enigma to her sometimes. Mostly so quiet and tentative, which gives the impression that his inner world is a painful mystery. She watches him as he sits with his back arched like a question mark, still looking afraid of himself. His lips are dry and orange chicken coating has stained the corners of his mouth. She feels an urge to protect him.

'Do you think that's a good idea, Math?' She hates disagreeing with anyone but the thought of drinking too much scares her, even more now than before. She tries to sound relaxed and kind. 'Because it's not been long since, you know. And we've got loads of stuff to sort out for the funeral still.'

'Leah, I'm fine. I want to go out,' he says. He holds his face to the sky, receiving the sun, keeps his eyes closed. 'I've been sitting in your flat for days now. I'm going mad. I've got to do something. They won't let me go back to work. They've covered all my shifts for a month.' He opens his eyes and looks at her. He can be stubborn with wine inside him, the only time he seems to truly back himself.

'Don't look at me like that,' Matthew says.

'OK,' she says quickly. 'Couple of drinks in town.'

Matthew smiles and closes his eyes again.

'Ask Nathan. And we'll have to ask Jay, I suppose,' he says.

Jay's name sends a small shock through Leah's body.

Matthew opens one eye and looks at Leah again. 'How are things with you two?'

'Fine.'

'Will he come, do you think?'

'Who knows.'

She is embarrassed about never knowing if Jay will be around. She can't work out if she is excited about the potential of seeing him or dreading it. She takes the warm bottle and swigs from it.

'I don't care either way.'

It starts at Nathan's pub. Leah walks through the door and Nathan drops a metal ashtray on the floor. Leah looks over at him crouched down, scooping cigarette butts into his palm. They catch each other's eye briefly. Nathan smiles. Leah looks away and wishes she hadn't, it seems cruel but it was instinctive. She is suddenly more aware of herself around him, has lost the easiness. Her actions seem to take on more significance. It creates a frantic feeling, makes her want to avoid him. At the same time, the way he looks at her gives her some kind of satisfying pleasure. Though she didn't enjoy Nathan's kisses, the attention made her feel more powerful than she has felt in ages.

Those kisses are hiding in everything. They drip from beer fonts, they gather with the ash in the garden, they linger with the remnants of pork scratchings in the edges of foil bags, they flash with the lights on the fruit machines and pound with the music. They are everywhere apart from where Nathan wants them to be.

'Le.' Nathan is walking over to her and Matthew, wiping his hands against each other. Leah's eyelids are heavy and her tongue is coated. She's drunk, she knows it, and now he's walking over she finds she wants to make him blush, to be coy and feminine and worldly, in control of him. She feels a little unsteady on her feet and instead she smiles at him, a huge smile, hoping it will defuse everything. They hug for a little too long before they break apart.

'We need a night, Nath. Us lot,' Matthew says. His eyes are shiny. Leah nods at Nathan behind Matthew's back by way of encouragement.

'All right, you bunch of ball bags.' Jay is walking towards them, the door swinging behind him. His voice clangs through the air like a massive bell. He's in high spirits, nothing like the Jay from yesterday, timid in Elena's living room. Leah is relieved but knows the night won't be the same now that he has arrived. It will be so much about Jay. She shares one quick glance with Nathan.

'You got the message then,' Matthew says.

'Well done, brains,' says Jay, ruffling Matthew's hair. Matthew's knees buckle a bit. Jay reaches across Leah and shakes Nathan's hand. He pulls Leah close to him by her wrist and gives her a kiss on the mouth. She's a little stunned but receives it and smiles.

'I didn't know you were coming,' she says to him.

He frowns. 'Why wouldn't I?'

Nathan finishes his shift, shoves one last tray of glasses into the washer, chucks his dirty towel in the corner. And then they are out of the dark pub and into the boiling afternoon.

Leah hangs back watching the three boys ahead of her. Nathan is up ahead, walking alone in the way he always does. Jay is striding, almost bouncing, breaking the approaching dusk with his body, talking loudly to Matthew and close to his face. Matthew is barely keeping up, tall and gliding, turning to look at Jay occasionally, but not saying much, his profile stark and sharp. There is a self-consciousness in his shoulders that Jay and Nathan don't have.

They are lit up, her boys, in the sunlight, Jay's broad back, his blonde hair shining, Matthew's glinting like a crow and then Nathan up ahead, the shape of his curls. Leah is overwhelmed with love, all different types of confusing love hitting her at all angles. She tries to untangle her feelings. She wants one of them to turn around and hold her but they are striding ahead, they won't look back and, besides, even if they did, she wouldn't have the words to explain how she feels right there in that moment, so full of love but so terribly lonely and scared – wanting to leave them all while never wanting to let them go.

Jay turns around and calls to her.

'The Bedford Arms, babe.'

She nods and can't stop herself from feeling warmth towards him at the term of affection he'd used, a word that marks her distinction from the others. He has barely spoken to her since they kissed, but being in his presence when his mood is bright like this is exciting, like the old days. She ignores the nagging anxiety, the argument yesterday, his rough hands on her, the memories of drunk girls with pity in their eyes telling her stories about him, the girls who say hello to him when they are out, who he explains to Leah are 'just friends', girls who went to the school on the other side of town who have glamorous lives that she watches play out on social media, who have decent shoes and small bodies, girls she is nice to whenever she sees them as if to prove to Jay how resilient she is.

They reach the Bedford Arms, an old favourite, the place they've been getting served the longest. It has a mock Tudor exterior, a low wall at the front where old Brighton Boys sit and smoke, a crew of ancient soft leather waistcoats, heavy-looking silver rings in tired earlobes, fantastic moustaches and red wine teeth. The place is run by two men called Dave, one a tall man with a mass of badly dyed black hair, one wide and small with a brilliant white quiff. Tall Dave has a giant pet rat who runs across the damp beer mats, dragging its thick pink tail.

Jay has sunk his third beer before half an hour had elapsed, cold shooting through his teeth. Lager blooms into glasses, frothy heads spill over rims like snow. Their faces become flushed.

Nathan is uncomfortable watching the way Jay and Leah are together. It isn't just the vibrant memory of her naked body. It is to do with the way she looks at Jay, like she's always aware of exactly where he is in the room, how she follows him and fusses, smooths the front of his shirt, picks the fluff from his hair, pauses to let him speak when he interrupts her, agreeing. Nathan can see her working away to turn his chaos into something she can safely love. Each time she puts her hand on Jay, he moves as though he hates being held. He carelessly regards Leah, his attention never fully on her. He moves free around the pub, taking up space, seeking out attention where he wants it, the bass of his voice slamming through everything.

There are moments between Jay and Leah that Nathan finds excruciating to watch. Jay asks her to fetch him things, a cigarette, his jacket. She rolls her eyes, but she does it and he kisses her after each task like a reward. When Jay rubs Leah's thigh as she sits at the bar, he tells the room she's been eating too much bread and looks around for a laugh. When she doesn't laugh, he nudges her with his elbow, a little too hard, asks her if she is OK, his question a warning. 'Look, Le, you've got a cracking body but you've always said you'd be happier if you were a little slimmer,' he says. 'I'm saying it for you, not me.'

Sometimes it feels like a game with Jay. He pushes so hard until it hurts her, badly, then makes it up to her with gestures, picking her up by the waist, spinning her around, kissing her in front of people, loving her again.

'Leah, did you put this shit on?' Jay says, walking to the speaker, hips first. Leah blushes.

'Think so,' she says.

Jay plugs his own phone in behind the bar as the two Daves have always let them, selects a different song, something loud and fast. A few people make noises of approval. Nathan is reminded how everything Jay likes always seems imbued with a sense of magnitude, simply because he endorses it.

Nathan watches Jay walk out front. On the way, Jay says hello to a girl, touches her on the wrist. Jay gets close to her and says something quiet in her ear. The girl looks young.

Nathan notices Leah is chewing her lip by her bag at the table, watching it play out.

Leah takes tight little sips of her cider, watching the pub to see who is watching her. A group of men in the corner stare blatantly at her chest. She feels both invaded and proud that she is worthy of some attention. She wants Jay to notice, to display some kind of jealously but she knows he won't. If she mentions it, it will seem obvious to him that she is searching for some protective instinct that he doesn't have. She keeps her eyes away from Nathan, and her eyes firmly fixed on Jay, regards everyone else but him with the sloppy half attention of someone completely in love. She'd told herself earlier that she would be indifferent to Jay, that this night would be hers and Matthew's, but since he kissed her in front of everyone, she can't.

She watches Jay with his hand on the girl's wrist, goes to the toilet because she doesn't know what else to do with herself. Recently it's like she's forgotten how to be in a social situation, like everyone is doing her a favour by spending time with her. She gets nervous introducing herself to new people in a way she never used to before. She can't respond to jokes as quickly, without feeling self-conscious. Words get stuck. She can't remember an exchange when she came out on top.

She smooths her hair and licks her lips, hoping to soften them, checks her shape in the toilet mirror as if it would have miraculously changed, morphed into something thinner in the last hour. The girl that Jay was talking to was so beautiful, it had made her want to go home and cry. There were certain women, she observed, who seemed to be born with an innate elegance that they didn't even know they had, an effortlessness. She wonders what sort of things they worry about.

When she gets back from the toilet, Jay is in the middle of a joke, the girl looking up at him; Dave is laughing, pouring two beers at once with one hand. When Leah walks back into the circle, Jay notices her but carries on talking. When he watches her, she feels ridiculous, massive, each movement exaggerated. The punchline comes. Jay is glowing with approval. The girl laughs. Nathan doesn't.

'Don't mind Nath. He doesn't say much,' Jay says, pushing Nathan in the chest. 'Nath, stop staring at everyone and say something.'

'I'm getting a drink,' Nathan says.

Leah lingers, then decides to join Nathan at the bar, feeling drunk enough now to talk to him but pretending she's in charge of herself. The pub has become very full. Nathan is standing with Matthew at the bar, talking close.

'You know, I read we all have a certain amount of heartbeats. So how quickly your heart beats determines how long you live. Like a fly lives such a short life because its heart's going ten to the dozen,' Nathan is saying to Matthew. Leah smiles at the two of them, leaning on the bar together. In the hot little corner with Matthew and Nathan, she feels like she could start enjoying herself.

'Nath, if that's true, you're gunna live forever,' Matthew says. 'You've got that big mammal heartbeat. Slow. Not like me, I'm always flapping.'

Nathan is drunk and his limbs look a bit unruly. When Leah arrives, he puts his arm around her shoulders. It feels nice, to be both held on to and to be able to lean into him. She lets him keep his arm there. He leans into her ear, breath sour and hot, a tiny wind against her neck. Her skin prickles.

'Let's go outside.'

Outside smells like piss and there's broken glass on the street catching light and throwing it right back up to the flat sky, like glitter. Leah sits on the low wall.

'You OK?' Nathan says, rolling his cigarette.

Leah blows out through her nose. 'Is anyone OK at the moment?' They catch eyes. She feels a pull behind her navel. They look at each other with a look reserved only for people who have fucked.

'I know, stupid question.'

They smoke for a bit, passing Nathan's roll-up between them. Nathan never feels the need to fill silences and Leah is thankful in that moment. They catch each other's eye occasionally and laugh, in on something just the two of them.

'You're being quiet,' Leah says.

'You know me,' Nathan responds. The secret between them makes everything seem like it's got a double meaning.

A group of girls in tiny dresses fall out of the bar opposite, laughing hysterically. Their heels clatter down the street, towards the sea. Leah watches them disappear. Lately, night times when people are laughing and without care always break her heart a bit.

'Leah—' Nathan starts. There is something underneath the way he says her name. Leah stops him.

'Don't say what I think you're going to say.' She holds the cigarette up like a stop sign. She wasn't expecting a confrontation from him.

'What do you think I'm going to say?' He always hesitates

before he speaks and runs his eyes over her face, which makes each moment more suspenseful.

'About us,' she says.

'I think we should talk about it.'

'Why? It happened. It's not going to happen again. Ever.' It sounds cruel out loud but she knows it's true.

Nathan has a blank look on his face.

'I don't believe you.'

'Nath. Don't. I can't. Not now.'

'I haven't stopped thinking about it,' Nathan says. 'I'm going mad over it.'

'Well stop.'

She flicks the cigarette into the gutter and tries to go back inside. Nathan grabs her shoulder and turns her to face him. His hands on her hurt, they dig in with too much pressure.

'Nathan.'

Two men turn around to look in their direction. Nathan doesn't release her shoulder. His grip tightens. The men are still looking but they don't say anything. Leah can feel more eyes spinning in their direction. She is surprised by how hard Nathan is holding her, how much it hurts.

'Nathan?'

She feels his grip intensify. She tries to shrug him off but he's holding her too tight so she bends down and sort of wriggles out from underneath him, her neck bent at an awkward angle.

'Nathan, what was that?'

'Leah, please. Listen to me. I've been thinking.' He's reaching out his arm as though he's going to grab her again.

'Nathan, come on. Let's get another drink. Please.'

Nathan is looking up at the streetlights and keeps inhaling sharply.

'I love you, Leah.'

'I know you do. But, there's Jay.' It feels ridiculous.

'You and Jay, it's over, it's been done for a long time. Why are you still pretending that's going to work out?'

'You don't know anything about it.'

'Really, Le? You don't think I know? About what he's like. He's not good for you.'

'Please can we leave this?' Leah puts her hand on his chest and it's warm, heaving up and down. Part of her has already gone inside, wondering what Jay is doing. She tries to walk away again. Nathan puts his arm in front of her chest.

'I'll tell him.'

'Nathan, don't.'

'You OK, darling?' a woman calls over.

'She's fine. Leah, I will tell him.'

'Fine.'

Jay walks out with a fag between his teeth. Nathan drops his arm.

Jay looks at the two of them. Leah thinks she sees something flicker over his face, something like recognition. Jay lights his fag, smokes it hard like he's not even enjoying it.

'What's happening?' he says.

'Nothing.' Nathan goes back inside. He bumps Jay's shoulder as he does and Jay staggers back a bit. Jay looks down at Leah and feels for a moment that he wants to protect her. Her cheeks are all red from being out in the wind, a bit of her hair is standing up, the streetlight behind her showing stray wisps. She looks so familiar to him, like a part of his own body.

'Everything all right?' he says to her and gives her shoulder a hard squeeze.

'Yeah.'

Looking down at her face, he is hit by the knowledge that he could do anything he wanted tonight and she'd forgive him.

Before it's midnight, their faces are stolen by drink. They are dehydrated and throbbing, their movements getting slow, clumsy, vestiges of the night all around them, empty glasses ringed with old beer foam like the scud of the sea. Everything starts to blur. Jay produces some rocky-looking coke that he spoons out to everyone on a key.

Matthew feels the tug of his bowels, heat rising through him, metal taste in the back of his throat, fingers irritable and needing something. He stops noticing how loud the music is, and how everyone's voices rise to match it, how they're close in each other's ears, talking.

'I just feel sometimes I could do more, you know?' Leah says.

'Like what?' Matthew shouts.

'Like, I dunno, teach or something?' Matthew sees her jaw clench and unclench. She's more drunk than she usually gets; her head looks too heavy to hold straight. 'I think I could be good at that.'

Jay is in the corner, finding music, skipping through songs too quickly, making Matthew's head pound.

'Head off to uni with the brainy lot, yeah?' he says from the corner.

Leah flushes red. Her chest is blotchy.

'I don't know. That's the point. I just feel old.'

'You'd feel well old there.' Jay is standing up now, shirt undone slightly, an unlit cigarette between his teeth the wrong way round, eyes closed and swaying to the music. 'They'd all be eighteen. And rich.' His eyes widen. 'Fuck me, this stuff is good. It's like speed or something.'

'Jay, why do you always have to piss on the bonfire?' Leah says.

'What? I'm not.' He opens his eyes and looks at her. 'Jesus,' he says. 'There's always something I'm doing wrong.'

Matthew looks at him witheringly.

'What?' Jay says.

'Nothing. It doesn't matter.' Leah takes a sip of her drink.

'You're so sensitive,' Jay says.

On the way to another bar, they pass pubs closing up, stacking chairs, the smell of bleach in buckets, everyone turfed out into the dark negotiating whether to stop and go home or whether to wring the last dregs of fun out of the night. Matthew watches. He's hit abruptly with the reality of what has happened. That Ron is dead. That he is out here drunk and trying to forget and that memory is not a choice but an onslaught.

Leah puts her arms around him, breathing hard and heavy. They sway together like trees as they walk up the street, Matthew's teeth chalky in his mouth. Leah's feet slap ungracefully on the pavement. She wipes something, ash maybe, off Matthew's cheek.

A couple walk past Matthew and Leah, blatantly in love, kissing while walking and tripping over, laughing together. Matthew thinks of Caleb.

'I met someone, Leah. Well, I found him again.' He says it quickly before he stops himself, glad he is not face to face with her.

'A man?'

'Be quiet. Yes.'

'What, they can't hear us!' Leah gestures to Jay and Nathan. 'They don't care either, Matthew. No one does.'

'I know. But I don't like it. I don't like them knowing.'

'OK. Well when did you meet him?' Leah is excited, child-like suddenly. Matthew still finds it hard to believe she's actually pleased for him.

'Before all this, obviously.' He's walking quick, his tongue thick and thirsty.

'And?'

'And nothing. I haven't spoken to him since Grandad died.'

'But you are thinking about him. Aren't you? Have you told him? About what happened?'

Matthew remembers the fumbling with the keys to Caleb's front door, kissing in between trying to open the lock. He thinks of his grandad taking off his shoes.

'I can't. I don't know how to say it.'

'Just text,' Leah says.

'And then what?'

'And then see him, no?'

'I'm scared to. I always manage to fuck everything up.'

'No you don't. And who says?'

'I do.'

'You won't.'

'How do you know that?'

221

'Well I don't. But you can't live like that.'

Matthew doesn't respond. He wants the conversation done, the exposure of it, the fact she can't change his mind.

They walk in silence for the entire next road. Leah's hands are firm on Matthew's arm. He can tell she wants to say something, she keeps opening and closing her mouth, a drunk little fish at odds with herself.

'I did something awful,' she says.

Matthew feels her starting to shiver slightly, it is the coldest part of the day, the moon melts into the sea behind them.

'What?' Matthew is grateful for the distraction.

'Me and Nathan.'

'No.'

Leah nods. She looks at him then with red-ringed lips and wide eyes, her jaw stiff.

'And Jay?'

'He doesn't know. Don't say anything.'

'Obviously.'

'Shit.'

'This is a mess,' Leah says.

'OK. Don't panic. It doesn't have to be a mess. No one's ever going to find out. Nathan's not exactly going to tell anyone. People do this kind of thing all the time. And then they just get on with their lives and no one ever knows. Or if people do know, no one says anything. Just keep quiet.' He waits a moment. 'Are you going to end it? With Jay, I mean?'

Leah shakes her head. 'I don't know. I need to think about it. Maybe. I don't want to. We do love each other.'

Matthew looks at her. She looks like a little girl. He's always kept his feelings about Jay to himself, scared to push her away. He's drunk now though.

'You deserve better, Le,' he says.

'Yeah, so does everyone.' She scrabbles in her bag for some gum. 'Relationships aren't straightforward. We've been together so long, we're bound to have problems.'

'This is more than problems, isn't it?'

'Well who's to say I wouldn't have this with the next guy I meet? Who's to say I'd even meet someone else?'

'Well you definitely would.'

'It's me too. I'm not a saint in all this,' Leah says. 'I can actually be very unreasonable.'

'I find that hard to believe.'

'I don't want to throw all this away. I do still love him. I've never woken up and just been certain, like right, I don't want to be with him. Even after all the bad stuff.'

'But you know, don't you. About the other girls.'

'Yeah. But I agreed to it. Our relationship is more than possessiveness or jealousy.'

'Did he say that?'

'Yeah, but I see what he means.'

'Do you?'

'Yeah, Like I love him for him, not because I can control his actions. If you think about it, it'll actually make us better people. It might even make the relationship last longer. Monogamy doesn't always necessarily work for some people.'

'This is coming from you?'

'No, it was his idea, but I agree. That it can advance our relationship, on a deeper level.'

'Did you think he would actually see other people when you agreed to this?'

'I don't know.'

'Are you seeing anyone else?'

'No. Apart from what happened with Nath.'

'Why do you think that is?'

'I just haven't had the time, I guess.'

'Or wanted to?'

'Maybe.'

'Well it sounds like you've convinced yourself.'

'You know what, this isn't helping,' Leah says. 'You don't understand, I don't know why we're even discussing it. You can't know. You've never been with anyone. Not really.'

'I'm allowed an opinion.'

'Clearly.'

'And my opinion is he treats you like a joke,' Matthew says. Leah tries to brush it off.

'Oh, you can't be fair because you two don't get on. You're not close.'

'It's not that. I see how he is with you. How you are with him, completely different like you're scared to speak or something. You're smart, Leah. You really think he's going to change? Wake up and be a different man? Once this experiment is over he's going to come back to you?'

'Oh shut up Matthew,' Leah says. She means it to shut the conversation down but it comes out confrontationally.

'You're not yourself around him. You do whatever he wants.'

'Yeah well I've been taught forgiveness. I've been taught love is about sacrifice, compromise.'

'You're compromising! He's not compromising.' Matthew

224

laughs to try and soften the argument. 'Leah, I've got this awful feeling you're signing yourself up for a lifetime of unhappiness if you don't get out.'

'Are you jealous or something?' Leah says. It comes out quick. Matthew stops in the street and looks at her.

'Oh fuck you. I can't be bothered with this,' he says. He leaves her there, walks ahead to Nathan.

A lump calcifies in Leah's throat. They've not argued like this before. Her head swims with the drink. She tries to trace backwards through the argument.

A group of beautiful people walk past her. She overhears something obnoxious about Tarantino. She wants to leave Matthew, Jay and Nathan up ahead and walk beside these new people, walk all the way to wherever they are going, hoping it's far away. Instead, she walks behind Matthew at a safe distance.

'I'm going home. I've had enough,' Nathan says. When he walks past Leah in the direction of home, he looks at her as though he hates her. For a moment, she feels so heavy and hopeless she wouldn't mind if a bus came tearing down the road and hit her right there where she stands. She allows herself the fantasy of being hurt badly enough for Jay to cry and fuss over her, hurt badly enough for him to realise he loves her, hurt badly enough for Matthew and Nathan to forgive her while still being all right in the end.

The bar they arrive at is loud and smells of sweat and men's deodorant. It's hard to move through the bodies. Matthew is short with Leah. She keeps trying to talk to him and he gives her one-word answers. In the queue for the bar a boy to Leah's right looks over and smiles. Leah smiles back.

'Fancy him?' Jay says, coming up behind her.

'What?' Leah says. 'No.'

'I don't mind if you do,' Jay says. 'You should talk to him.' He's pushing her again. She can feel him probing her for a reaction. The boundaries he has created are so blurred, so different from hers, it unmoors Leah from her former basic principles of what is normal and what she actually wants. She tries to go along with him but she knows she can't win. Whatever way she reacts will be the wrong way. Jay will always be dissatisfied, either unconvinced if she goes for it, or disappointed if she doesn't. She often wonders what he would actually do if she openly slept with someone else. She suspects it would depend on his mood, and if it suited him that particular day. Either way, it is unlikely she would come out on top. She wishes she wasn't so drunk, she can't think straight, hates the thought of him knowing she's had too much.

'I'll meet you outside,' she manages over the music, goes to the toilet and leans her head against the cold cubicle wall.

Outside, Jay and Matthew stand among the bodies behind a red velvet rope. Jay offers Matthew a fag from his packet first, the decent thing to do, and then the lighter. Matthew appreciates this mark of respect that doesn't require them to communicate verbally.

'When's the funeral, then?' Jay says.

'Next week.'

'Oh yeah, that's right.' Jay nods. 'How you feeling?'

'I'm OK. It depends. Leah's been amazing.'

Matthew gives Jay a look that he hopes he will correctly interpret. Jay is unfazed. He's smoking deeply, not looking.

'Yeah. Not surprised. She's good at all that.'

'Organising funerals?'

'Like, helping people.'

'Like helping you?' Matthew is still emboldened by drink. Besides, he's not scared of Jay in the way other people are. He can see through him.

'Yeah, she helps me. Sometimes.'

'Sometimes?'

'What you getting at, mate?' Jay says, holding his cigarette, seeming to forget to smoke. He fixes Matthew with a practised look, like he's trying to get him to back down. Matthew goes for it, uses some of the anger he has grown inside of him this last week.

'What's going on with you and her, Jay? It's messed up. Do you love her?'

'Yeah. Of course I do. Of course I love her. She's family. She's like . . . home to me.'

'Home?'

'Yeah.'

'Like cosy . . . comfortable? Reliable, that sort of thing?'

'Yeah. And she takes care of me.'

'And what do you do for her, do you think? I'm actually genuinely interested.'

'I don't know. I'm there for her. I love her.'

'Are you there for her? I've not seen that lately. She's not happy. She tries to hide it because, you know, she's strong, doesn't make a fuss, she cares about you, well she loves you, but she hates it. All of it. You and her.' Matthew feels the quick rush of telling the hidden truth. Jay is still standing wide, taking up room.

'What?'

'With you. She's not happy with you. It's clear you actually make her very unhappy.'

'Well I've told her how it is, Math. Made it clear she can see other people if she wants to,' Jay says, holding his hands up. 'It's her decision at the end of the day. It's not really my fault if she's not said anything about not being happy.'

'God, you're even stupider than I thought.'

'I'm stupid?' Jay's eyes are icy, carved out.

'Yeah, Jay. You shouldn't have asked her to do that. It's not right.'

'I'm not going to take a lecture from you on how to treat people.'

'Me?'

'You can't talk, mate. You couldn't even look after your own flesh and blood, when you lived under the same fucking roof all those years.'

This makes Matthew take a step back. The smoking area seems to have gone quiet.

'That's not fair.'

'OK. But it's true. And I'm probably the only one who will say it, but how the fuck could you not have known something was going on there? How do you go about just ignoring something like that?'

'I wasn't ignoring anything.'

'What?' Jay leans in towards Matthew's face.

'Don't you think if I knew I would have done something?'

Leah is outside now, standing by Matthew's side, watching the two men talk.

'How you didn't see something was wrong I'll never fucking know,' Jay says.

'Well you didn't either.'

'I didn't fucking live with him.'

Leah jumps in.

'Jay!'

'No, not now, Leah. He needed you. And you did nothing,' Jay says to Matthew.

'It wasn't like that.'

Jay is heaving his chest up and down.

'Go home, Jay,' Matthew says.

'No. Fuck you, Matthew. Telling me to go home? You think you're better than me. Smarter. Shit, you think you're more interesting. You and Nathan, chatting your shit together all the time. And then you tell me how to treat Leah? Like you know her better than me?'

'I think I do actually.'

'Stop,' Leah says. 'Please.'

'You don't know anything,' Jay says to Matthew. It sounds juvenile and Matthew smiles.

'It's not funny,' Jay says. 'He was good to me, your grandad. You don't know anything about him. Do you know about Billy? About what he was going through?'

'What?'

Leah looks pale, watching on.

'Yeah, you don't even know about that,' Jay says. 'I spoke to him all the time. Every day.'

'Good for you. I did too, by the way.'

'I actually listened to him.'

'I listened to him.'

'No you didn't. Clearly you didn't.'

'Just because he told you stuff that he didn't tell me doesn't make you a better person.'

'He loved me.'

'Oh shut up, Jay. Why is this a competition? Why does everything have to be about you all the time? You are obsessed with people liking you. Billy Big Bollocks marching around. Not everything is about you.'

Jay pushes Matthew in the chest. It knocks the wind out his lungs.

'Faggot,' Jay says. He spits on the floor. A bit adheres to his chin.

'Don't!' Leah shouts.

People are starting to look. Matthew staggers and as he's straightening back up, Jay pulls back his arm and hits him in the face. It makes an ugly sound, flesh connecting with flesh and bone. Matthew doubles over and whips his hand up to his face, his nose streaming blood. Jay freezes, looks at what he's done, Leah cupping Matthew's hot blood in her hands, spilling through her fingers, dark and thick and hitting the floor. She's saying 'oh my God' over and over. Matthew's hair falls out of place, hangs in thin strands across his forehead. His body is turned away but Jay can see he is in pain, the blood dropping in silky circles on the floor. Jay looks at his knuckle. It's red, trembling slightly. He hears a roaring, everything around him loud and chaotic, like he's standing beside a motorway. Bodies jostle like molecules, reacting to the fight. He hops over the velvet rope and walks off into the night before security come over, doesn't look back.

Matthew is swaying slightly on the spot. Someone brings out a roll of blue paper towels and he presses a wad to his face. The pain starts after the shock has gone, booming all through his head. Blood bubbles in his throat and his voice sounds strange.

'I'm sorry,' he says. His eyes are streaming.

Leah takes him by the elbow.

'Come on. Home,' she says.

Friday

Matthew wakes up too early, feeling terrible. His heart is banging quickly, his chest tight. His mouth tastes awful and ashy. A hangover is spreading around the whole of his body. The air in Leah's room is fat with the smell of hot, drink-filled bodies. Matthew cracks the window, letting an aggressive slant of light fall in. Leah stirs on the floor in her jumper and pants.

He looks in the mirror. The bridge of his nose is thicker, a slight yellowish bruise has spread under each eye. His skin is pale and he looks half dead. The night comes back to him in pieces. There are gaps in his memory but he keeps getting slapped by the argument with Jay and is filled with a bleakness. He wishes he'd never gone out.

How is it possible, he thinks, to feel so invincible a matter of hours before, like you could say or do anything, and after some snatched, agitated sleep, feel so completely awful? It seems only minutes ago that they were bang in the middle of last night, feeling reckless, like their lives were changing, saying whatever they wanted. Now, the daylight fills Matthew with regret, the meekness that arrives after the boldness caused by

232

drink. Everything feels sinister. He keeps moving to stop himself thinking. He flicks on the kettle in Leah's small kitchen, hoping Jenny won't come in and try and talk to him. He reads the back of a cereal box to distract himself. His hands on the kettle and cups comfort him; here is something he knows how to do.

He remembers making coffee for his grandad, how he was particular about how he liked it and how Matthew will never again be able to perform this small act of kindness. It used to feel so tedious. Now he would do it again and again if he could.

He wonders how many coffees he has made for his grandad over the years. He tries to comfort himself with the thought. Perhaps that could have been enough for him to know how much he was loved. He keeps thinking of Jay's voice, that maybe Jay is right, Matthew was complacent, thinking that what they had, the two of them, in that little flat, was enough. *Who were you?* Matthew thinks, now that Ron is not around to answer. *And what was it that made your life so unliveable?*

The guilt begins again, a hot guilt for every time he went out for days, for all the times he was sad or despondent and lay in his room with the door shut, for not asking more about Ron, for failing to somehow coax it out of him. He imagines his grandad alone in his room, in his vest, turning his sadness over in his head. Matthew slams his fist down hard on the kitchen counter to try and get rid of the image.

The kettle boils. Matthew pours the water, tries to remember the good things. The tidying of their flat together, the chores they shared each week, cooking good simple meals like mince and onion, peas and mashed potato. They watched old Westerns and at Ron's request, *The Third Man* or *Casablanca*, depending on his mood, though he would always fall asleep before the end. Matthew knew the words off by heart but never got bored of watching them, the familiar scenes holding him tight in an old comforting routine. They talked about how the sea looked depending on the weather, the different boats on different days, the oil tankers and cruise liners and sailboats. Ron listened to the shipping forecast at night, which Matthew could hear through the thin walls. After Ron had given Matthew his first camera, after they had fixed it together, Matthew took photographs of his grandad's hands and his face, his noble jutting brow, and showed him the negatives with a little square viewfinder. These portions of his quiet life with Ron arrive like butterflies, landing and pausing.

Matthew hears Leah groan from the bathroom then her footsteps on the way to the kitchen.

'I could barely piss, I'm so thirsty,' she says and slumps herself into one of the kitchen chairs. Matthew puts a cup of tea in front of her. She's staring at the table, picking inattentively at her eyelashes and pulling a couple out by accident.

'I feel as if my head's been kicked in,' she says. She puts her head on the table with a dramatic thud. Matthew can tell she's exaggerating her hangover to defuse the tension between them from last night.

'Mine practically was,' he says, sipping his tea.

Leah looks up at him guiltily. Matthew smiles to soften the room. He lacks the energy to hold any grudge.

'I can't believe he did that,' Leah says. 'I'm so sorry.'

'Why are you sorry? You're not responsible for him.'

Leah blows air out of her mouth with such force it makes the newspaper on the table lift. She plucks at a tight elastic hairband around her wrist. It's left a deep, red groove.

'I'm so done, Math. I can't believe I've let it go on this long. I can't believe he did that to you.'

'It's gone too far now, Le. You and him.'

'So people keep telling me.'

'Surely you see that for yourself?'

'I do.' She pauses. 'I just can't think about cutting it off before the funeral.'

'I'm not asking you to.'

The atmosphere shifts a bit.

'Have you spoken to him?' Matthew says. 'This morning?'

Leah shakes her head.

'Listen, Math.' Leah takes a deep breath in. 'Those things he said. They're not right. You couldn't have fixed everything alone. Jay's an idiot. He thinks he's right. About everything. He's not.'

'Thanks, Le.'

'Do you believe me?'

'I will eventually. I hope.'

'Let's go to Joe's,' Leah says. Even her voice sounds hungover, low and hoarse.

On the way to Joe's, the local greasy spoon with fake wooden walls and tables covered in plastic cloths with fag burns still present, Matthew stops by the flat. Billy's name keeps nagging at him, like a fingernail on a pair of tights. He wants to scour the flat and find him there in the objects Ron owned.

Leah waits outside, resting against the balcony railing, watching huge boats made tiny by the distance.

Though it's been his home for years, standing in the living

room, it feels like Matthew has never lived in the flat. The whole space seems to have taken on a distant quality. An urge arrives, to pack everything up, to clean it all.

He knows what he wants: something to read, some evidence of life that will bring him closer to Ron. He crosses the living room and starts looking through the small desk. It's mainly receipts, old change, bills, pages of the paper ripped out, crosswords. In a small drawer Matthew finds a soft brown leather address book. He holds it tightly in his hands then puts it to his face. It's soft against his nose. He breathes it in, the rich leather.

'We can get rid of everything in there, Le. I'm only going to keep a few bits,' he says. 'I want you to have the books though. He'd want you to have the books.'

'God, they won't fit in my flat.'

'Fine. Pick ones you love. And take them with you. Wherever you go next.'

Matthew and Leah look at each other for a moment. Something has dislodged in them both, something wordless which they seem to share with one look. They don't know when it happened, perhaps last night, the cheap coke, the same old pubs, the night out, the punch, the blood pooling onto the concrete, activating something in them. They're ready for something else. Matthew takes Leah's hand.

'I'm sorry about last night,' Matthew says. 'I was harsh.'

'Don't be. I was an idiot. I've been so stupid.' They keep their hands linked, heat trapped between their palms as they walk away from their block.

In the café, they cut through the smell of bacon with the stink of their skin, tobacco and sweated-out drink. They sit in a corner, shoulder to shoulder. The smell of cheap ketchup makes Matthew want to throw up.

'I feel grim,' Leah says to a dried mustard stain on the table-cloth.

After strong tea that makes their saliva thick, Matthew puts the little brown address book on the table.

'I want to have a look at this. Jay's right. I didn't know much about his friends. He was private about them. And Billy. I've heard his name before, just thought he was a mate from school.'

'What did Jay say?'

'He said "you didn't even know what he was going through with Billy." Maybe he's sick or something.' Matthew rubs the soft leather with his thumbs. 'Did you know how much they talked? Jay and Ron?'

'Yeah. More after his dad died. Sometimes I'd think he was using it as an excuse not to see me, but a lot of the time I genuinely think he was with Ron. He was always going on about how much there was to learn from him.'

'Hmm. That's so Jay.'

'What do you mean?'

'Wanting to get something out of people.'

Leah blows air through her nose, a tired laugh.

'I didn't think they would talk about this kind of stuff,' Matthew says.

'I guess we didn't know the extent of it.'

'Yeah. I thought we could, I don't know, like contact Billy.' Matthew waves the address book at her gently. 'I should invite him to the funeral if he's important.'

'Well go on then. Open it,' Leah says.

'I can't. I don't know. I can't see his handwriting. It's too sad or something,' Matthew says.

Leah nods and takes the book from Matthew. He watches her run her finger down the tiny paper tabs at the side which divide the book alphabetically. She stops on 'B' and opens it at the right page.

Matthew looks over Leah's shoulder. Every entry is in delicate, soft pencil. Ron had a beautiful, swooping hand, his Ls and Ss particularly gorgeous. There are names and addresses, landline numbers, the occasional mobile, and birthdays written neatly. Some of the older entries are so faded Matthew can barely read them. Leah scans the pages in the 'B' section.

'There's nothing here.'

Matthew feels hope leak out of him, suddenly directionless.

'It might be done by surname,' Leah offers.

'I don't know what his surname is.'

'Well, I'll just have to start at the beginning and find the fucker.' Leah doesn't look up, eyes hovering over each line. 'You better get us some more tea.'

Matthew gets up and walks to the counter. 'And a Snickers.' She winks at him.

'It's not here,' Leah says, after a while.

'Why does Jay know this? Why was he telling Jay all these things and not me?'

'Why don't you ask him?'

Matthew gives her a look. 'Ask Jay?'

'Fair,' she says. 'Shit. I've got to go to work, but take my keys, yeah? And go sleep. You need it.' She kisses him on top of his head.

After Leah leaves, the prospect of an entire day alone feels flabby and unbounded. Matthew's tired but knows he won't be able to sleep. He is urgent, restless, sick of the limbo and the pointless days that surround grief. He wants to do something.

Instead of walking to Leah's he goes back to his flat again. He nudges the door to his grandad's room and steps in. He expects it to feel ghostly, but it just feels flat, like no one has lived there for years. He lies down on the bed and stares up at the Artex ceiling. It dawns on him that he can touch anything he likes now. He props himself up on his elbows, leans over to the bedside table and picks up the picture frame that's stood there. It's a wooden frame that Ron had carved himself, intricate, ornate. Inside is a photo of Matthew's nan in a beautiful fuchsia dress, her hair white, and Matthew standing thin, even as a toddler, at her feet. They're in a neat garden somewhere and she is smiling. The sky in the photo is faded slightly and there are a few orange spots in the corner, like it had got wet once, a few tiny dead bugs trapped behind the glass.

Matthew wants more. He looks in all the drawers and cupboards in his grandad's room. There are woollen socks balled in pairs, screws, little pieces of old watches, pencils, a battered tin of watercolours. There are books of maps, notebooks full of scrawls and hand-drawn routes, old cans of motor oil, some beautiful bow ties in a wooden box. There are plaid shirts and there are bright raw silk shirts he never saw Ron wear. On the floor of the wardrobe are boxes, plastic storage containers. They are full. Some hold things from Matthew's childhood, topic books from school, colourful posters he'd made about the environment and history projects on the Tudors, the papers stained with tea to make them look old. Matthew can't believe that Ron had kept these things for all these years. It reminds him how Ron used to sneak into his room as a kid, replacing the milk teeth under his pillow with fat pound coins. He searches deeper inside the boxes, finds more photographs of his nan, his dad as a wary-looking toddler in a sailor's outfit, black and white photos of Ron at school. In a shoebox he finds letters. The letter on the top is the most recent. It's headed and signed: Billy. Matthew leans against the wall and reads.

Dear Ron,

As I write this, I am sat on a bench on the Malvern Hills, looking out over the Severn Valley. It's a beautiful view but a little windy and overcast, bracing. I've always felt at peace on the hills. You got tired of me telling you that each time we drove to the South Downs with my flasks and your waterproof maps. What walks we had! These hills, though, I find particularly spectacular, so much more dramatic than the Sussex coast. I had hoped we would come here together one day, and I could show you myself. There is a natural spring, water simply shooting from the earth, a taste like you wouldn't believe, so much better than our chalky water down south. You may remember me telling you that my grandmother lived here, in a small village a few miles outside Malvern. I came here as a boy to stay with her. She was a wonderful woman and she loved me very much, always without complaint. I think probably much more than anyone else ever did. I have always found, being the man that I am, such kindness from the women in my life. I know you feel this too, having spent so many years with such a wonderful patient wife. To be truly loved is to be accepted for exactly what you are. What freedom.

The wind is blowing up a right gale so you'll excuse my handwriting. Ron, I have to write this letter. I can't put it off anymore. I am full of thoughts of you. What better place to write it than here, where I have some resolve, some clarity, where I have so many happy memories living in the very soil of this place.

I can't continue what we have, this friendship, this thing that you can't name. I can't carry on never knowing what we are. To live with you so near to me in miles but so far away in all other senses is too painful.

I know you would have things carry on as they are, but I can't live with the uncertainty, with you turning up in the middle of the night and then vanishing again like you do. I don't know whether I'm coming or going from one day to the next. I am going to ask, for the sake of my heart, that we stop all this now. I won't write anymore, or ring.

When I asked you on the beach for one last shot, I thought for a moment that you might say yes. And that we might live together, that we might find some happiness in our last few years of life (who knows how many more we have?)

I've learnt to accept myself for what I am. I was hopeful you could have done the same. In truth, it felt cruel when you said how wrong it all was, that is to say, how wrong we are for loving each other.

I'm not going to ask you to change your mind again because I know now that you can't. I understand that you never will. That for you it is impossible. I wish it wasn't but that is what you said. I don't want to go into all of that now, not with this view out ahead. I suppose I just want to say the things I couldn't say that day on the beach, that final time.

That is I love and admire you. The time we spent together, these years of friendship, have been the happiest of my life. And I forgive you for not loving me in the way I need to be loved. I hope you understand the reason behind this letter.

I listened again to 'Cigarettes and Coffee' this morning, before I took Nelson out. (He's just been groomed so looking very smart!) I imagined all our late nights smoking, drinking coffees and putting the world to rights. But I think I better stop with all that now. You know how sentimental I can get.

I hope Matthew is well.

Please know I think of you every day, I will always think of you.

Always,
Billy

There's an address. An East Sussex postcode. There's a landline number. The sight of Matthew's name on the paper is strange, like something is reaching out from the letter. Matthew takes out his phone, types in 'Cigarettes and Coffee' and the song comes up immediately on YouTube. He plays it through his phone's speaker, listens to the soft, slow snare drum, the sliding horns. Then the vocal comes in:

> *It's early in the morning,*
> *About a quarter till three,*

Little Boxes

I'm sittin' here talking with my baby
Over cigarettes and coffee

Matthew lies down on his grandad's bed and stays there for a long time.

Friday

'A love letter,' Nathan says.

'That's what I thought,' Matthew replies.

'Christ. Did you know?'

'No idea.'

'What are you going to do?' He's folding the letter up carefully and passing it back to Matthew.

'I want to speak to him,' Matthew says. 'I want to invite him to the funeral.'

'Sounds like they . . . fell out?'

'Mm.' Matthew looks down at the folded paper in his hands.

'Call him?'

'And say what?'

'Just tell him who you are. He clearly knows you. Did you ever meet him?'

'No. I've heard his name a few times. I thought they were just friends.'

'Definitely not just friends.'

'Clearly, Nath.'

'Call him. Definitely. Do it now.'

'I can't. What do I say?'

'You can,' Nathan says. 'Hang on, mate.' He leaves Matthew at the bar to serve a customer. Matthew feels his throat go dry. He can see Nathan watching him as he pours a pint. He unlocks his phone and copies the number from the letter, presses the dial button. He has no idea what he wants this man to say. Part of him prays he won't answer. Part of him wants to ask every single question he can think of and bring Ron back for a moment. Part of him wants the man to tell him nothing is his fault, that everything will be OK. He runs his tongue along his teeth. The phone rings and rings.

'Well?' Nathan says. He's standing back in front of Matthew.

'Nothing.'

He rings the number several more times. Each time his calls go unanswered he wants to speak to Billy more. His mind won't focus on anything else.

'I'm going to go there. To his house. See if he's there,' Matthew says to Nathan.

'Just show up?'

'Yeah. It's not far. Lewes, I think.'

'When?'

'Today. He might not even know about what's happened.'

Nathan puts his hands in his pockets and looks at the clock.

'I'll come with you.'

At the station Nathan buys the tickets. Matthew feels uncomfortable and wonders if people will just carry on doing that now, buying things for him in sympathy. The air-conditioned train is a welcome relief on his hot skin. He and Nathan sit opposite each other on the stiff green seats.

It shouldn't take long to get to Lewes. It's only three stops but to Matthew it feels like hours. Twice the train lingers in a tunnel. He still has a headache and the announcements over the Tannoy are too loud. He can feel his pulse in each toe within his shoes, his blood surging around. He looks at himself in the window. Thin and barely there, he tries to remind himself this is real, he is real.

When the train pulls into Lewes station, Matthew doesn't feel like getting off. He wishes he could ride it all the way to the end of the line, looking out the windows.

'Where are we heading?' Nathan says. Matthew gets his maps up on his phone.

'Fifteen-minute walk, apparently.'

The town is quiet. Nathan buys them two sandwiches from a bakery.

'Fourteen fucking quid,' he says and passes Matthew the roll wrapped in brown paper.

Someone is playing a violin on a bridge with black railings that arches over a brown river. They walk through a precinct which narrows into a small high street. At the end there's a second-hand bookshop in a small old building with a lane on a hill veering off behind it. There is a sign to a golf course. People walk their dogs. The leaves shiver in a sudden breeze.

'This place is full of rich people,' Nathan says.

The incline is steep and they are out of breath. At the top of the hill is a row of about five houses. Number seven has a yellow door.

'This is it,' Matthew says. Nathan crouches over with his hands on his knees, panting.

'You OK Math?' he says.

'I'm fine,' Matthew says but his stomach is turning over.

'You want me to come in with you?' Nathan says.

'Course.'

Matthew looks through the frosted glass panels but sees no movement, just the outlines of furniture in the half-dark, one sharp blade of light illuminating a table full of books, some sunflowers past their best, bowing in on themselves. He takes a breath and knocks, looks around at Nathan, who smiles in encouragement. He thinks he hears movement inside but it's hard to tell. It may be the houses next door or the way old buildings crack and breathe like bodies. He waits for a while then knocks again, harder this time. Another sound makes his heart surge but no one answers the door. He knocks one more time, this time until his knuckles hurt.

Matthew looks behind him again at Nathan, who has a look of pity on his face. His mood slumps. He lingers by the door for a minute, but it remains unopened. He turns around and starts walking down the hill. Without the distraction of tracking Billy down, his hangover intensifies, he's nervous and shivery.

'I guess it was stupid really, thinking he'd be in.'

'We could go somewhere. Wait. Come back?'

Matthew smiles at Nathan's optimism.

'I'm tired. Let's just go.'

Walking back down the hill, they hear a man call for his dog, 'Nelson!'

The name is familiar to Matthew, like he's recently heard a story about it.

He sees the dog then and it makes sense. A brown poodle, short curls cut tight to its body, running up the path towards Matthew and Nathan, his pink tongue swinging from his mouth.

'Nelson, come here!' The man comes walking around the corner.

Nelson stops running towards Matthew and Nathan, turns towards the command.

Billy holds up a large hand up in greeting.

'Sorry!' he says. He's got Nelson on a short lead, wrapping the excess around his fist, hunching down slightly and walking right towards them. 'He's a mind of his own.'

Billy's manner comforts Matthew instantly, like a character from a countryside drama that someone might watch to help distract them from real life, someone with a completely different existence. He's very tall, wide-shouldered with a grey moustache, generous but not untidy. He's wearing a pair of round glasses and Matthew notices that his eyes are the same rich brown as Nelson's, two stars of light reflecting off their glassy surfaces. There is something warm about his eyes, they move Matthew instantly. He's old, his face weathered by the sun and his earlobes big and thick but he is, it strikes Matthew, beautiful. He's got a strong crooked nose and the sleeves on his blue shirt are rolled up to the elbows. The tendons in his neck stand out, skin sagging in between the scaffolding of them, grey hair pokes out of his shirt and up to his Adam's apple. Billy starts to walk away, up to his front door with his keys in his hand.

Matthew is about to let him go. Nathan steps in.

'Excuse me. This is really random but are you called Billy?'

Matthew looks at Nathan gratefully, waits for Billy to reply.

'That's me, yes,' Billy speaks slowly. He's what Ron would have called well-spoken. Nathan gives Matthew a look, eyebrows raised.

'I'm Matthew. Ron's Matthew.' He finds that it's hard to say Ron's name, that it clings on to the inside of his mouth.

Something flickers across Billy's face like wind over a lake, his eyes widen a fraction. He looks a little scared.

'Ron,' Billy says. It's not a question. He's very delicate with his mouth when he says the name, purses his lips slightly after. 'What are you doing here?'

Nelson is pulling at the lead, interested in a squirrel in a nearby tree.

'Nelson, sit.' The dog obliges, his lovely eyes looking up to Billy.

'I wanted to meet you, I suppose. Shall we get a drink? It would be good to talk.' This suggestion feels surreal or like he won't be taken seriously, but Billy nods. Matthew's hands feel stiff and cold at his sides.

The pub Billy chooses is at the bottom of his hill. It has a low ceiling and a stone floor. The walls are panelled with dark wood and it stinks of ale. They're served by a large man with a gold chain resting on his crêpe-paper chest wearing a white vest, shirt and high trousers with a smart belt. He nods at Billy in greeting and takes a glass from the shelf, ready as they walk in. The pub is empty. It's early afternoon. Pale yellow daylight streams in through the windows, shows the dog hair on the flagstones. Matthew wishes there was some music playing.

Billy gives a tug on Nelson's lead and Matthew notices his hands shaking. As Billy buys the round, his movements are slow, gentle.

'That man gets fatter every time I come in,' Billy says, gesturing over his shoulder at the landlord. 'Rests his gut on the bar, I swear.' He takes a big sip of his red wine, looking at the boys over the rim, slightly impish.

'Don't even get me started on his missus, the old witch,' Billy says. He's playful, his eyes glitter.

'Perm almost touches the ceiling and a face like a torn pocket. You hate to see it.' He winks at Nathan.

The three of them settle around a dark wood table, perching on old squat barstools that wobble against the uneven stones of the floor. Nelson sighs and lies down at Billy's feet. Matthew realises he wants Billy to like him, to become fond of him. He wants to appear intelligent, funny.

'Did you drive over?' Billy asks. 'Roadworks on the A27 are a bore.'

'We got the train,' Matthew says.

'Ah. There we are then. Quick, isn't it?'

'Fine, yeah,' Nathan says. He talks a bit about the logistics of the journey. Matthew is nervous, and grateful Nathan is there. Now he's found Billy, he has no idea how to say what needs to be said. He looks at his lively golden lager dancing in the glass. The fact they are together around the table is dream-like. Matthew feels like he could just close his eyes and sleep.

'I wasn't expecting to meet you,' Billy says. He looks up from the dark depths of his drink and meets Matthew's eye. 'Ron's very private about you.'

'Yeah, I'd not heard much about you either.' He pauses. 'I don't know how to do this,' he says. He looks at Nathan for some reassurance.

'It's OK Math. Um. The reason we've come,' Nathan says, 'is we need to tell you something, unfortunately.' He looks at Matthew. 'Math, do you want me to?'

'No. It's fine.'

When he tells Billy, Billy nods a few times, opens and shuts his mouth and makes a kind of tutting sound. Then he closes his eyes and lets out a long breath, lifts both hands to his face and covers it entirely. From behind his hands, Matthew hears a kind of soft groan. Matthew wants to do something with his hands, take a sip of his drink but he feels he should stay very still.

'Dead?' Billy says.

Matthew nods.

'How?'

Matthew and Nathan stay quiet. Billy's eyes are wet-looking, the whites slightly creamy.

'Not deliberately?'

'Yeah,' Matthew says.

'Oh God,' Billy says. 'Oh God.' Matthew and Nathan can see him thinking, his eyes quivering from point to point on the table.

'Well. He suffered. All the time I knew him,' Billy says. Tears are leaking down his wrinkled face; one travels down the deep curved line around his mouth. He looks honourable crying. He lets all the tears fall, doesn't wipe them away. 'He struggled with his moods. He could get very low. He found it hard to talk about.'

Nelson shuffles his feet, stands up and rests his chin on Billy's knee like he knows he needs it. Billy reaches down and buries his face into his fur. He stays there for a while, breathing heavy. He rises up, pauses for a long time. With one sigh he seems to compose himself. Matthew and Nathan watch him take some nicotine pills from his pocket. The packet bends and crackles as he pops one from its casing and slips it into the corner of his mouth.

'I'm sorry,' he says. 'This is very hard.' They can hear the pill in his mouth when he speaks. He exhales warm air that Matthew can feel on his face, the faint smell of mint and spice of nicotine.

'Silly old bugger. What did he have to go and do that for?' he says, not addressing Matthew or Nathan but rather the air all around them.

'I don't know what you know about me and Ron,' he says. 'We had a special friendship. Did he mention me?'

'Not much. I'd heard your name a few times,' Matthew says. Billy looks unsurprised and a little resigned.

'He was quite a guarded man,' Billy says.

'Yeah.' Matthew nods. 'I just wanted you to know and also to tell you that the funeral is next week and that of course we'd love you there.' He feels like he's impersonating an adult. Billy smiles at him.

'Oh yes, I'll be there. I loved him,' he says simply. 'We loved each other.'

'I'm glad,' Matthew says. 'I'm glad he had you.'

'I met your grandad at school.' Billy takes a swift sip. He pulls a handkerchief from his pocket and dabs at his face with it.

'It was a difficult friendship. After school, we were always losing touch. We argued a lot. When I went to university in Scotland, Edinburgh, he was very upset. I didn't see him for years. My mother and father died young sadly, so there was never any reason for me to come back down here. We wrote, a little, for the first year. I met someone. I lived with them for a great many years.'

Billy looks at Matthew as though he's considering how to say what he is going to say next.

'A man. I always knew who I was. I was happy. I was loved.'

Matthew and Billy hold each other's gaze for a long time. Matthew feels naked, like Billy can see right inside his head, can see Caleb perhaps.

'Then your grandad got married. We weren't in touch. I remember hearing it through the grapevine somehow,' Billy says. 'He and your nan had your dad and I thought that was the end of it all. How is he? Your dad?'

'He's coming over,' Matthew says, 'for the funeral. He works abroad.'

'That's right. The rigs,' Billy says. He runs his two fingers over his moustache and tugs at the ends. 'Fathers,' he says. 'So many find it so hard. And your mum?'

'Still in Spain. She's happy. We speak.'

'He did love your nan, you know,' Billy says. 'They were good pals. I remember, he told me, they used to get kicked out of the church hall for dancing too close.'

Billy pauses. The sound of a fat bluebottle.

'This must be strange for you,' Billy says.

'Kind of. But it's OK.'

Billy wipes his cheeks with the heel of his hand and sniffs.

'You got back in touch then?' Matthew says. It feels good to ask these questions, like they will help him find the truth of things, the truth that seems all murky and cold. He wants his grandad sharp in his head again, bright, warm.

'Ah, eventually,' he says. He takes another hefty swig of wine, drains the glass, some sediment is left in the bottom. A few droplets adhere to his moustache.

'When we were in our late twenties. He found me somehow.

I got a letter. This was before the internet, of course. Can you imagine?' Billy manages a small smile.

'So we met. I was living in London by this time. In the East End. Had a tiny place on Roman Road. Fuck me, it was a dive! Ron was still down south, he was doing well, Sonny had been born, he was running the business. But he was sad. Incomplete. Those were his words. He wrote. We started meeting up again after that. Regularly for a few more years. Happy years they were. We had very happy times together. We rented little places, the Lake District a few times. We'd walk a lot. I had a different dog then, Juno. Another poodle. Always brown standard poodles with me, I'm very fond of them. We'd get back after days out in the wind and rain and sleep by the fire with the dog and hot coffee. And I'd look at him, sleeping there, my man, with the rain coming down outside and I'd think, "He's come back to me. Is this heaven? Am I dreaming?" And then the trip would come to an end and we went back to our lives. And I'd have to wait weeks to see him. He'd head out in the night and ring me on payphones. The letters were what kept me going. And then it was the eighties.' Billy lets out an enormous sigh. 'And I lost five friends in a year. It was not a good time to be men like us. Perverts and mentally ill, apparently. Ugly business. And anyway, there was so much going on for the both of us. Your grandad was struggling with his marriage. Your dad was playing up a bit, I remember. The world felt like quite a cruel place to be.'

The lines around Billy's eyes twitch. There are so many, they make his face soft and kind, comforting, like a tree. Matthew can hear a lump sat right in Billy's throat. He pinches the bridge of his nose. His eyes fill up again. 'He came back again, much later. Turned up at my door one night. Didn't even phone! It went on like this for years. And recently, we ended it again. Well, I ended it. I couldn't go on like that anymore. I'm old. I want a peaceful life.' Billy shakes his head and holds his hands up like some admission. 'It felt very final this time,' he says. 'We argued. I wanted him down here. I wanted him to move in, I've plenty of room and, forgive me for saying this, but you're in your twenties now, I told him I thought you'd be fine getting your own place. He didn't want to move out of his flat though. Set in his ways.' Billy keeps going, his nicotine pill crumbling, chalky on his tongue.

'I even said I'd come and live in his place with him, up on the estate,' Billy says. 'But he hated the thought of that. Wouldn't hear a word of it. He said two men living together in the block he raised his own son in . . . he thought it was absurd. Hated the idea of people talking. But he wouldn't live with me either. Which obviously I found very cruel. He said I didn't understand. Said it's easier for me down here with my money and my liberal friends. That's how he put it. So it sort of got to the point where I didn't have much choice. We were at an impasse. I told him I wanted it to be over and that was that. But I did always think we'd find each other again,' Billy says. Droplets of drink are still congregated in his moustache. He swallows firmly.

'He couldn't live with himself. He couldn't be with me in the way he wanted. And there was nothing I could do. I think he realised when we ended it that, no matter where we lived, where we moved, what we did, he still wouldn't be able to reconcile it. And it wasn't just me, us, the way he was. The fact of our. . . relationship. He had always endured these bouts.

Even before I met him. But we didn't talk about any of those things back then. We just got on with it all. He was treated so badly at school. By his father. It did him in really. He was his own biggest secret,' Billy says finally.

'But God, there was so much to enjoy about him, wasn't there?' Billy looks up to his left, with the faint smile of someone remembering, like he's recalling something of great beauty. 'We had such adventures. He was meticulous, thorough. If we were ever going to go anywhere, he'd know everything about it. He'd know it all. He'd have read up on it, taken notes. Maps! And he'd love to talk you through it all. Even bloody motorways!' Billy is crying and laughing, holding his hands up, gesturing, like they're all in on it together. 'His own steak knife whenever we went to a restaurant, with the handle he carved. It used to embarrass me!'

Matthew and Nathan laugh, tears in their eyes now too.

'He knew what was right, didn't he? Decent. Never a violent man. He had advice about how to live, how to be kind. He listened so well. Said he never made his mind up about anyone or anything until he'd slept on it. Always good at tipping waiters,' Billy says. His eyes shine, ferocious.

'And handsome,' Billy says. 'Always dressed smart. Polished shoes.' More tears are falling rapidly from his eyes, running down the tributaries of his face. He ignores them, talks through them with joy.

'He didn't have the words for it, Matthew. He didn't know the language. He was never taught to understand it, least of all accept it. The world made him hate who he was. He was so tired.' Billy shakes his head, smears away the last of his tears.

Matthew feels an urge to open his life up to Billy, to draw himself closer.

'I'm the same. I mean, I like, I don't like girls. I like men, too.' It feels lumpy coming out of his mouth, but it comes out and he's glad. He goes further. 'I'm gay,' he says. 'Do you think he knew that?'

'He might have, I suppose,' Billy says. 'But he didn't want you to feel his fear. He wanted you to have a better life. He would never have told you, Matthew. He couldn't.' He's gentle, lets the words land like wet petals on a lake. Matthew can see the shape of his head reflected in the wetness of Billy's eyes.

'I did always fear this. I've lost so many men to themselves,' Billy says. 'In a way, I'm relieved,' he says. 'That he should no longer be suffering. But I suppose that's the wrong thing to say.'

'No, I know what you mean. It's the honest thing to say.'

'Of course he shouldn't have had to suffer at all.' Billy smiles at Matthew then blinks a few times. 'Anyway, I feel like I've been talking at you forever.'

Matthew wants to stay with Billy. Leaving him feels like another form of leaving his grandad.

'The funeral is next week. Please come,' he says.

'I wouldn't miss it.' Billy takes out a piece of paper and a pen from inside his jacket. Matthew gives him the address of the church.

'I am here. If you need to talk, Matthew,' Billy says. 'Listen, Matthew. There's nothing wrong with who you are.'

'Thanks.'

'And Matthew, the fault. The fault never lies at anyone's door.'

Matthew feels released by Billy's words. When they say goodbye, Billy holds the back of Matthew's neck with his warm hand.

'Come and visit me, Matthew. You're always welcome.' He pauses. 'And safe in my house.'

When Matthew gets back to Leah's, no one is home. He sits down at the kitchen table for a very long time, until the room gets dark. He flicks the lamp beside him on, then off, then on again for something to do, he likes the feeling of having control over something, a small god for a moment.

He starts to picture the secret he and Ron kept from each other as another person living in the flat with them, another body, living and breathing and moving about, squeezing past them in the corridors, forcing space between them. How extraordinary, he thinks, to have shared this commonality but to have never been able to name it, these two men under the same roof.

It makes sense to him now, his grandad's final words to him. A plea for Matthew to try and live differently, to act before he teaches himself so much hate that it can't be unstitched. He thinks of Caleb, of a life of hiding him in the night, whispered doorstep conversations and secret letters, and he knows so profoundly that he does not want that, that his future could be different from the suffering Ron was made to endure, the terrible alternative. He can almost feel the loss shaping him entirely, like hands touching him all over. He is so tired of being silent. He dials Caleb's number. He feels the warmth of the phone against his ear. Caleb picks up on the third ring.

Saturday

Nathan wakes up early. He thinks as always of Leah. Then of Billy's old face weeping. Lately it feels like he's being internally pulled in two directions, a tugging. There is the part of him that feels a low-down bottomless sadness, a dark grey mass inside of him, the cruelty of the world. He can't stop thinking of Ron walking along the beach on the last day of his life. He pictures an alternative life where Billy and Ron walked hand in hand to get the paper in the morning. The other part of him feels so alive, grateful, alert, so relieved that this is his bedroom, his life. Nathan walks into the kitchen where his mum is standing, halving a bowl of strawberries. He holds her for a long time.

Sometimes Ron came into the pub when Nathan was working. He always had half a cider and paid in the exact change. He'd lean against the bar, drink his cider standing up and ask, 'What's on your mind?' and Nathan would tell him.

Once he sketched Nathan in a small, soft sketchbook that he kept in his top pocket. He showed Nathan about perspective, the line of the bar getting further away, the slope of Nathan's left shoulder facing towards Ron.

'It's like most things in life, Nath,' Ron said. 'Pretty hard to wrap your head around at first, but once you've got the knack, it opens it all up. Start with the horizon line and work from there.' He seemed to enjoy teaching others what he knew, practical things that they'd remember for life. Nathan keeps the sketch on his corkboard, the dusty grey lines of it among photos of Leah, Matthew and Jay.

Ron asked after Nathan's parents always, asked if they were healthy. 'Decent folk,' he'd say. He'd always buy Nathan a drink for after his shift, 'Make sure you keep that for yourself. Don't put it in the tips jar. Are you all right for cash, Nath? You'd say if you weren't, wouldn't you?'

Nathan got the impression that Ron made it part of his weekly schedule to check on him, on Leah and Jay, on all the people who cared for Matthew, on the families who lived on the estate. It never seemed like a chore for Ron, an imposition or anything even very deliberate. It was regular, day-to-day, a simple duty.

Ron's final visit to the pub a week or so before he died stuck with Nathan, kept repeating in his head as he lay in bed waiting for sleep.

'One day, Nathan, people will look back on their lives and they will appreciate you for letting them be who they are. You're a good boy,' he said. As he was walking out of the door he turned. 'I hope Jay will fix himself up. Keep an eye out for him. And Nath, thank you for taking care of Matthew.'

At the kitchen table Nathan sips a coffee. The radio babbles about a heatwave, a crisis to public transport, the elderly dying, a possible hosepipe ban. Nathan puts a strawberry in his mouth.

Elena gives Benny a look with raised eyebrows. Benny folds his newspaper.

'Nath, do us a favour and go and check in on Jay. Your mum's a bit worried about him.'

Nathan is reluctant, apprehensive about Jay's mood. But he goes, dutiful as always to his parents.

Jay answers the door looking as though he's just woken up. A dusty shadow of stubble is cast all over his jaw, his eyes swollen from sleep and hair standing up. His tracksuit bottoms are stained.

'Hi mate,' Nathan says. Jay raises his eyebrows.

'What do you want?'

'Just thought I'd come round. See how you're getting on.'

Jay shrugs and pulls the door open wider to let Nathan into the flat.

'Have you eaten?' Nathan asks.

'Can't remember the last time I did.' Jay yawns.

'I'll make some eggs?'

Jay throws himself down on the sofa.

'Fine.'

Nathan pulls a frying pan from the cupboard. He knows Jay's kitchen as well as his own.

'Where's your mum?'

'Work.' Jay flicks through the channels on the TV at speed then turns it off abruptly and throws the remote on the floor.

Nathan is grateful for the sound of the eggs spitting in the pan which interrupts the vast silence between them. Jay is staring at the ceiling. It's strange to see him like this, still, despondent.

Nathan sets the eggs down on the coffee table in front of Jay.

'Is everything OK?'

'She's not at work. We had a row. She told me I was like my dad and then she fucked off to Bournemouth, to my auntie's.' Jay doesn't look at Nathan, sits up over his eggs and grinds the pepper mill furiously.

'What about?'

Jay holds up his right hand and shows Nathan his knuckle. It is angry looking, purple and swollen. He shovels a mouthful of fried egg and bread into his mouth with his free hand.

'Told her about what I did. To Matthew's face. She went off on one. Started saying all this stuff about my dad. I told her she was mad and then she really lost it. Said that's what he used to say.'

Nathan thinks about the time he saw Jerry headbutt a man at a football match and his food starts to make him feel a bit sick. He looks at the jelly of his egg white.

'Have you spoken to Matthew? Said sorry?'

'No.' Jay throws his fork on his plate and it clatters against the china.

'He's not angry. I saw him yesterday. He's fine.'

Jay doesn't respond.

'Eat your eggs before they get cold. Nothing worse than cold eggs.'

Jay starts to cry then, quietly, his shoulders shaking. Tears hover on the rims of his eyes, little divers ready to fall. Nathan wasn't expecting this. He puts a hand on Jay's back, feels the heat and the damp humanness of him. Jay gets up and walks to the window. The curtains are partly drawn so only a bar of daylight shines into the flat. He turns his face away.

'I've fucked it all up, Nath.'

'Come on. You haven't,' Nathan says, though he knows he sounds unconvincing.

'I don't know what to do.' Jay pauses. 'I bet Leah won't talk to me. Won't understand why I did what I did. I didn't mean it. You seen her?' He sniffs, like a toddler after a tantrum who knows they have pushed something too far.

'No. She's been working, I think.' Nathan thinks about the last time he saw Leah, his hand hard on her shoulder. He winces within. 'Just speak to them. Apologise. Move on,' he says.

'They won't understand,' Jay says, turning from the window to where Nathan is sat on the arm of the sofa. 'No one understands. I'm so fucked up, Nath. I just end up hurting people. It's not my fault.'

'Jay, just say you're sorry.'

Jay stands up taller, broad and dishevelled, stares right at Nathan. For a moment, Nathan thinks he might punch him straight in the mouth. Instead he just looks at him, his jaw clenching and unclenching.

'Do you feel lucky?' Jay says.

'Lucky?'

'To have what you have.'

'I guess. Yeah. Of course.' Nathan wishes Jay would turn a light on. The flat is gloomy and everything is cast in cold shadows.

'Your mum,' Jay says. 'Your dad. The whole fucking thing.'

'Yeah. I'm lucky. I know.'

'I just wanted to live at yours. When we were kids, you know that?'

'Yeah?'

'My mum doesn't say much. It used to make my dad so angry.'

'Your mum's just shy.'

'Yeah. Not like your mum. You can say anything to her.'

'Yeah, I suppose you can,' Nathan says. 'She can be a bit much though.' He's trying to be kind, to shrink his good fortune. He laughs. Jay doesn't. They look right at each other until the room blurs around them.

'You're just happy, aren't you?' Jay says.

'Yeah. Most of the time.'

'Happy with your life.' It feels more like a statement. Jay pauses. 'I'm so sad, mate.'

'I know.'

'I miss him.'

'Your dad?'

'Ron,' Jay says. 'I swear to God, I don't know how to say the things I need to say. I can't say things to people like I could to him.'

'You can. To me.'

'I can't.'

'Well you're going to have to learn.'

'I can't,' Jay says. 'I feel like I think differently. He took his time with me. I need that,' Jay says. 'He wanted to know things.'

'What sort of things?'

'Like, about me. About who I am. About my dad. Nothing was ever stupid or embarrassing. Does this make sense?'

'Yeah.'

'My mum can't stand to look at me.'

'That's not true. She loves you.'

Jay snorts.

'I told Ron I was scared because I look like my dad. That I'm turning into him.'

'What did he say?'

'He said I had it in me to be good.'

'He was right.'

'You know whenever I would give him a lift anywhere, I would pray for traffic jams.' Jay looks small. 'Just so we could chat.'

'That's nice.'

'I owe Mickey so much,' Jay says. 'He's phoning every day.'

'We'll sort it, Jay. Somehow.'

'Somehow. Yeah.' Jay breathes in and out very slowly. 'I don't want to lose Leah. I need her to understand. She's not going to leave me, is she?'

'She won't,' Nathan says sadly. He knows she won't be able to leave him if she sees him like this. And that he only ever wants her when he is at his lowest.

'And Matthew, he'll be all right, won't he?' Jay says.

'He'll be fine,' Nathan says. 'Just say you're sorry.'

Jay's face is folded in on itself. He looks like he would rather do anything else. Nathan wants to comfort him while wanting to walk out and leave him there, alone, pitying himself. He doesn't know if Jay is capable of apologising, if Jay can change beyond what he has grown into, his rigid self. Jay turns away again, the back of his neck a pale gold. His eggs go cold on the table.

Saturday

Caleb is waiting for Matthew when he arrives. He's sat at a plain pine table, a black coffee in front of him, lavender in a beer bottle. The whole place smells of lavender. It's busy, full of families enjoying a Saturday. Everyone around him in the café looks happy, talking lots. Matthew approaches. Caleb's tongue seems to soften in his mouth with sympathy the minute he looks at Matthew. His eyelids swoop shut like two swallows diving. Matthew doesn't want the pity. He feels uncomfortable for Caleb, who is now part of it all. Caleb stands, reaches for Matthew's body, tries to hold him. Matthew feels himself stiffen instinctively, then he relaxes. He keeps having to remind himself it's Caleb in front of him.

'I'm sorry. I'm sorry I haven't called,' Matthew says.

'Don't be sorry.'

'But I am. I just didn't know what to do. I didn't want to involve you.'

'Well I'm involved,' Caleb smiles. 'How are you?'

Matthew exhales. 'Up and down.'

'That's fair.'

'That's all people say.'

'What is?'

'How are you?'

'Sorry. I don't want to be like everyone else.'

'No. Don't be. You're being nice,' Matthew says. 'I'm getting used to it.'

'I missed you,' Caleb tells him.

'Did you?'

'I did.'

'Did you actually?'

'Matthew, stop. I promise. I tried calling.'

'I know. I'm sorry.'

'Stop saying you're sorry!' Caleb reaches and grabs Matthew's wrist. 'OK?'

'OK.'

'Do you want to talk about it?'

'Not really.'

'You sure?'

'What is there to say?'

'Well, what happened?'

'He killed himself.' Caleb flinches slightly when Matthew says this. Again Matthew feels as though he's implicating him in something.

'I would have been there if you'd needed.' Caleb says. 'I wanted to be.'

Matthew is defensive suddenly, made aware of his own impotence.

'We don't really know each other, Caleb,' he says. He feels the mood shift.

'Wow, OK,' Caleb says. 'Do you want me to go then?'

'No,' Matthew says. Caleb looks frustrated, rolls his eyes to show he is exasperated but in an affectionate way. 'I don't know what else to say to you if you're going to be like this,' Caleb says. 'I'm trying to tell you I care about you. And we had that night.'

'One night?' Matthew says.

'But it was significant. To me,' Caleb says. He seems so adult-like, knows just what he wants.

'I know. I'm sorry.'

'Stop saying sorry. You shouldn't be sorry.'

'For fuck's sake, Caleb, I can't help it,' he says. He pauses, calms down. He looks at Caleb, his forehead wrinkles, front teeth overlapping. 'It's not easy for me. It doesn't come easily. I'm trying,' he says.

'Listen, Matthew. I like you. A lot.'

'You do?'

'I do.'

Matthew swallows. He thinks of Billy, his head buried into his dog's fur, weeping for a lost man.

'I really like you too.'

'Let me help. I'll be at the funeral.'

'God. No, don't.' The thought of Caleb watching the spectacle of a funeral makes Matthew itchy.

'OK. I get it. Can I still see you though? After, I mean?'

'Yeah. Obviously,' he says. 'I just need some time.'

'OK.'

'Listen, I'm going to Spain. For work,' Caleb says. 'For a while' he adds. 'A year maybe.' He looks nervous, chews at his lip a bit.

'You should come out. For a few weeks. See how it goes, get a change of scene.'

'Oh,' Matthew says. 'Yeah. I mean, maybe.' It seems unrealistic and indulgent.

'I mean it,' Caleb says.

Matthew changes the subject. They talk a little about what Caleb has been doing until Matthew's phone starts ringing.

'I'm going to have to go. My dad's flying in today,' Matthew says.

'You're doing so good, Matthew,' Caleb says. 'Call me after the funeral? I mean that. And think about Spain. Seriously.'

Matthew leaves the café and feels like he can't grip on to anything that's just been said. He remembers the feeling of Caleb's damp hands on his, the smell of the lavender, the trapped air of the café, the way the light fell on the silver band around Caleb's wrist, the small shiny scar nestled in his eyebrow. He'd intended to tell Caleb how he felt, how even despite everything, he still woke up smiling from dreams of him, how his face, voice, smell was still vivid, his touch still hot on Matthew's skin days after. He had wanted to tell him everything there was to tell about Ron, who he was, what he'd been made to hide. But somehow when he'd got there, his mouth had failed him, the words wouldn't come. Caleb was there, breathing, living, harder to speak to. He felt embarrassed for not being in touch, for thinking he could be honest. He found it hard to believe Caleb cared. He cringes at the bumps in the conversation, his defensiveness, the tension, his own incapability, wants to go back and do it all again. The funeral is tomorrow, hanging over him, an ugly blimp. And there is the matter of his father who has just landed at the airport.

His phone goes in his pocket. A text from Caleb.

I'm here whenever. x

Matthew thinks of Billy again, looks down at Ron's rings on his fingers and then forces himself to type a response.

Thanks. Spain sounds lovely. Let's talk after funeral. xx

Saturday

Leah picks the skin around her nails. The wooden stool she is sitting on is uncomfortable and wobbles slightly. She wishes for a straight-backed chair so she could lean against it and steady herself, compose her posture. Eccentric staff with colourful hair buzz around her. She wishes she'd chosen a different café.

It happened last night, the call from her dad. At work her phone had rung, an unknown number, she nearly didn't answer. It was him. The first time he had called in years. Back for Ron's funeral. Her mother had told him, which irritated Leah. She felt it was inappropriate for him to position himself in the intimate business of their grieving. And Jenny telling him meant he was coming back, which Leah now had to deal with. She didn't have space in her head to grapple with it. She was worried too about Raph and the way he might react.

He is late and this annoys her. She had wanted to be the one to walk in so he could see her, recognise her, look at her full grown-up form, her tall body. She wants him to gasp at how much of an adult she is, how he's missed it all. But he is late. He is always late for everything. On the way down, she'd imagined walking in coolly, ordering a black coffee and greeting him by his first name. 'Hello Stephen,' she'd say, and he would say, 'No love, call me dad,' and she'd say, 'I'd rather not, if it's all the same to you.'

She waits for twenty minutes, sits hunched on her stool, her spine feeling sore from curving it over the table. Her coffee is cold by the time he walks through the door, small, bald, old. It has been years, but he still looks the same, maybe slightly thinner. Leah stands up.

'Dad.'

He smiles and approaches. Up close, his frame is tiny. Leah remembers when she used to sit on his shoulders and she wonders, looking at this small man, if that had ever really happened.

Instantly, Leah feels a wetness in her eyes. She wasn't expecting this, blinks furiously to rid herself of any tears collecting. Her throat tightens.

'Do you want a drink?' she manages. 'I'll get it.' She hopes it makes her seem in control.

'Oh yes thanks, darling. Just whatever fruit tea, please.'

Leah walks through the clutter of stools and benches and over-familiar waiters to get to the counter where she orders, turns and navigates back to where her father is sitting, looking comfortable and blending into his surroundings, one leg crossed over the other, helping himself to some tap water from a jug full of fresh mint, floating. He's wearing an oversized silk shirt and it feels practised, makes him look a little like someone on their way to a party, dressed as an artist.

'Wow, Leah. You're all grown up,' he says as she approaches.

'That's what happens, over time.'

Stephen laughs happily, though she hadn't meant it to be a joke.

'Stay there, let me look at you,' he says. She hovers awkwardly between standing and sitting.

'You look beautiful, darling.'

'Thanks.'

She wants to sound detached but she is slightly flattered.

'So this is very out of the blue,' he says.

'Kind of.'

Stephen does the laugh again. 'I have to say it's lovely to see you. Even if it is for such a sad occasion. How's Raphael?'

'He's fine.'

'Oh I am glad. Great boy, Raph. Very special energy about him.' Leah hates him mentioning Raph's name, how general his description is. She doesn't want to tell him anything else about her brother.

Stephen's tea arrives, carried by a young waitress with a nose piercing. He looks her up and down, his eyes lingering over her, clinging on.

'Thank you,' he says. The waitress smiles. Stephen watches her until she's back behind the till. Leah's toes curl up inside her shoes.

There is a short silence during which Stephen dunks his tea bag several times, pulls it from his cup and puts it on his napkin. Leah watches a deep red stain spread out. She can't look up at him. She can smell her father's scent from where she's sitting. Slightly old clothes, something like lemon. It sends her back to being in his arms. She fights this.

'How's your mother?'

'She's really great, actually. Really happy.' Leah wants to divert any pity coming from her father.

'Oh she is? How wonderful!' Stephen seems surprised, which makes Leah want to throw the wet tea bag in his face. 'Has she found a partner?'

'No. She doesn't want one.'

He takes a small sip of his tea.

'I think you put her off for life,' Leah adds.

'Yes. Well. Things between your mother and I were . . . complicated.'

'OK,' Leah folds her arms across her chest. 'By complicated do you mean you complicated it . . . by fucking several other women?'

Stephen looks a little caught out. He hesitates for a while. Then smiles, wide, sits back a bit in his chair.

'You were such a vibrant little girl, always something to say. Always performing, singing your little songs.' His arrogance seems unaffected by the years he's spent apart from his daughter. There's something almost flirtatious about him. At the same time, he comes across vaguely threatening, looking at her over his cup, sat back in his chair, confident, unbothered. Leah doesn't reply.

'Look, I'm not sure we were the right match. Me and your mum.' Stephen runs his open palms over his bald head, a gesture Leah sees Raph perform sometimes. Her hands are light on her cup and quivering a bit. She feels untethered. She has a brief fantasy of tipping the table over and running off. But she doesn't move. She looks down into the black circle of her coffee cup.

'It was hard, you know. Hard for me. Your mother, she changed, when we had Raph. When he came along, she was so tired all the time. Always wanting to stay in the flat. It didn't suit me,' Stephen says. 'I'm being honest now.' He looks at Leah candidly. 'I wasn't happy.'

'Me and Raph made you unhappy, basically?'

'No, you're not listening,' Stephen says through his teeth. Leah sees a moment of anger in his eyes, like his mask is slipping.

'What, then?'

'Well, your mother, she was different when we met. We were younger, we had more freedom. She wasn't interested in getting married and conventional things like that.' Stephen waves his hands in front of his face at the mention of this. 'But like I say, when Raphael came along, and then you, she began to be more restricted in her outlook.' Stephen continues. 'She began to favour the domestic realm. She wanted stability. We got the flat, we raised you.'

'She raised us.'

'Well, I raised you for a bit. I did nappies and night feeds, I remember. But I wasn't myself. I looked around at my life one day and I thought, this isn't me.'

'Right. So you got her pregnant and then you changed your mind?'

'No, that's not what I'm saying.'

'What are you saying then?'

'I'm not the sort of man who likes to stay in one place for too long. I find it restricting. Your mum, she knew that when she met me. When I left, I think deep down she understood. She found her peace with it. She let me go.'

'Why did you keep coming back then, Dad?'

'Well, to see you.'

'And her?'

'And her, yes of course to see her.'

'And then you'd leave again.'

'Leah, you're young. It was complicated.'

'Oh don't give me that.'

'We did things in our own way.'

'She was miserable, Dad. For years.'

'Well, I'm sure there have been some challenges,' Stephen waves his hands dismissively. 'But would you have really rather had me there, unhappy, limited, unable to fulfil my true potential?' He looks at Leah intently, as if to imply that to disagree with him would be outrageous.

'Why haven't you been in touch? All these years?' she says.

Stephen looks uncomfortable, brushes nothing off the front of his shirt.

'Things have been a bit thorny.'

'How do you mean?'

'I met someone. She wasn't exactly comfortable with the fact I had children. We spent a few years travelling, moved about a lot. I've had some financial troubles, all sorts of reasons. I always sent cards though, did your mum make sure you got them?'

'Yes.'

'Oh good.' He looks pleased.

'So where is she? Where do you live?'

'She's at home. With our son. Well, it's her home now. We've decided to live separately.'

'You have a son?' Leah feels her scalp getting hot.

'His name is Noah.'

'Right,' Leah says. Stephen runs his hands over his head again.

'And you've split up?'

'We have separated, yes. For the time being, at least.' He laughs again but it feels flat. 'I'm actually feeling very good. Light. Staying with friends, living out of my backpack. It feels good.'

Leah feels a brief note of pity.

'Well good for you, Dad. I'm glad to hear that. So why do you want to meet me now. Have you spoken to Raph?'

'I haven't reached out to Raphael yet, no. But I will. I'd like to.'

'Right.'

She can feel herself becoming mocking and unkind, can hear it in her voice. The thought of how Raph will react when he finds out his father is back makes Leah feel cold.

'I'd like you to meet your little brother,' Stephen says.

For a moment, Leah entertains this picture, playing with a small child she is related to. She knows she would take it on. But the thought doesn't move her. It's hard to imagine. For so long it has been just her and Raph. In truth another brother to take care of terrifies her.

'Are you ill or something, Dad?' she says. 'Why are you back really?'

'No, I'm in remarkably good shape,' Stephen says. 'I feel amazing. I wanted to pay my respects. To Ron. And well, I've missed you,' he says. 'You're my little girl.'

For a moment, Leah lets herself believe her father. She wants to be normal, to not to be the reason he left, to go back in time, dancing around the living room on his shoulders.

'I want to know you, Leah. Catch up, hear about your life.' Stephen leans in conspiratorially, as though they are two old friends sharing gossip.

'So you're just not going to say you're sorry,' Leah says. 'For disappearing for all these years?'

'Oh for Christ's sake, Leah,' Stephen snaps. He slaps his hand down hard on the table. The light voice he's been using falters and it comes out as a shout, loud and low. Leah remembers this temper. A couple of people glance over. Stephen catches them looking and takes a breath. When he speaks again, he's back to a serene voice, softly raised eyebrows.

'Do we really have to talk about this? Why can't we just have a nice time? I'm your dad. For God's sake leave it alone.' He places his palms together like a prayer and leans his slightly purple lips on the tips of his fingers. Leah wants to look away, can feel herself going red, an old instinct after anyone shouts, but she forces herself to hold his gaze, her father, a hang in his cheeks despite his biting blue eyes.

'It worries me', Stephen says, 'that you seem so intent on dwelling on the past.'

Leah feels a headache starting at the back of her head.

'Dad, I've got to go. Please don't call Raph. I don't want him to know about this until I've spoken to him.'

Stephen frowns. 'I need to explain to him you're back,' she says. 'Please.'

She rises from the table, knocking her cup off its saucer.

She moves through the buggies and people on the way to the door. Stephen pivots around. He watches her go and doesn't say a thing. She is glad of it. She doesn't want to have it out. She is too tired for all of that. She pushes the heavy door and steps into the milky early evening, gasping in the air like she's just saved herself from drowning.

Her walk home is an obstacle course. She can't stop thinking of her dad when he left, running lightly down the stairs and to his car, an old Volvo diesel that growled, looking up at her and slamming down the boot.

By the shopping centre, she bumps into two girls from school and stands bored as they perform arbitrary small talk about their partners and children. She realises she doesn't glow with pride when they mention Jay's name, in fact it makes her cringe. There was a time when her association with Jay had made her feel special, when she had been totally defined by being his girlfriend. Now she feels a peculiar feeling, an embarrassment of sorts. She doesn't want to tell him about the meeting with her dad. She doesn't want him close.

She walks on through the town, the whole place pulsing with people she doesn't care about. People loom and surge around her, her head spinning. The air is full of flying ants. The sea is a deep flat blue.

Back in her flat the air is burly with something bad. She knows it as soon as she puts her key in the door. She knows how to tell, she'd got used to it, attuned to identifying Raph's thick moods. The kitchen is a mess, a golden train of cereal running from countertop to lino, puddles of glassy milk on the floor. It smells of drink. The subliminal thud of low music comes from Raph's bedroom. Her heart rate quickens immediately.

In Raph's room, the lights are out. The curtains have been ripped down and are half hanging off their pole. Unsettling techno music chugs from the speakers. The exercise bike has been destroyed. Kicked over, pulled apart as best it could be and Raph is in the corner, in his filthy looking dressing-gown, sat with his face between his knees, a bottle of something at his side.

He looks up when she enters, red-raw cheeks and volatile eyes.

'What have you done?' Leah says.

'Dad called,' he says.

For a moment, Raph looks as though he might reach his arms out to be hugged. Instead, he picks up a silver aluminium ashtray by his side, stuffed to the rim with butts and ash, and throws it at her head. She dodges reflexively but the side of it still grazes her cheek and stings, a bright, sharp sting. The ash falls like snow in a black and white movie, beautiful, romantic, fractured with the light coming in from outside through the half hung curtains. Cigarette butts cascade like bombs and dot the carpet. Leah presses her palm to her cheek and feels the wetness of blood, a bruise already working away under her skin. She breathes in sharply, coughs on the ash. Raph flops his head back down onto his knees. She backs out and closes his door softly.

In the hallway mirror she stares at herself. She can see the bright veins that criss-cross on the tender skin of her upper eyelids, her face is so pale. The ashtray has penetrated her skin. She touches her fingers to it lightly and winces at the slightest pressure. The cut is deep, and the blood is thick and gunky. A wafer-thin flap of skin decorates the edge of the cut. Leah thinks of rice paper and confetti, weddings. The perimeter of the gash is a deep, beautiful purple. Calmly, she takes a wipe from a packet in the bathroom and cleans the blood from her face. Then she wipes all her makeup off, splashes herself with cool water. It feels as though she is uncovering someone else, someone new. When she has no makeup on, her eyelashes are red like her hair and they make her green eyes look ringed with light.

She squeezes her eyes shut until her skull hurts. She puts

her fists in her hair and grabs on tight and pulls until she can't take it anymore, until her scalp burns.

In the kitchen she mops up the milk with paper towels and sweeps everything that has been spilled by Raph into the bin. She glances at a note taped to the fridge from her mother with instructions about what to heat up for dinner. The note is cheerful, golden with optimism, a little heart drawn on the bottom in her mother's preferred green biro. Leah notices it is just the same as her handwriting and wonders how it is possible to feel so far from the woman she calls Mum.

She prays Raph will stay in his room and not come out. She waits up until stillness comes and he is no longer crashing around. When peace settles, she pushes his bedroom door and sees him passed out on the floor, breathing heavily. She counts ten of his long breaths.

Leah sits on the very edge of the sofa, her body weak. She knows it is time to leave Raph, this town, this life. She sees it all play out in front of her. The future. Raph getting better, the juicy hope of that, then the crash of another relapse. No money for doctors, endless waiting lists. Her mum ignoring it all, whistling through her teeth as the front door slams. Her mum getting older. Her dad turning up from time to time. Her mum holding hands with her prayer circle in the living room.

Jay. Charming when he wants to be, down on one knee in a chain restaurant on the seafront, a modest silver engagement ring, a stag do during which she worries what he is up to, then a small wedding reception in the church hall, the acid of cheap wine and the dancing to disco, men with undone bow ties and sweaty chests, geared up and loud-mouthed, chewing the ears off of aunties. The thrill of the attention, of the party, loving him so much for that one day, the feeling of an expensive dress under her hands, worn only once, hung up in a wardrobe, heading to a charity shop twenty years later, old-fashioned-looking in the window of the British Heart Foundation on some high street. A short, hot honeymoon on a Greek island where Jay would sleep too late and they wouldn't do much apart from eat and fuck clumsily. Then the years after. The loveless fucking. Drifting apart like two sticks on a lake. Never knowing where Jay is. Waiting by the phone like her mum. The prodding from her colleagues, saying 'tick tock, body clock, you're next', the passing of time and her waning fertility made obvious and excruciating by people she doesn't care about. Then the alien stretch of her stomach once the inevitable happens, purple stretch marks and her belly button popping out, sleepless nights and baby shit and screaming and Jay, tired and angry and itchy, leaving during the night. Leah moving back to her mum's, repainting the small room she slept in as a child. The paint on the balconies of the block peeling even more, no one coming to fix things, forgotten up there on the hill, by the sea, rubbish spooling from split bin bags and old three-piece suites damp from rain growing mould around the back. New flats springing up nearby with expensive cars parked outside. Another sweltering summer, frothing and teeming with wealthy people with summers to spare, another overcast winter with an iron sea mashing itself onto land. Then again, then again. Raph at the front door, saying he will quit again. Jay. Telling her he will change and come back. And among all of that noise, her in the middle, not thinking or knowing who on earth she is.

She used to think she wanted Jay to look after her forever. When she was a kid, she would put the white bathroom hand towel on her head and act out wedding ceremonies to a congregation of toys. She was brought up on the promise of love, of marriage, and for years she has thought she wanted it. But looking out at her future she has never wanted to be alone more.

When her mum comes back to the flat the next day, laden with plastic bags of shopping, fussing and whistling in the way she does, Leah can't bear to tell her about the limp, disappointing reunion with her father. Jenny looks happy, calm. Leah takes the bags off her and starts putting the shopping away.

'Mum?'

'Mmm?' Jenny is stuffing the used plastic bags into the cheerful cloth tube that hangs on the door.

'Are you glad you had us, me and Raph?'

'Of course. What you on about?'

'It's been hard though, right?'

'It's not been as easy as it could have been. But that's life. I've made sacrifices, yes. But that's what you do when you're a mother. And a wife. I always made sure you had a full belly. We made do with what we had.'

'Why does motherhood have to be about sacrifice though?' Leah says.

'It just is. You'll understand when you have your own.'

'You had to give up your life though. Because of Dad. Why did you give it all up for him?'

'Oh Leah,' Jenny says, filling up the washing-up bowl and manoeuvring her freckled hands into her pink marigolds. 'It's love, isn't it. You don't know what you're doing when you're in love. Surely you understand. You've got Jay.'

Leah swallows and it hurts.

Monday

The sky is blue like in a child's drawing. There is no need to set an alarm clock today, their minds wake them early with the knowledge of what is to come. Matthew and Leah drink strong coffee at 6 a.m. sitting at the kitchen table in silence. The room fills with a thin light as the sun rises higher into the day. They are quiet, static, in a liminal time when most people are sleeping, and the calm that this allows is a balm to their aching heads and bones. There are no words while you are waiting to bury a body.

Jay is awake and in his bedroom, metres from where they sit.

Nathan knocks softly at Leah's door at seven, bringing with him a loaf of bread, warm and dense, baked by his mother. He and Leah manage a thick slice with butter, but Matthew can't move his mouth to speak or chew. Leah looks down at the bread in her hands and counts its calories then hates herself for this instinct.

Nathan is wearing a suit that is slightly too big for him. He shrugs and says, 'It's my dad's, do you think it will be OK?' Leah loves him intensely in that moment, his sweetness, then shrugs it off. Today is not the day for questions like that.

It is like they are in a dream. They have each imagined this morning many times and now that it is here, their projections of it have made the real thing slanted and skewed.

Leah's mum emerges from her bedroom looking soft and warm and sleep-stained in a blue dressing-gown. She makes more coffee, she cuts more bread, she places her pillowy palms on Matthew's shoulders and tells him anything he needs, he is only to ask.

The gulls start and they grow in volume until it is 8 a.m.

In the shower, Matthew sits down for a bit, legs folded underneath him like a baby deer. It feels good to sit and let the water wash over him. Yesterday, he had seen his father. He'd waited at Ron's flat for Sonny to arrive, killing time, packing boxes.

Sonny knocked at the door, as tall and thin as Matthew but with wrinkles and bags under his eyes, rough skin on his neck, a different colour to his face, nicked from shaving. He was wearing a battered-looking leather jacket that Matthew remembered from at least twenty years ago, jeans faded at the knees and heavy boots. His eyes were obscured by a pair of reflective sunglasses, the type that cut across the face in one long strip, like a cyclist would wear. Matthew could see his own warped reflection mirrored back at him.

Sonny gave Matthew a rough clumsy hug. They stood awkwardly for a few minutes before Matthew cleared some boxes out of the way and they managed to find somewhere to sit.

'Got anything to drink?' Sonny said.

'There's no milk. But you drink your coffee black, right?'

'I don't.' Sonny cleared his throat and scratched at his neck. 'And I meant a proper drink.'

Matthew fetched the box in the kitchen, full of Ron's old whisky tumblers and bottles. He poured two fingerfuls and they drank, feeling the heat in their chests.

'I used to do this for Grandad, every evening. He'd always want a whisky and water at about six,' Matthew said.

Sonny coughed again. He looked around the flat.

'He always had so much tat,' he said. Matthew thought his face looked redder. 'You tell me what I owe for the funeral and I'll write you a cheque straight away,' he said, draining his glass and holding it out to Matthew for some more. Sonny didn't stay long. On his way out of the door, he paused.

'Thank you for being here, Matthew,' he said. 'For all you did for him.'

In the shower Matthew sits, rests his head on his knees and moans, testing his voice to see if he has one left. He pretends he is in a music video from the nineties, sitting in the rain, and it is a nice distraction until there is a kind knock on the door and Jenny is telling him that she's very sorry but there's never enough hot water in this house.

Nathan is alone in the kitchen when Raph walks in. He can't look Nathan in the eye. They've not seen each other since Nathan wrestled him from the boat into a taxi home. Raph is wearing a white shirt, boxer shorts and socks, trying to tie a tie around his collar.

'Do you know how to do these?' he says after a while.

Nathan is not an expert but he wants to make Raph comfortable so he says he can help.

Nathan realises for the first time he and Raph are exactly the same height. As they stand face to face Nathan takes a breath and meets Raph's eyes. They are green-blue, ultraviolet, like Leah's but never as open. The lids look as though they are made of something heavier than skin. Nathan notices that Raph looks scared and looks away to spare him. He struggles with the tie, can't get it right. It feels like it is taking forever.

Leah is standing in her bra and pants. She's worn black ones because it is a funeral and because she thinks it will make her feel more reverent. She ignores the way the elastic of her waist-band cuts into the flesh around her hips. She pulls some lint off the cup of her bra and wishes she had newer, nicer things. Her hair won't do what she wants it to do. She convinces herself her face looks fat. Leah doesn't like dressing up. She finds it embarrassing that people know she has made an effort to look nice because she thinks she still only looks passable.

Matthew walks into her room with a towel wrapped around his slender waist. Little pearls of water still speckle his body. Leah walks to him and tells him to come here, she's got him. She's still just in her bra and pants. She pulls Matthew into a hug and feels cold stings of water against her skin. She holds him until it doesn't feel cold anymore.

Jay convinces himself to get out of bed. He takes his mum a cup of tea and tells her the time, how they'd better be leaving soon.

'I know, baby,' she says.

Jay notices his suit, neatly dry-cleaned and still in its plastic, hanging from her wardrobe.

'Thanks for doing my suit, Mum.' He is hit by an instinct to look after her.

'It's OK.' She takes a small sip of tea, propped up against her headboard in her plain, clean bedroom that smells so much of laundry powder, it hits the back of the throat. There is an intimacy to being in her bedroom this early, as she is still under the duvet, a closeness that Jay hasn't experienced for a while.

'Don't you think you ought to go round to where they all are?' she says, looking ahead at the blue suit, perfect against the white wall.

'I don't know,' Jay says. He can't bring himself to go. He's not spoken to Matthew or Leah since the night out. His mother raises her eyebrows.

When Jay puts on his suit, the silk lining feels cool against his skin. He spends a long time brushing his teeth, brushing until the foam becomes too much and drips down his chin, slaps onto the sink. He holds mouthwash in his mouth until it burns. He washes his hands and doesn't know why. He looks at himself in the mirror. The thought of turning up at Leah's, the reproach from his friends makes his throat flush red. He turns his phone off, tells his mum he will see her at the church and leaves the flat.

Matthew's suit is a beautiful deep green. He can't help but feel when he puts it on that he looks like a bridegroom. He studies his nose in the mirror, realising for the first time that it's his grandad's nose. In his mind, his grandad's face is already blurred by time. But lately, he has noticed little things he says, that he has learnt from Ron. 'I should think so too' and 'Right then.' Every time he says these things, he misses Ron with a clear pain, proud to have known him, to be a part of him. He combs his hair and fixes it with some wax. It seems so bizarre to be there himself and for it all to be happening.

Leah gasps when she sees him and tells him he looks handsome. Jenny clasps her hands in front of her face when she comes out of the kitchen and looks at him.

'You could be a model,' she says.

Nathan pokes his head out from behind him. 'You look lovely, mate. I've made more coffee.'

'Any more and we'll all shit ourselves,' Leah says, and they all manage a small laugh.

Leah grips Matthew's arm before he enters the kitchen.

'Everything is sorted, OK? You don't have to worry about anything,' she says. 'Cab's booked.'

Matthew imagines the soft blue and dirty white of Brighton's taxis. The thing that used to transport them back from drunken nights.

There is a knock on the door.

Leah goes to answer it. Her dress feels too tight, it rides up her legs with each step. When she answers it, Jay is standing there, shoulders slipping forward, lips pursed in tension, eyes like two stars.

Leah imagines all the things she would like him to say to her. *I'm sorry. You look so beautiful. You are strong. I love you. I am lucky to have you. I understand you.* Instead, he says, 'hey' and she says 'hey' and then she says 'you came' and he says 'I thought I should.' Leah thinks he looks like he would rather be anywhere else but she is grateful to see him. He kisses her on the cheek.

'They're in the kitchen,' Leah says.

In the kitchen, Jay and Matthew look at each other and smile. Then the taxi honks outside the block.

The thought of being shoulder to shoulder with Jay in the car makes Leah strangely satisfied. It's important to be near him today, she wants to do this with him, one last thing to prove their significance to each other.

They drive to the church. When they arrive Sonny is waiting outside with the undertakers in suits. He is wearing a shirt and smart trousers but still has on his leather jacket and reflective sunglasses.

Matthew goes to hug his father. Sonny sticks out his hand to shake Matthew's.

'Oops, sorry, son,' Sonny says, his hand crushed against Matthew's abdomen.

'How you doing then?' Sonny says briskly, rubbing his hands together. Matthew feels an urge to sound adult, masculine. 'Hanging in there,' he says. He notices his tone change to match his father's, quick, light, casual.

Benny and Elena arrive in bright colours. They get out of a cab with Jenny, Raph and Pauline. The undertakers quietly explain the logistics of shouldering a coffin. Benny, Jay, Matthew, Nathan, Sonny and Raph nod. No one remembers when this was all decided but everything seems to just be happening. They each take up their role. Traffic rolls by on the road beside them. People go about their shopping.

Leah watches the men lift the coffin onto their shoulders. It wobbles a lot more than she thought it would. For a moment she is scared they are going to drop it. It seems smaller than she thought it would be and the cardboard too flimsy. The flowers she has chosen clash with the finish of it and look insubstantial on top.

Jenny comes forward and puts her arm around Leah's shoulders. Leah wishes she was holding the coffin, she wants to do this one last thing for Matthew and Ron. The men look unusually smart and so different from one another.

The church is small and modern. It hasn't got a spire and

it's in the middle of the town among shops and houses. Matthew is at the front of the formation. As he approaches, he sees Billy stood by the door. Matthew turns to Sonny, who is shouldering the coffin on his right. He can't see his father's eyes behind the sports sunglasses.

'Dad,' he says.

Sonny looks around, a glare of purple visor.

'Yes?'

'Can we stop for a minute?'

The procession stops and the coffin wobbles again. Matthew calls Billy over. 'Take the coffin. On your shoulder. Take my place.'

Billy shakes his head. 'You should.'

'I have,' Matthew says and begins to slip his shoulder out. Billy approaches, trying hard to hold his face, it seems, in a neutral position. He pushes a shoulder under the coffin and turns to his right to look at Sonny, who is frowning.

'It's all right, Dad. He's a friend.'

Sonny turns back to the front and starts walking again. Matthew follows behind with Leah and they enter the church. The pews are made of a light wood with simple red squares of cushion. There are no stained-glass windows. A huge patchwork banner in soft pastels hangs at the back of the building. 'God is love', it says. The pulpit is a simple plastic lectern. A young vicar wearing a suit and Doc Martens with yellow laces stands watching the procession walk in. There is shuffling and quiet classical music playing as everyone takes their seats.

The coffin is placed on a plinth at the back of the church. The smart-looking funeral director tells everyone what to do, the running order of things. There is a small piece of white paper on everyone's seats with a simple order of service designed tastefully by Leah.

The vicar begins to speak. He is wearing a radio mic and it sounds a little harsh. He talks for what feels like a long time about death not being the end. He says he knows this must seem unfair, but it is part of God's plan. He starts to become passionate. Leah tenses, she and Matthew look at each other, almost laughing. Jay isn't looking, seems distracted. The vicar's spit is visible. Leah wishes Jay would hold her hand. She looks at her mother, whose face is fixed in determined faith.

When the vicar is finished they stand up and sing 'Bread of Heaven'. Leah hears Benny's voice booming from behind her. Matthew doesn't sing but Nathan and Jay do and she is touched by it, their soft, low voices.

After the singing is over and everyone has sat back down, it is Matthew's turn to speak. He feels physically ill, like a flu is taking over. He manages to make it to the front.

The microphone amplifies the spit collecting under his tongue, the quiet groan of his swallow, the sound of him opening his mouth, the sounds of his body feel as though they are drowning him. He can't speak. Leah rises from her seat and comes to stand by his side. He begins.

'Firstly, I want to say thank you for coming here today.'

Leah puts a gentle hand on his back.

'How do I start to speak about my grandad?'

Matthew hears Sonny cough from the audience.

'How do I start to speak about a man who kept himself to himself? Well, I asked Leah and she said, how about we ask everyone who knew him what they thought. So we did. And the thing everyone said was that he was kind.' Matthew's voice cracks at this. He swallows again and carries on.

'He was kind. I haven't met anyone who had a bad word to say about him, actually. I can't tell you the amount of stories I've heard about him fixing people's cars. Putting up their shelves. He was one of those men who just knew how to do it all. Not like me.' The congregation laugh a sympathetic laugh.

'He was who he was. Simple, really,' Matthew goes on. 'He liked his whisky, his crosswords and his cricket. His horses, his walking. He liked a chat. Most of all he liked a large cod, chips and mushy peas on a Monday night. To get a bit pissed and listen to a radio drama.'

Everyone laughs, louder this time.

'I'm not sure I can ever really understand what happened. But I can say, he loved me. It shouldn't be like this. But I hope he's found some peace. And I, for one, will miss him.'

The last three words are hard for Matthew to say. They come out in a barely there whisper. Leah walks with him as he sits back down on the front pew. His legs are weak and tingly like they're made of spun sugar. He is so relieved. And then it is time for Billy to speak. He walks to the front, regal and elegant with his shoulders held back.

Stationed at the lectern he breathes in deeply. He pulls a folded piece of paper from his top pocket. His hands don't shake. A ray of sun comes in bright and sharp through the window and lands on his rings. He begins to read. Words drop slow and steady like morning arriving from his lips.

'Firstly, I wish to extend my gratitude to Matthew, who has invited me here to share my knowledge of Ron with you all, to celebrate the man that many of us in this room loved deeply.'

Sonny coughs. Matthew can hear the phlegm rattling up in his throat.

'I met Ron when we were at school. He was a shy boy, as quiet in childhood as he was in life. He was gentle.'

Leah notices Jay's fists are balled up tight in his lap.

'It seems, more often than not in this world that people are self-interested. Speaking over one another, always trying to outdo what's already been done. Ron didn't have time for any of that. He liked to listen to people. He was careful with their feelings. He was a good friend around a kitchen table, a good ear. He never wanted to offer an anecdote that was grander, more exciting, better. He wasn't always waiting for his turn to speak. He didn't want to show you how interesting and intelligent he was. At school, he excelled, an avid reader, always a book in his back pocket or skulking around the library after classes. He was a keen historian, a geographer. I imagine he could have gone on to university, that seemed to be on the cards for him. But I know how much he loved this town, the ocean. He wanted to make a life for himself here. And he did that, running the garage for all those years, from 1972, training up apprentices, some of whom join us here today, getting to know all of you, whom he held so fondly in his heart. I hope you all know that. He said this place was where he belonged. That he wasn't a remarkable man. Just a man who wanted to work and live an easy life. But I believe him to be remarkable. Ron raised a hard-working son and cared for Matthew with compassion. There's an indication of the kind of man he was. We all knew him for his hands, hands that could fix anything. For the notebooks he carried around with him, his love of maps and routes and roads. How he never drank water, just tea and ale.'

Billy pauses, glances up from the paper as though considering whether to go off script. 'He was always the type of man to sit on an uncomfortable chair for hours, you know? Without complaining. To spend his last twenty pence on someone.'

The congregation laugh and some shake their heads and nod in recognition.

'It seems too painful now to talk about the circumstances of his death.' Billy runs his fingers over his moustache and the gritty sound travels throughout the church.

'But I want to mention it only to say this: You can be a kind man in this world but this world is hard and it is cruel and some people simply cannot manage with things the way they are. Some people have too much they cannot face. The world is geared against people like this. Ron faced it all for as long as he could with a golden generosity in his heart. But he found things harder than us, in a way he couldn't put into words. But do not misunderstand. Yes, a life lived in silence, a life with overwhelming pain, is a tragedy, of course. But do not think of this man and think only of pain and sadness. Think of all he had and shared. There were some moments in his life that were filled with a happiness so intense that even living that for one second could make it all worth it. I know. Because I was there. He loved and was loved. He was one of the lucky ones too. I saw he could love. And I loved him in return. I invite you all to see him in the tides, in the birds, in the static between your radio stations. I hope you look down at your toolboxes and think of him, look into your chip wrapper, your cryptic crosswords, your book-shelves, your coffee, and see him in all these things. Raise glasses to him, remember him. And try to be as kind as you can in everything you do. In this way you will fix your broken hearts. Don't turn to sadness for this life lost, but instead fight for a kinder world, a world where men like Ron are welcome, are safe. That, for him, would be the greatest tribute.' Billy pauses. 'Thank you,' he says.

Matthew's chest loosens and he closes his eyes, pictures Ron with a cup of coffee, smiling at him, listening to him talk about his day. He feels something hot where his heart is, like something is being fused together with a white-hot burst of light. He thinks of Caleb again, of a reality in which he can walk on the beach with him, their hands full of each other's hands. He feels a relief, a forgiving, a surrender.

Billy's hand is shaking as he stuffs the paper roughly back into the top pocket of his coat. He walks back to his seat and sits down and his shoulders fold in on themselves. Leah sees a vein on Jay's head stand out like a brief monument to all the pain. His face tenses. She only catches it for two seconds before he stops himself. He sniffs and wipes his cheeks and then he is back to how he always is. She loves him for those two seconds of feeling. The vicar is back and he's saying prayers but no one is really listening. Jenny holds her hands together and closes her eyes. At some point, everyone says 'amen', some music begins to play and then it's all over.

Walking out of the church Elena takes Leah in her arms. Leah thinks how safe she feels in Elena's grip, how confident Elena is, how much strength she has always had, this woman who has not been broken down by a man.

'I hope you know how special you are, Leah,' Elena says. 'Matthew, he couldn't have done this without you.'

'Thanks El.'

Elena leans in closer towards Leah.

'You deserve the world, honey,' she says. 'Listen, I love Jay. But there's more out there for you.'

Leah nods, squeezes Elena's ringed hand.

In the graveyard afterwards Leah, Jay, Matthew and Nathan stay by the grave long after the coffin has been lowered down. They watch the mass of bodies making their way down the hill, little black dots becoming smaller. The four of them stand swaying slightly.

They talk about the logistics of it all because they don't have the words for anything else. They talk about the weather, who has turned up, the old woman who tripped walking up the hill, whether the sandwiches will be decent. They speak in clipped sentences with long pauses in between. The heat clings to them all.

Leah can feel how much has changed. She glances at Jay, who has barely said a word all day. He keeps sniffing. His fists are meaty clumps hanging at his side. They have an air of cruelty about them but contrast with his smart suit.

When she looks at Jay and can't even imagine sleeping with him, can't remember what he looks like with no clothes on or any of the private, intimate times they shared. She feels so far away from who she was, a distant, less sensible version of herself, obsessing over him, wanting him so much.

'I'm hungry,' Jay says.

'There'll be food there, Jay,' Leah says, before she can stop herself, recognising her instinct to appease him.

'Good,' Jay says. He begins to walk off down the hill, alone. Nathan, Leah and Matthew all glance at each other. Matthew follows.

Nathan and Leah stand alone at the top of the hill. She turns to look at him and they both sigh deeply at the same time then laugh.

'I'm sorry,' Nathan says. 'About what happened with us.'

'It's OK.'

'I shouldn't have said what I said that night. I lost my head for a bit.'

'It's OK Nath. Another lifetime maybe?'

He smiles. 'A whole other lifetime.'

Walking down the hill, Jay puts his arm around Matthew, slumps it over exaggeratedly. It feels heavy on Matthew's shoulders and it's hard to walk, but he appreciates the gesture, Jay's own form of apology. Matthew looks at Jay all tight and screwed up. He pities him just as much as he dislikes him.

'Glad that's over,' Jay says.

'Same. I think it will be the after bit that is hard. Just normal life without him.'

Jay looks at their feet moving in unison.

'You never tried with me much. After he died,' Matthew says.

'I was angry. About it all.'

'I get it.' Matthew pauses. 'Why do you think he told you all those things and not me?'

Jay considers. 'We got what we needed from each other, I guess.'

'That's the most philosophical thing you've ever said.'

Jay grins.

'He loved you, Jay. You know that, right? He talked about you. I know things have always been a bit weird between us, but he loved you.'

'Yeah. I know. I think.' Jay looks grateful.

'He told you about Billy. You never judged him.'

'Not my style.'

'Thank you. I'm glad he had you.'

'I'm glad I had him. He was like a dad really.'

'Turns out he's left me some money, my grandad. I want you to have some of it. To pay off what you owe. Leah told me.'

'No. Absolutely no.'

'I want you to. I know I never had your certainty, but I am sure about this.'

Jay shakes his head.

'Please take it, Jay.'

Jay sighs. He swallows and nods once, a tiny nod, and that is all that is said on the matter.

In the small church hall the air is limited. It's a boozy affair. People gather holding warm glasses of wine. Leah walks in first. Little sprigs of yellow flowers are dotted around in jam jars but the room seems to swallow them up, the dated curtains and stacks of extra chairs in the corner. Leah has printed Matthew's photographs of his grandad, blown them up and hung them on the walls. There are close-ups of his hands, a beautiful portrait shot in profile where he is laughing, a head and shoulders shot of him eating a big doorstop of a tomato sandwich, light glinting off his glasses, a full body shot where he is captured, suited and serious, walking along the path that joins the pavement to their block, umbrella under his arm. The photos are arresting and alarming in their beauty. They show his deep wrinkles close up. They show him alive in the real world.

Matthew walks to the close-up photo and stands in front of it for a long time, tracing his fingers across the black and grey grooves of Ron's frown lines.

Raph is standing by the trestle table where all the bottles are lined up uniformly. Leah notices he's holding a large water glass full to the top with red wine. She sees Jay across the hall. He's avoiding her, she knows that much. She can't help it, she approaches him like he is a big magnet, sinking the rest of her wine as she does. It's still Jay, she thinks. That must mean something.

'Steady on with the booze,' he says as she walks to him.

'I'm fine,' she says, but she knows she sounds defensive. They talk briefly. It's clinical.

'How've you been?' she says.

'Fine.' There's an awkward pause. Leah burrows around for some love, some recognition, just for today, like a desperate animal. But he is distant and cold, and it is so painful. She imagines being kicked in the stomach.

Matthew passes his father an aluminium tray of sandwiches which crackles beneath his grip.

'Thanks, Matthew.' Sonny clears his throat and Matthew smiles at him.

'Thanks for holding it all together. While I was getting back. It's a long way,' Sonny says. 'You look good.'

'Do I? Grandad always said I look like you.'

Sonny smiles weakly. 'I suppose we've got the tall gene.'

'So how is work?' Matthew says, clutching at things to talk about.

'Oh, you know. It keeps me busy. I'm in charge of a lot of men out there, and there's always a lot to be done. We travel a lot.' He bites into his sandwich. 'And you? What plans for the future?'

'I might do some travelling myself.' Matthew says. It feels strange to say it, like he is going to be told to stop being silly.

'You should, Matthew. You should see the world.'

Matthew nods.

'I'll miss him,' Sonny says. 'He was a good dad. He did right by me. Always said he'd take care of you.'

'And he did.'

'For as long as he could,' Sonny says. 'Come here.' Sonny hugs Matthew with his sandwich in his left hand. 'It's going to be OK.' He's brisk, rough, but Matthew can feel the good in him. When his dad's away he feels such an indifference towards him, like he doesn't actually exist. But now, it is good to be in his company again.

'Maybe I can come out and see you,' Matthew says.

'Always welcome, son.'

Leah steps outside. Raph is hunched against the peeling wall of the building, attempting to light a wonky-looking joint. The speed with which he flicks his thumb on the lighter is alarming, concentrated. He finally gets it lit and inhales, a huge, deep mournful breath. His face relaxes and he tips his chin to the sun exhaling, leans against the walls like a giddy milk-drunk baby.

'I had it in my pocket. For emergencies,' he says to Leah when he notices her.

Leah smiles weakly.

'Just this one though yeah? Promise?' she says, looking into his eyes.

He looks at the ground, surveys the fag butts and the litter and the blocked drain of the church hall.

'Yeah.'

Leah can't help but notice Raph's small, watery eyes intensely fixed on the pub across the road, like he's yearning for the men outside with full drinks, bang in the middle of a session, woozy and shouting. She rests her head on his broad shoulder, resigned, and he takes another pull.

She sees Jay leaving then, walking quickly out of the church hall and away from it all, pulling on his suit jacket. He hasn't said goodbye to her. It likely hasn't occurred to him, she thinks. Still, she doesn't want him to go. She wanted one last moment with him. She is light and weak from booze and wants to call out his name.

Her dad comes out of the church hall then. Raph's expression changes, his face plummets.

Stephen approaches with open arms. 'Kids,' he says.

Raph looks him up and down, turns his back and walks back inside. Leah thinks about following him but the presence of her father somehow prevents her, she can't quite bear to.

'Never mind him. He'll come around. How are you, love?' her dad says.

'Tired.'

'Mmm. You must be.'

For a while it feels good to talk to her dad. When he asks her to sit on the low wall in front of the hall with him, she is grateful to take the weight off her feet, enjoys the new experience of talking to him as an adult.

'Today was hard,' she says.

'It's terribly sad,' Stephen says. 'I remember Ron from when you were babies.'

A little fly has landed in Leah's wine. She stares down at it twitching.

'Hey, since we're here we may as well have a catch-up, Leah. Why don't you tell me some things about you?' Stephen says. 'How about we start with that?'

Leah sighs, too tired to pitch herself and who she is to her father. It makes her prickly. She has no idea what she likes and dislikes, what she has done in her life that is meaningful.

'I don't know,' she says.

'Well, what do you do in your spare time?'

Leah feels completely boring and pointless.

'I don't know, Dad. Read sometimes. Watch films.'

'What's the love life like?' He gives her a nudge with his elbow.

Leah rolls her eyes.

'Dad, please.' She allows herself a smile. He smiles at her too, showing his teeth which look like they need some attention.

'All right. I'll stop. Are you working?'

'Of course I'm working. I just do admin stuff, receptionist.'

'See, it's good to talk. You're so grown up now. Working. Wearing this lovely dress.'

Leah can tell he's preparing to say something.

'I wondered if you might be able to help me with something, Leah.' Before he's said any more, Leah somehow knows what he's going to ask.

'You're an adult now so I want to be honest with you. I'm in a bit of hot water, financially. Just temporarily. I've made a bit of an investment which is taking a while to pay out and just need a little cash injection as a stopgap. The banks aren't too keen on giving me a loan, pure bureaucracy and, besides, I don't trust them anyway.' If Stephen is uncomfortable, he doesn't show it. 'Seeing as you're all grown up and working, I wondered if you wouldn't mind helping your dad out with a little loan. Obviously, I would pay it back, as soon as this investment comes good, which it will,' he adds.

Leah turns to look at him, a bit stunned. Instead of anger, she just feels weighted down.

'Oh,' she says. 'Right. Well, I'll need to look at my bank and stuff. See if I've got anything I can spare.'

'Well as I said, I'd pay it all back.' Stephen smiles at her.

'Yeah, OK, Dad. I'll have a look.'

'So would that be OK?' he says, pressing her.

'Maybe. Yeah. I've got to go back in probably. Things to sort, food and stuff. Sorry.'

She leaves him sitting on the wall, wanting him to disappear again forever.

In the hall she pours herself more wine. The day darkens and people start to leave. Leah doesn't want it to end, it feels sad somehow watching people go off to their homes, like the time for remembering Ron is over. Matthew is swaying to the music that's playing from the little amp, it's Johnny Cash.

When everyone has gone, he sits with Leah on the steps by the door. The clatter of Nathan and his parents cleaning up and talking in low voices soundtracks their cigarettes.

'Thank you so much, Le. It was special,' Matthew says.

'So. What now?' she says.

'Home, I suppose.'

'Or beach? Like the old days.' Leah looks at him with a look that seems to encapsulate their whole friendship.

Matthew smiles.

'Did you ever call that boy?'

'His name's Caleb. And yes.' He is so sleepy, scraped out but sort of satisfied. 'He's leaving. Wants me to go too. Spain.'

'And?'

'I don't know. I want to. I'm scared.'

'Me too. But freedom isn't free, is it Math? You've got to be scared. That's the price. I'm going too. I've decided.'

'Where?'

'Don't know yet. But I'm doing it.'

'I've always had this feeling that nothing particularly important or exciting is going to happen to me. I've just always known. That nothing will ever really be as good as imagining how good things could be.'

'I know what you mean. I'm the same. But we won't change that if we stay. I'm done with this.' Leah smokes. 'Go to Spain, Math.'

She leans over and kisses his cheek. Matthew feels the heat and wetness of it.

'Hope is the best thing we've got, Math.

'I'll miss you so much,' he says. 'You're my best friend.'

'I'll miss you too.'

'What about Jay?'

Leah makes a small gesture with her hand like she's slicing her throat to indicate how done it is. She laughs but it sounds sad and empty. Matthew nods.

'I've been kidding myself. I let him do whatever he wanted with me. It's embarrassing. How I put up with it for so long. I couldn't see what was happening.'

305

'It's not your fault, Le. He knew what he was doing.'

She smiles at him.

'You've been so . . . quiet,' Matthew says. 'I couldn't stand to watch it.'

'I've been so lonely. I've loved him all my life. What shit luck,' she says.

Nathan comes out from the double doors behind them and crouches between the two of them.

'We're all done in there,' he says.

They walk to the beach and make a fire like in the old days. The city is alive with night. On the beach, the sounds of Brighton murmur behind them. The dark creeps in on them and snakes its cold around their bare arms, robs the colour from the day. The flames spit into the sky and smoke billows. There are stars bright overhead, so alarming they're like spots of blood on a handkerchief. The sea is calm in the distance, but they hear it surge and retreat on the pebbles, white foam and scud visible in the dark. It feels good to be by the sea, something powerful and primitive about it, part of their ritual. The pebbles grow colder beneath Leah's legs. She feels so small and so afraid but ready.

They watch the flames and drink until they're drunk and then they shout things into the sky.

'Goodbye, you fucker,' Matthew says. 'I'll miss you, old man!'

He is spent, glad he made it through the day. He is full up to the eyes with pain. But this pain is bearable, he thinks. It is different from the numb feeling he's had before. It is better somehow. It makes him feel sure of something, close to his grief. It qualifies his love for Ron. Somehow he knows it will get easier. Though the brutality of it all is still so sore, already he is starting to find small moments of peace, to see his future. He is frightened of forgetting, frightened that the pain will come for him one day when he is not expecting it. But he feels fiercer somehow, more ready for the outcome. Each time he tends towards guilt, he is able to talk himself away from the dark, hearing Leah's voice, or Billy's. Matthew walks close to the water. He feels like he has been holding his breath forever. He wants the bliss of letting go.

He calls Caleb.

'I've decided,' he says. 'I'll come.'

They talk for a little while, he and Caleb on the phone, Matthew watching the lights on the water, hearing the gentle thud of nightclubs. Caleb is in bed and Matthew can hear the rustle of his sheets. They talk about the funeral, agree on coffee tomorrow morning and when Matthew hangs up the phone he closes his eyes, breathes in the smell of the sea and starts laughing.

'This is for you, Grandad,' he says under his breath. 'I'm doing it.'

They walk home. Leah opens her front door. Raph is passed out on the sofa, fully clothed. He's got a kebab wrapper on his chest and the flat smells of onion. There is a letter on the table for her, thick and A4. A brochure she ordered on a whim for a university out of town. She's too scared to open it, like opening it would commit her to something. She puts the radio on and smokes the rest of her cigarettes. The sensation of a different life arrives, a different routine, the unknowable pulsing out ahead of her. This time coupled with a calm resignation, a certainty. She imagines Jay metres away in his flat and wonders what he's doing in his room. She doesn't want to call him or be near him, she is sure. She knows what she has to do.

Tuesday

Leah has asked to meet Jay on a bench looking out to sea. She is wearing a red dress. It is cut low and wrapped around the waist. Her nose is covered in freckles and the tip is pink. Jay notices the cut on her cheek has the beginnings of a scab forming. She looks a bit wild, Jay thinks, she looks particularly beautiful. He knows what is about to happen. He's pushed it to this, deliberately, but seeing her now makes him want to hold on to her.

He watches her walk towards him and wishes he could watch her for longer. He still doesn't know why he loves her and that makes him feel like he is out of control. He wants her pity now, to beg her to stay and make her feel sorry for him instead, for her to absolve him of everything.

Leah walks towards Jay. He looks beautiful, as though he is carved of wood, hunched in the lager-gold light of a Brighton afternoon. Half of his face is cast in the shadow of the old-fashioned covered bench. His eyes look grey, like the sea spread out in front of him. He's wearing a big sweatshirt, rolled up over his arms, which are folded against his chest. He gives a sad, knowing smile when he sees her. She returns it and wishes that could just be the end of it.

Leah sits down and Jay's eyes fill up with tears. She's derailed, feels an acute tenderness towards him. She can't be angry with him, she hasn't made it there yet, so she wraps her arms around him and holds his heaving shoulders. She comforts him. She knows he wants her to pity him and because she is kind, she does. She wipes his face with her two index fingers and strokes his cheeks. He takes her finger into his mouth and holds it in its warmth, pulls her close and kisses her. The feeling of the kiss rises through her body, she pulls herself away.

'Don't do that,' Leah says.

'Why not? It's us.'

'It's not us anymore. You know that. We've got to stop this, properly this time.' They speak in short coded sentences because there is too much to say.

'Leah, please. Please don't end this. I'll be better.'

She hadn't expected this.

'I think it's too late for that.' It is hard to drag the words from her mouth.

'Please, Leah, I love you.' *How can you?* she thinks.

'Don't do this to me,' Leah says. Jay looks desperate. Tears are falling down his cheeks. A couple walking past slow down and look at him.

'Jay, don't cry.'

'How can you tell me not to cry?' he raises his voice. The couple look back again. 'Leah, don't leave. I need you.'

'That's not fair.'

'I'm going to get help. You can't leave me when I need help.'

'That's good that you're doing that. That you want to do that.'

'I want to marry you. Like we always said. I want you to have my kids. Remember?'

He's begging properly now. Leah feels sick. He looks like he's surprised himself but he can't go back. He sees she's more resolute than she has been and he keeps trying. She's still not crying like she thought she would. She feels sad for him then, sees him as a small boy, knows that what they had was so far from normal.

Leah has imagined this moment so many times before it happens. In her daydreams he makes it all better, he fixes it and makes her feel so vital that she takes him back. But looking at him on the bench, she doesn't see what she used to see.

'I don't think I want that,' she says. It feels strange to say the opposite of what she had thought she had wanted all these years.

'You do.'

A group of midges consort in front of Leah. She bats a quiet hand in front of her face.

'I don't know if I want that with anyone. See this is what I mean, Jay. I don't think you know me really.'

'No. I know you, Leah. Better than anyone else.' Jay is indignant, frowning, body turned towards her as she looks out at the sea. She worries if she looks at him too much she might just forget it all and do what he wants.

'I really don't think you do, Jay. I've been pretending.'

Two seagulls swoop past in unison as though they have planned it. Leah notices a small purple bruise on her thigh. Then she's full of a memory of her and Jay in soft dress-ing-gowns together in a little hotel he'd once booked for them on the seafront. They were fresh from a bath, clean and sleepy and happy, eating chocolate in bed, watching a film. Leah presses the little bruise on her thigh with her finger. The skin around it goes white. She thinks of Raph and the ashtray sailing towards her, the look in his eyes. She thinks of Jay with his arm around another woman, bounding through the front door of a party.

'I'm going to leave. After this summer is over,' Leah says.

'Leave Brighton?'

'Yeah.'

'And do what?'

Leah imagines a city far away with different coloured stone, landlocked and grey where she is anonymous. She pictures herself getting home to a small flat, exactly the way she left it that morning, a fat ginger cat to talk to, a bottle of wine in the fridge untouched by anyone, a big bowl of pasta, calm. She's been fantasising about getting on trains, long journeys that last whole days. She is full of a yearning for places she has never been. They feel familiar to her, not remote or terrifying, but comforting. She thinks of the sound of foreign traffic, small, tiled European flats with spiral staircases between floors, white-washed walls, washing hung out of windows. Something tells her she would be a different person in these places, that these places would disrupt her old life and reset her completely. For the first time it doesn't seem impossible that she will make it there.

'Anything,' she says to Jay.

She looks at him now, a mystery so total to her. She knows it's time to leave but it is hard to get up. She still wants to run her fingers through his greedy hair. There aren't enough words to cover all the years, all the love and the good, the times he has let her down, the things he has done but will not admit to. There are things she wants to say, things she wants him to understand, to atone for, but they seem too cruel and she can't bear to. After everything, she still hates seeing him cry.

She tells Jay she has to go. He stands up, tries to hug her and bumps her breast awkwardly. They manage a weak embrace. It seems so limp, this hug, after all these years. This makes Leah linger a bit longer than she should and so he kisses her again. She expects it to be gentle and full of meaning but it is rough and toothy and she doesn't enjoy it. He's walking away before she knows it.

It occurs to Leah that Jay didn't say he was sorry.

And that is it. The ending was ugly and sad, but it is done. They are walking in different directions. Leah wonders for a moment where Jay is going but then lets the thought slip from her. They are free of each other, life is carrying on, the street around them noisy and inconsiderate and gorgeous.

Walking home alone, Leah smiles. She is looser, no longer part of a couple fighting to keep some sort of love. No more ignoring the truth of him, no more going back. She puts one foot in front of the other, she keeps going.

The prospect of her flat feels more unbearable now than it ever has, Raph pacing around, so Leah walks for a while and drinks in the town with new eyes, eyes that savour it all a bit more now that she knows she is leaving. In her mind she is already gone. Her conviction is so complete that it almost makes her laugh. It seems alien now, all that doubt. She knows now, clear as day, that she will make sure she is as far from Jay and Raph as she can be, that she'll never speak to her dad again.

Leaving strikes her as a radical act. It all comes into focus again, sharper this time, the fact that she has been living for others, living for Jay, trying to be the woman he wants her to be, easy and malleable and safe. She has been living for Raph, tidying up after him, like she tidied up for her dad after he jumped from their lives. The men have been at the centre for the longest time. Leaving feels like she is reclaiming her life for herself.

She finds herself at the doors of Nathan's pub and watches him through the window for a while, carrying out little jobs freely like a person who doesn't know they're being watched, his good-natured, slow self, leaning on the bar chatting to an old man.

It is hard to know what shape her love for him takes. Watching him softly respond to an old drinker with thick glass between her and him, she feels an urge to lie on his chest again. Perhaps she just loves how much of a different type of man he is. He looks up and he sees her and her brief love disappears. She remembers with brilliant clarity that she is leaving, and she is alone and she is fresh and silver with newness.

He waves her in. It's getting cold and she can feel a heavy wetness in the air.

'You all right?' he says when she reaches him.

She realises her face must be sea salt speckled, hair unruly from the wind.

'I really am,' she says. 'I just broke up with Jay.'

He frowns.

'Jesus. Are you OK?'

'I'm actually fine.'

'Well then. I hated you two together anyway.' He smiles to let her know he's not being fully serious, passes her a cold bottle of beer. She takes a sip, an indelicate gulp that makes her oesophagus spasm. The beer is freezing.

'Bliss. That might be the best thing I've ever tasted.'

She still feels so safe with him, knows their secret will be squashed and lived with forever.

'So it's over then? Between you two? Mad.'

Leah nods.

'I spent my whole life chasing him. I don't know why.'

'Ah, Jay's got his virtues.'

'Ha. At least he was never boring, I suppose.'

'I can understand, Le. Why you stayed. Jay's persuasive.'

'You're always so fair, Nath.'

They both laugh. When she tells him that she is leaving he nods.

'I'm happy for you. I'll miss you.' She so appreciates that he is letting her go, keeping his love for her firmly to himself once again.

'Yeah. I'll miss you too.' She means it so much. 'You're a really good person, Nath.'

'Come back lots. I'll have my own pub one day. Promise. Little flat for Mum and Dad above. Free beers all day long.' He touches her shoulder gently.

'I'd love that,' she says.

'And Raph? How will he take it?'

'Yeah Raph. I have no idea. But I'm not staying for him.'

'He'll be fine.'

'I think I hate him sometimes.'

'No you don't. You really don't.'

She walks home happy and exhausted. When she gets in she wants to sleep instantly. She takes off all of her clothes and stands in her bedroom, looks at the shape of herself in the full-length mirror, feels as though she could do anything.

Two weeks later

Matthew's old flat is empty. He'd never noticed before that the walls are a light mint colour, the flat was always too crowded to recognise. Where the pictures used to hang there are squares of darker green. Most of the furniture has gone to the British Heart Foundation on Western Road. Leah's taking the books with her when she leaves. Matthew's kept his grandad's notebooks, a birthday card from Ron with a message inside written in watery blue ink, Ron's maroon sweater and razor with the wooden handle, but nothing else. He wants to be light. Everything he owns now fits into the large blue suitcase that's waiting outside the front door. His camera hangs around his neck.

'Math. It's time.' Leah knocks on the glass panel of the open front door. 'Benny's going to drive us to the station.'

They haul Matthew's suitcase into the back of Benny's van. Matthew has butterflies in his stomach, nervous about navigating the airport. He's never done it on his own, his only trips have been to see his mum a couple of times, always with Leah or his aunties. He wonders if it'll be obvious what to do, what protocols to follow. He worries crowds will swarm around him, confident frequent travellers. There have been times when he's considered not going but he has pushed on.

At the station Benny hands Matthew his suitcase and pulls him into his arms.

'We're so proud of you Matthew.'

Leah emerges from Budgens with a bottle of white wine and some chocolate buttons.

'Breakfast.' She smiles at Matthew.

They buy tickets and board the red Gatwick Express, find some seats with a table. Leah cracks the wine open and pours generous helpings into paper coffee cups.

They both drink.

'That's sorted me right out,' Matthew says.

They're both a bit frantic, neither knowing what to say. Everything feels like a line from a bad film.

'I can't believe you're going. Are you excited?'

'I just want to get there now. Thanks for coming with me.'

'Don't be silly,' Leah says. 'Is he picking you up?'

'Yeah. He's got the flight details.' It feels unreal to Matthew that Caleb knows exactly when his flight lands, that he'll be planning his own train journey to the airport to make it on time to arrivals. A different type of train, a wide, air-conditioned Spanish train hurtling past dry countryside. He wonders what Caleb will be wearing.

'Do you think it's going to be awkward?' Matthew says. 'What if we have nothing to talk about?'

'You will, you idiot.'

After Matthew had decided to go with Caleb they'd met up a few more times in Brighton, day dates that melted into the night, walking around the Laines with coffees and cakes in paper bags, then pints, a spontaneous showing of an old nostalgic Disney at the independent cinema down on the corner of London Road. Caleb showed Matthew pictures of the flat they'd be staying at in Spain, they looked up the cheapest flights, they started to get excited. They walked with their arms around each other, which started to feel more normal to Matthew.

Caleb left a week before Matthew was due to fly out so that he could settle into his new job. Matthew spent that week packing up his grandad's flat with Leah and worrying that any moment there would be a phone call from Caleb calling off the plan. That phone call never came. Instead, Caleb sent texts with plans for meeting at the airport, links to galleries he thought Matthew might like and a reservation for a restaurant that he'd made for Matthew's first night.

The day before Matthew left he and Leah took a walk around Brighton, their favourite parts, arm in arm. They walked up to their school and looked through the green-link fence, then down to the Level and all through the Laines. They stopped in on Nathan, who gave them drinks on the house, and they finished up at the sea, watching the sun plunge down into the water. They waded out with their jeans rolled up, felt the freezing ground beneath their feet, pushed their toes into the sand, a texture so familiar to them, little stones against their soles. They both took a pebble from the beach to take with them. Matthew imagined it balancing on a white windowsill, a view of a different town out ahead.

'Everything used to matter so much,' he said.

On the train Matthew relaxes. He starts to feel in control. He is actually going, it is actually happening, and he has decided on it. Caleb is waiting for him. It's real and he has made it happen. He bought the plane ticket. He packed his things, neatly, chose his outfit for the journey. He cleaned up his grandad's whole life from the flat, hoovering every corner on his hands and knees. He met with an estate agent and put the flat on the market. He rang his dad without feeling he was imposing. He has more money in his bank account than he has ever had. He has paid undertakers. He has visited Ron's grave with a bunch of red tulips.

He closes his eyes and pictures a square full of people eating lunch in the sun, walking unfamiliar streets, each corner brand new and full of promise. The train goes fast past the small stations outside of Brighton and with each blurred village Matthew feels stronger. Brighton and his life, the pedestrian day-to-day, the anxiety, seem to drop away as the train pushes on.

He will look back on this week, this journey to the airport, and think how amazing it is, the things he can now do. He will recognise it as the start of his life as a man who knows who he is and what he is capable of. He will look back and be proud of himself. Grief is not what he ever imagined. It is less dramatic, quieter, an adjusting of his reality while the world carries on noisily around him. He fits his grief around his daily life. It is not a straight line. There will be times where the pain, the injustice of it, feels impossible to bear. Often he will wish that his grandad, who never went abroad in his life, could have walked the same heat-baked streets as Matthew and Caleb, but with Billy by his side. He will keep going, reminding himself of the good days, of his grandad's voice asking him to give himself a chance. There will be days of such peace and accept-ance. He will carry on, scruffily, imperfectly, with doubts and fears and days where it feels hard to get out of bed, days where he can't believe he is there with Caleb, but he will carry on.

At Gatwick, Leah queues with Matthew to drop his bag. They're a little drunk now and hold on to each other in the queue, laughing as Matthew tries to compose himself, shows his passport to the man at the desk. The man asks Matthew questions and Matthew feels himself slipping into the role of someone who knows what to say, someone confident. It's like he's watching himself from outside himself. The man hands him back his passport and smiles.

Before security, Leah stops.

'Don't do a weird goodbye,' she says.

She walks backwards towards the train station, waving. Matthew looks at her one last time then turns to the noise of security, walks through the turnstile.

Six months later

Leah is sat in a hot room above a pub. The walls are painted black. The floor is also black and scuffed with foot marks and dotted with old bits of tape. They call it a theatre. She is watching a man act. He talks about his life. He is talking in a low voice with a delicious, gloopy Midlands accent about a time he wanted to die. Leah feels as though she's in his head. It feels too real to be watching. From where she is sat she can see his eyelashes, she can see the sweat gathering above his eyebrows.

After the play is over, Leah talks to the girl who wrote it. Leah is holding a glass of red wine, big as a bowl, to her chest. Her hands are shaking.

'I've never seen anything like it,' she says. 'How did you write it?' The girl looks just the right type of modest and proud. She's smiling and wringing her hands together.

'I don't know. I just write about real life.'

Leah introduces herself to the actor. She feels embarrassed in his presence, like she knows him too intimately. His voice isn't the same as on stage and he's changed his clothes. He is a different person. Leah feels like a different person lately too.

She is doing things she has never done before. The actor tells Leah she has beautiful eyes.

'People say that,' she says.

He asks if he can see her again. She smiles. She realises she doesn't want to say yes, though she doesn't quite know how to tell him.

'I've just got out of something,' she says, 'and I'm new here.'

'So?' he says.

She wonders who she was before she loved Jay, what she wanted, and how to begin again now it's done. She doesn't change her mind about the actor's offer. The men are gone, she tells herself. At least for now. On the way home she reads a headline about a married actor's affair with a very young woman.

Leah is in a seminar. When she started university she'd imagined red bricks covered in ivy. In reality, her seminars take place in a standard-looking block on a busy main road. She's read the book that this seminar is about. She read it twice before she even applied for this university, but she read it again in preparation. Boys much younger than her are putting their hands up and offering opinions. The book is about a young girl who dies after an older, married politician she is seeing crashes into some water. He survives, she drowns. Leah disagrees with some of the boys putting their hands up but she doesn't say anything. She wonders if her opinion counts without someone to confirm it. She writes a note to herself in the margin of the book, reminding herself: *Trust your gut.*

In the campus afterwards she watches a couple argue. You always overreact, the man says, and she watches the girl try not to show she's hurt. She is glad to be sitting alone with her book and her sandwich.

At parties she meets people with regional accents. They ask about Brighton, say how cool it must have been to grow up there. She smiles and nods and says 'yeah.' And it was, she thinks, it was a treat, remembering nights on beaches with her friends watching the sun recede, the particular fresh cold that comes only when you are by the water. Sometimes she feels like saltwater is still pumping through her blood. The smells, the waves and pebbles, the pubs, the reckless boys. But hers isn't the Brighton people think of when she tells them that's where she's from. Hers is different. It's not the theatres, the restaurants, the tourist-packed parts of the beach. It's home. Imperfect, frustrating but good enough. Up there in their flats they were both part of Brighton and separate from it, normal people getting by. She is both protective of it and glad to be away.

Sometimes she misses her people, the people who would say she has done very well for herself. The people she saw every day for over two decades. People scraping snow off their cars, grappling with black bin bags, smoking on their front steps, complaining, laughing, talking together, all knowing intimately all the joys and all the problems in that little patch of flats. The people who knew every neighbour's name, the safety, the comfort and cosy community of that, the children she used to play with in her block. They were people to whom the reality of living in the town doesn't need to be explained, who affirm everything about being from there with one smile, one nod. She gets the feeling the people asking her about it will never have a true sense of it, she won't be able to translate it. She meets lots of people who don't feel as though they are from anywhere in the way she feels she is from Brighton and she is glad to call it home.

Leah meets people who have been to places she has never been, people who spend summers in other houses abroad, large farmhouses in the south of France with huge families. Sometimes she feels envious of them. She meets people who look genuinely shocked when she talks about her life, which makes her feel a bit alien, proves her distinction from them is wider than she had once thought. She meets people who seem so confident in who they are it genuinely baffles her.

She drinks with people who have never been drunk before. She politely declines when people offer her coke at parties, trying not to sound uptight or judgemental. She usually wants to go home earlier than anyone else but feels it might be anti-social, worries what people will think of her.

She's always keen to get back to her books and her TV and her own food in her kitchen that she can take time cooking, a room that she can lock, that no one will burst into, far away from any danger of Raph coming home drunk and needing her. More than anything, she likes eating in bed. Huge bowls of food that are exactly what she fancies when she fancies it. She's put on weight but she cares less. She's started swimming and she feels strong.

There are only certain people she wants to stay out with when she does go out, two women she has met in one of her classes. They're older than her. They talk with purpose. They like Leah, she thinks. She feels seen by them, they ask her questions. She feels enthusiastic around them, like she is growing. She can sit with them, comfortably. She can be unsure around them and vocalise that. They drink pints and order chips and never mention what impact this might have on their weight. They laugh at men and fold pages down in books that they think Leah will like. At school and in Brighton Leah felt like she was retreating from her intellect. Jay resented it in her, he could be sneering and unkind. Here she feels as though it is being drawn out of her. It's almost a physical feeling. They talk about their homes and their exes and their families. They come from families held together by just a mother too, different small flats in different large cities. She tells her friends some of the things Jay used to say to her and they react concerned. Being around them is like the feeling of stepping into a blade of sun on a cold day.

Leah's old life feels far enough now that she can approach it with a degree of hindsight, she can talk about it with them and feel as though she has learned something, that she was right to leave. It feels strange how everything that mattered so much has now concluded, that everyone has simply moved on.

Every night and sometimes in the mornings when she's drinking coffee from her own small cafetière she bought for herself, she writes in a leather notebook that was too expensive and before long, the pages are full up with stories and ideas and descriptions of things she has noticed. Seeing her thoughts written down makes them feel realised and important. Time seems to pass differently when she writes, like she is hanging in a doughy, liminal space.

Leah finds herself on a train back home. Her mother has been calling lately and saying things like 'you can't stay away forever'. When her feet touch the platform at Brighton station, she feels a real panic like something very bad is about to happen. She walks down under the bridge. She feels separate from the town, very aware that she is a visitor. Leah calls Nathan's phone. He answers and says that yes, he is in the pub. She walks the route she knows, using all the shortcuts that are still entrenched within her muscle memory, the piss-reeking back alleys, the parks to cut through. It makes her feel like she must be from here but it still feels different. It's winter. The sun is out, the trees are bare.

Nothing has changed in the pub. It's not quite evening and it is quiet. There are a few men speckled around nursing pints. Nathan is leaning against the bar. When Leah walks through the door he looks up. His face lights up, the lines his smile makes are familiar, still. Those heavy eyes are still sweet to her. They walk over to each other and hug like old friends do, a long and deep hug where they rub each other's backs with generous strokes. He asks how she's been and she says, 'Oh you know,' and he nods and says she looks well. There's a song playing softly in the background that she recognises as something that might once have been important to them. She wonders if it's a coincidence.

She considers too how long would be appropriate to stay here in his company. Part of her feels as though she might like him to hold her, kiss her, scratch some itch of loneliness in that old, safe place. The other part is keen to get out of the door, to not indulge this feeling, remind herself that she mostly enjoys her solitude now. He is wearing a beautiful deep purple jumper and after they hug she rubs his chest with an open palm and tells him he looks nice. He looks shy and embarrassed but he is still smiling.

Leah asks him how he's been and he says he's been happy.

'There's a book I've been reading,' Leah says, once she has a warm tea in her hand. The minty smell of it snakes its way up to her nose.

'It's all about this boy who's just like you.'

'Oh yeah?' Nathan says.

'Yeah. He's wonderful.' She wants to say more, thinks she ought to explain why she couldn't love him but she leaves it alone, there is no need.

They talk about their families. Nathan asks after Raph but the truth is Leah doesn't know. Not yet anyway. She feels a tightening in her bowels at the mention of his name and the question of where he might be. Nathan sees something flash over her eyes and he reaches out and hooks his thumb and first finger around her wrist. He gives it a little squeeze.

'You seem calm,' she says.

'I am,' he says. 'Life is good.' He pauses. 'I do think of you.'

Though Jay is not there with them, he is everywhere. The question of him may as well be ringing the last orders bell, swinging from the fairy lights on the ceiling, smashing all the glasses off the shelf. Leah brings herself to ask after him.

'I think he's OK. Truth is, I've not seen him in weeks. It's different without you around,' Nathan says. 'When will you be back then?' Leah drains the last of her tea. The teabag hits, wet and squidgy, against her lovely teeth.

'Christmas, I guess,' she says.

He nods.

'And how's Matthew? Do you know? His pictures look incredible.'

'He's in love,' she says. They smile at each other and Nathan sighs deeply.

'Thank you for everything, Nath. I'd have been lost without you,' she says. Then she tells him she needs to leave.

Outside there are dead leaves all stuffed up in the gutters, wet and stagnant. There is red in the sky. The tyres of the buses on the wet ground crackle. The light is fading, and windows are beginning to steam with breath. Leah treads on broken glass. A boy racer tears down the road beside her and makes her jump, an L-plate hanging from his fender. Bodies swaddled in raincoats and scarves bob along the high street.

As though she is in a dream Leah sees Jay fizzle into view, like the thought of him has summoned him from some place he lay dormant all the months she was out of town and trying to keep him from her mind. Brighton is like this, ghosts gliding around every corner. Jay is walking towards her, moving through the bodies of London Road. There seems to be a different quality of light on him, he is shining differently. His hair is longer and he is wearing a tie. She can't believe it's really him, in physical form. Leah's gut feels like it's racing to her mouth. Everything in her is tingling and precarious. Her teeth don't feel like her own. She is hot and cold and completely unmoored. He feels both a stranger and everything in the whole world to her all at once.

He nods with a knowing look and says, 'Hey.' He is unfazed, as though this was prepared.

'Hey,' she says it back but the word comes fast out of her mouth with too much breath and it doesn't really sound like language.

He pulls her to one side with a firm arm so that they are out of the way of the business and the noise of the street. She's suddenly aware of how dark it's getting and how cold it's becoming. She doesn't want to do this here. She wants warmth and safety in which to speak to him again but she is also afraid of what that might mean, or what it could make her want. She knows she won't be able to help but be kind to him. She also wants him to know he is a thing of the past and that her new life is better. She wonders how best to communicate this in a casual, succinct attractive way, right there in the loud street, a way that will make up for all the mess and hurt of the past and tie it up in a neat bow, a way that will allow her to leave this encounter with her dignity intact. She considers whether he still finds her attractive.

'How are you?' she says.

Jay nods a lot, perhaps a little too much.

'I'm doing good, I'm doing good,' he says. 'Working.'

She raises her eyebrows. 'Not like that,' he says. 'I spent the summer doing the deckchairs on the beach. It was good. Lots of time to think. Now I'm doing sales. Actually doing it this time.' He gestures to his tie and his shirt.

Leah notices the tiniest spot of coffee next to one of the buttons. She wonders if his mother still does his laundry. She remembers the comfortable mass of his body sleeping beside her, the knots in his shoulders that she used to massage.

'I'm really happy to hear that. That sounds good,' she says.

Jay laughs, a little cruelly.

'You want me to tell you it's better than what I was doing before, yeah? So it proves your point, right? Well it's not. I'm skint. And I hate it. But it is what it is.'

'Maybe it will get better,' Leah says. Jay laughs again, blatantly scathing.

'Maybe.'

'How are things otherwise?' she says.

'Fine. Things go on, don't they. People move on. Start to care less.'

330

'I suppose.'

'I may as well tell you. Before you hear it from someone else,' Jay says. 'I met someone.'

Leah feels a jolt. Like she's nearly dropped something precious. She makes a point to smile and her chest hurts. She feels queasy.

'Oh yeah?'

'Yeah.'

'You're together. Properly?'

'Yeah. I was going to message you. I don't know why I didn't.'

'That was quick then,' Leah says. She wishes she hadn't.

'Yeah. She's . . . Well she's good for me. I think I'm finally learning how to be intimate, I guess. She said I had intimacy issues when we met, so I'm figuring them out.'

'Good for you,' Leah says. It sounds cutting. He doesn't seem to notice.

'Still living with your mum?'

'Yeah.' He is looking behind her now like he has somewhere to be.

'Things are good with me, too,' she says, although he hasn't asked.

'Good, I'm glad,' he says. He's distracted.

Leah considers telling him more. She wants to impress him, tell him about the things she has learned, the people she has met. Something stops her though. Something makes her shrink herself to make him feel bigger. So much of what she knew with him involved saying nothing when she should have said something. There's a pause.

'Well I see you've finally learnt how to dress,' Jay says with a smile, though he's being cruel, undermining her in his old way.

Leah looks down at herself. She's wearing a new jumper, moss green and wool with a high neck and gold hoop earrings, hair on top of her head. She remembers getting dressed this morning and feeling good. She looks back up at him. He gives her a wink. She knows then how little he's changed. She won't get an apology. She's disappointed but not surprised. She suddenly would literally rather be anywhere in the world than standing there in front of him.

He is the one to say he needs to get off. She thinks about asking to see him again, some old pattern, but she remembers she doesn't want to. It's hard to believe herself, to stand her ground, but she knows firmly that she is right in this instance. She wants her life untouched by him.

'OK,' she says. 'It's really good to see you.'

'Same,' he says. And then he's gone. The back of his head disappearing into the street, the sky turning a lavish dark overhead.

The exchange is flat. They are both fine, there is no affection in their interaction, not even a knowingness, a nod to all the past. For Leah, it cements for her that their love was not, in fact, what she thought it was. She endured it all because she thought their relationship was beyond reason, vast and poetic. The notion of her and Jay as sacred seems silly and childish now. In the end, it was easily disposed of.

Walking home after seeing Jay, a realisation enters her and solidifies with a clarity she's not often had, but a clarity she experiences more often now that she is learning to trust herself. She has always told herself Jay was different, damaged and misunderstood. He didn't know he was hurting her. But she sees it now: he had wanted to destroy her. Some mornings she still wakes up and he's been in her dreams again, saying something terrible. She wakes up frightened, has to look around her new room full of her own things to remind herself she is free of him. Occasionally his name appears on her social media feeds and she feels as though she's been slapped hard in the face, tears forming spontaneously.

Leah is sitting in her mother's kitchen and her mother is fussing over her, saying Leah looks thin and aren't her ankles cold with her jeans rolled up like that? Leah is happy to hear she seems thin even though she knows it can't be true. She still eats the chicken pie her mother has cooked and has second and third helpings. The gravy is salty and she is full and happy. Raph is in decent spirits and mercifully doesn't touch the wine. Leah can't help but feel that the way Raph is looking at her is hostile though. His eyes seem narrowed and when he speaks to her, they're tinged with sarcasm.

'When are you back up to uni?' he says.

'Tomorrow.'

Raph rolls his eyes.

'Flying visit then.'

'More mash?' their mother asks, and she rises from the table, making more noise than is necessary. During dinner, Leah's mind wanders away from the flat, from Brighton, drifting back to her other life. It's true that for so long she stayed here because Jay and Raph mattered so much to her but now she is back, she is unmoved by them, detached.

Later when Raph is asleep on the sofa, Leah asks her mum how he has been. Her mum turns her back and begins scrubbing the baking tray violently with wire wool.

'There's been a few . . . incidents.'

'What kind of incidents?'

'Oh you know. He just takes things a little too far sometimes.'

Leah stands behind her mum and puts her arms around her waist. She wonders what to say, whether to offer to stay.

'I love you Mum,' she says instead.

'I love you too, love.'

Leah stands on the balcony holding a tea to her chest. She glances over at Matthew's old flat. The door is a different colour, no longer a bottle green, now a cheerful geranium red. The terracotta pots are gone and so are the boxes of junk that had piled up outside over the years. She watches for long enough for a young man to come out of the front door with a small baby strapped to his chest. The man looks clean and happy, he's wearing a white long-sleeved T-shirt, comfortable and easy with the baby. He notices Leah standing opposite him and he waves, smiles widely.

Leah is carrying three plates with one hand, balancing them on her forearm in a way she'd seen done on the telly but never imagined she would be able to do herself. She's got a pencil in her hair and her legs are screaming from standing up for the duration of a double shift. Someone asks her for a gluten-free option. A rich-looking man accuses her of giving him the wrong change. In the kitchen, she does an impression of him to her new friends. They laugh and pass her a small bottle of vodka they've been sharing between the waiting staff, the busboys and the chefs. She feels the warmth of it dance down into her belly and heads back out onto the floor. She can't make friends at university in the way she thought she might. Everyone is too young and too self-centred. But she likes these people, the ones who make twelve hours on a restaurant floor fun. After her shift, they lock the doors and eat sticks of leftover bread, drink more, share the tips. Leah is grateful for the cash in hand and the bread. Her bursary is running out and she's been living on thirteen-pence freeze-dried noodles from the basics line at the supermarket.

Leah goes to see a band with the women from her seminar. The ticket price makes her feel guilty but when the music starts she has a good time. The singer is French and the music grips Leah so much, she almost forgets to breathe. The singer talks about letting someone go and it feels like she is singing straight at Leah. Leah lets tears fall down her face but she is happy to be heartbroken, it means new things are waiting. The music makes her picture what the south of France could be like, all golden. She imagines driving down a farm road with the windows open, no makeup and an old T-shirt with some comfortable shorts, listening to this music. It feels so close. One of her friends silently weaves a hand around her waist and they sway together.

Leah is invited to dinner by one of her new friends. She lives with a man she calls her partner in a tiny flat in the centre of town. The floorboards are painted white and there are green, luscious plants everywhere in lovely heavy-looking pots. They don't have much but they've made it feel like it's a home. All around the flat is evidence of their love. The shelves in the kitchen are lined with ceramic mugs and bowls they made together at a pottery class in the student union. There are notes they've left each other on the fridge. They serve Leah coffee from these sweet little uneven mugs and she holds it in her cupped palms. Her friend's partner cooks that night using herbs he snips from a pot on the windowsill. He says thyme will be nice in the sauce. That night they drink and talk a lot and they offer Leah a bed on the sofa. In the morning she hears them talking in the kitchen. She can smell coffee. They're talking about what they will do that day. The man suggests a walk and lunch, perhaps the cinema later. The woman discusses the logistics of visiting the man's mother the following afternoon and he agrees with her and thanks her for helping. They speak softly to each other with voices full of love and compromise. Leah hears them kiss. She walks in and they are standing up, a pot of coffee between them on the countertop, eating soft-looking bread and jam. They both look pleased to see her.

Walking home that day there is frost beneath Leah's feet. A bonfire smoulders in an allotment, fills her with its smell. The sky is milky, ready to snow, like it's a giant net holding thousands of pale balloons. The day feels empty and blank, a hollowed-out thing. Leah loves the seasons, the shock of them when they're extreme.

Everything she knew is far away as though it's been exploded, turned into little fragments that are all floating separately, doing their own thing elsewhere. She is nowhere near the sea. She is hours away from home by train. Jay is no longer Jay, he has diluted, he's not as real anymore. There are times she imagines him at night, somewhere out there in the dark, thinks of calling him to tell him about new things that have happened to her but this, she tells herself, is nothing but a habit that she will learn to break. She's glad she loved him, glad he's gone. She wonders if she will ever have the gentleness of what she's just seen between her new friends. She thinks of her past life as something abstract, a fog she once passed through, so much less painful now.

Sometimes she is guilty for leaving. Some days she feels like she's an imposter in this new life. But she has waded through the days that feel like tar. Weeks have led to months. She's gone to bed each night and woken up each morning and somehow it's started to get easier. She's gone to seminars and worked double shifts. Everyone else seems to have more than she does but she feels, for the first time, she has everything she needs. She has a student pass for the cinema. She rents old DVDs from the library. She learns to have conversations where she doesn't apologise for herself. She's starting to feel more certain about things, not tripping herself up all the time. She starts to be able to say no. She identifies times where she has been unkind to herself. She starts to get a better sense of who she is, the things that make her happy. Things like being alone and quiet, buying wine from the shop at the end of the road where they wrap each bottle, even the cheap ones, in deep green tissue paper so it feels special. She likes colourful paper files and reading things that move her to tears. She likes buying the newspaper of a weekend and carrying its heaviness home. She only reads some of it but the ritual feels special. When she tries the crossword she thinks of Ron. She likes reality shows and sour sweets. She likes making people laugh and having the freedom to do that. She likes that people see her as good company. Somewhere between working and writing and sleeping and eating and drinking, she has started to feel something near to contentment, and underneath all the bulging past, are small moments of sharp happiness.

She gets home later that morning. It's true winter. She lets herself into her small terrace house, the one she shares with other students. They've bought a little Christmas tree from the market and it's leaning against the hallway wall, ready to be decorated together that evening. The smell of rich pine fills the air. Leah sees a postcard on the floor. She notices Matthew's familiar handwriting, writing she's known since school, tight and neat. On the front of the postcard is a photograph of a bustling Spanish town with high walls, sea and hills in the background. The sea is a brilliant blue. Leah leans against the wall in her hallway and closes her eyes, imagines him, near some different ocean, far away, with his own living, loving man in his arms.

Acknowledgements

This book wouldn't exist without the support of the following people; Steve Camden for lighting the fuse. Abby Parsons for suggesting I could ever write fiction. Eva Lewin and everyone at Spread the Word for helping me find the time and means to do this. I am also grateful to Anne Vegnaduzzo for offering me a residency in Paris to finish the first draft of what became this book. And Kerry Hudson – without your voice on the end of the phone, I would have given up many times over.

Thank you to the folks at The Roundhouse and Apples and Snakes, to all my mentors and teachers who opened up the world of writing to me and showed me this was possible, when it sometimes felt impossible. Thank you to libraries and to everyone who is committed to creating opportunities so that people like me can do things like this, it is truly wild to have made it here.

I want to extend my gratitude to those who have shared a kind and encouraging word about my work and given me that nudge that I needed to carry on. To the writers and artists I am fortunate enough to know; you have become some of my best friends and I owe much of this book to you.

A special thanks must go to my diligent, brilliant and glamorous agent Becky Thomas who's been there right from the beginning and who I'd be lost without.

Thank you to Ann Bissell and the wonderful team at Borough who believed in this book, and in me.

To my friends, you know who you are, for the times you have scooped me up, loved me, accepted me.

Thank you, Dad, thank you Hallam, my small family, for your friendship.

Lastly, thank you forever Luis. You showed me what real love is.